Memories of the two nights he'd spent with her came flooding back.

How he'd gently undressed her on their marriage night. How his hands had felt on her skin that night in Bath. The sensations that had erupted—

She bit her lip to keep it from trembling. She'd promised herself never to think of the nights she'd spent with him. *Never.* He'd thought her wealthy then.

How like a gamester. When holding Aces and Kings all full of bonhomie, but if the hand contained twos and threes…

She would show him she was more than a widow hand, the hand dealt but left on the table for no one to play. She would be in the game at last and she would win.

The widow hand would win.

Diane Gaston

the Wagering WIDOW

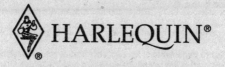

HARLEQUIN®

TORONTO • NEW YORK • LONDON
AMSTERDAM • PARIS • SYDNEY • HAMBURG
STOCKHOLM • ATHENS • TOKYO • MILAN • MADRID
PRAGUE • WARSAW • BUDAPEST • AUCKLAND

ISBN 0-373-29388-7

THE WAGERING WIDOW

Copyright © 2004 by Diane Perkins
First North American Publication 2006

www.eHarlequin.com

Printed in U.S.A.

Please address questions and book requests to:
Harlequin Reader Service
U.S.: 3010 Walden Ave., P.O. Box 1325, Buffalo, NY 14269
Canadian: P.O. Box 609, Fort Erie, Ont. L2A 5X3

This book is dedicated to my mother-in-law, Marie Grady. Unlike the mother-in-law in this story, Marie embraced her son's wife as if she were her own daughter. She has always showered me with her love and support, especially when I needed it most, when my own mother passed away. Marie, this one is for you!

Chapter One

September 1816, Scotland

Guy Keating straightened his spine and glanced about the blacksmith shop that he'd wager had never seen a forge. The voice of the anvil priest rang throughout the room. 'Repeat after me…I, Guy Keating, take thee, Emily Duprey, to be my wedded wife…'

Barely able to make his mouth work, he finally responded, 'I, Guy Keating…' His words sounded like a funeral dirge.

What the devil was he doing in this place, speaking these words? The final vow nearly caught in his throat.

'…'til death do us part.'

The priest, who Guy would hazard was neither priest nor blacksmith, turned to the young woman dressed in a plain brown travelling garment, standing on the other side of the never-used anvil. 'Repeat after me,' the anvil priest said. 'I, Emily Duprey…'

The young woman answered in a soft, but clear tone, 'I, Emily Duprey…'

Guy tried to give her a smile, this woman whose appearance was as unremarkable as her personality. She was neither short nor tall, thin nor stout. Her hair, worn with curls framing her face, was in the popular fashion, though its colour was the same bland brown as her dress. He could never quite recall the colour of her eyes, but whatever they were, her eyes did not enliven her always-composed face.

She gazed at him, almost a question in her expression, but not quite that animated. He ought to be flogged for bringing her nearly four hundred miles, to court scandal for them both at Gretna Green. Oh, he might tell himself she was better off wed to him than having her fortune gambled away by her wastrel father or plundered by one of the rakes who had lately been courting her. Guy had a much better use for her money. Did that not make him less reprehensible than those gentlemen ready to exploit her for their own gain? Certainly less reprehensible than her father, Baron Duprey, who was as addicted to the roll of dice as Guy's own father had been.

She continued the vows in modulated tones. 'I take these folks to witness that I declare and acknowledge Guy Keating to be my guideman.'

Guideman, indeed. Pretender, perhaps. Deceiver?

Rogue.

The anvil priest, who looked more like a prosperous merchant, come to think of it, took both their hands and clasped them together. 'Weel, the deed is done. Y're husband and wife.' The man laughed, jiggling his considerable girth. 'Kiss the bride, mon.'

Guy jerked up his chin. He'd forgotten about this part of the ritual. He had kissed her once, upon proposing, because it seemed what he ought to have done, but he'd not thought of kissing her since.

She coloured and glanced shyly at him through her lashes. He leaned down and placed his lips on hers.

God help him if her lips did not seem expectant, as though she anticipated more than this sham of a marriage could deliver. She deserved more, after all.

'Now shall we go on to the inn, then?' The anvil priest raised his brows. The inn was another of his enterprises, no doubt.

Guy swallowed. He had not forgotten they were required to consummate the marriage. Would she be as hopeful on that score as with the kiss? First they would have a leisurely supper and then… He offered her his arm. 'Shall we go, my dear?' What he meant to say was *I'm sorry*.

He escorted her around the puddles left in the street from the afternoon's rains. What sunlight there had been that day waned in the sky, slipping as low as his confidence. He'd once thought this the wisest course, but now he felt like the veriest blackguard.

A wide puddle of water blocked the entrance to the inn, not a problem for his boots, but deep enough to dampen the hem of her skirt. He scooped her up and carried her over the threshold. Her face remained subdued, but she trustingly settled in his arms, feeling to him almost as a wife ought.

He made a vow more genuine than the ones he'd repeated after the anvil priest. He vowed to be a good husband to her. He vowed she would never know the truth of why he'd married her.

Their meal was a stilted affair, the two of them confined together in a private parlour. He tried his best to be as solicitous as a new husband ought.

'Would you like some fish, my dear?' he asked.

'Do you care for another piece of tart?'

'Shall I pour you another glass of wine?

She responded with similar politeness and managed to dredge up conversation, mainly about the food.

'This tart is delicious, do you not think?...The pastry flakes wonderfully...The raspberries are sweet, are they not?'

And he responded as he ought. 'Very delicious...very sweet.' In truth, he could not taste the food at all, and he'd availed himself of the innkeeper's whisky far more than was prudent. Surely all their future meals together would not be so excruciatingly dull.

After they finished the last course, no other choice remained but to climb the stairs to the bedchamber the anvil priest/innkeeper had promised them.

Guy's boots beat like a drum against the worn wood of the staircase, matching the loud tattoo of his heart. He'd bedded his share of women. Any man in regimentals was bound to, after all, but those simple exchanges were honest ones. How could he bed Miss Duprey—his wife, he meant—when he'd kept the truth from her? He'd feared she would not marry him if he had been totally honest about needing her fortune, though many a *ton* marriage took place for that very reason.

The innkeeper led them down a hallway to the bedchamber where a cheerful fire flickered in the hearth. The oak floor was covered with a figured rug, and a large bed, its linens turned down, dominated the room. A bottle of wine and two glasses sat on the small table next to it, and a branch of candles further illuminated the charming scene.

Miss Duprey—his wife—wandered over to the window and stood peeking through the gap in the curtains. She still held her hat and gloves as if not certain of staying.

'I weel leave y', good sir.' The innkeeper gave Guy a broad wink and grinned wide enough to expose the gap between his teeth that had not been visible during the brief wedding ceremony.

The thud of the closing door broke the silence, while Guy's disordered emotions continued to rage inside him. Miss Duprey—his wife, dammit! he *must* recall—turned at the sound.

Her eyes were wide, but her countenance composed. She clutched at her hat, crushing its ribbons.

He tried to smile. 'Do you care for some wine, my dear?'

'Thank you,' she said.

He poured two glasses, wishing it were the good Scottish whisky instead. She glanced around and finally found a bureau upon which to place her hat and gloves. With hands clasped like a schoolgirl, she walked over to the bedside table. He handed her a glass and took one himself, almost raising it to his lips before he caught himself. He ought to make a toast.

His mind raced to think of something, hoping he did not appear as witless as he felt. Her expression conveyed no hint that she guessed his thoughts.

'To our future…' he managed, clinking his glass with hers.

'Yes,' she replied in a whisper.

Their wine consumed, he stared awkwardly. She made no move. He supposed it was his responsibility to decide how to go on.

'Do you desire me to call a maid to assist you?' he asked. 'I could step downstairs to allow you some privacy.' And consume how many whiskys while she readied herself for her wedding night?

She shook her head.

A wave of panic rushed through him, the latest of many on this day. Would he be able to perform his husbandly duty? How ironic. If he could not perform, he would provide her the means to have the marriage annulled. One could almost laugh at the thought.

She was a well-enough appearing female. There was nothing to object to in her. So why could he not dredge up some modicum of desire?

Guilt prevented him, of course. Lying to her, telling her that her father had refused permission when, in truth, he'd never approached the man. Guy had tricked her into this flight to Gretna Green, leading her to believe there was no other way for them to wed.

He tried to conceal his emotions. 'We do not have to…to consummate our vows this night, if you do not wish to,' he said. 'There is no one to know but ourselves.'

The hint of concern flitted through her eyes. 'The bed sheets?'

Ah, the bed sheets. Some chambermaid or another would be changing the linens and might notice the lack of evidence. Would that create any difficulty? He failed to see why any of these people would care. They'd been well paid. What's more, she could easily be a widow or something. He shrugged. He'd come too far to take a risk now.

'I could contrive something.' Blood was a ready commodity, as any soldier knew. He might pierce his arm above his sleeve, bleed on the sheets and no one would be the wiser.

'I am willing to proceed,' she replied.

How was she able to keep her tone so temperate? She might as well be conversing with afternoon callers, but he, on the other hand, felt his voice might crack and fail him at any moment.

Her expression remained equally as mild as her fingers reached for the buttons of her spencer. He watched her free each button and pull off the garment. Placing it neatly on a chest at the end of the bed, she reached behind her back and struggled with her laces. He closed the distance between them.

Feeling as if he were perched on the ceiling observing himself, he undid her laces and slipped the dress off her shoulders. She remained as still as a statue as it slid to the floor. His fingers trembled when he set about removing her corset, but he soon had her free of that garment as well.

She turned to face him dressed only in her shift.

Perhaps if she conveyed some emotion, he might be more easy in this moment, but she was as colourless as she ever had been. He held his breath, watching her take the pins out of her hair and wondering how the devil he was going to be able to perform.

She ought to have a husband who greeted this moment with joy instead of obligation. She ought to run from him now and deny there had ever been a wedding. Bribe the avaricious anvil priest to destroy the marks in the register and hire the fastest post chaise back to Bath.

Such spirit, he would not blame—he might even admire it—but her compliance made him feel like a cad.

Taking a deep breath, he sat down on the bed to remove his boots.

Emily stood by, watching her husband as she smoothed her hair neatly behind her shoulders. She could not recall ever seeing a man remove his boots, even her father and brother, but certainly they would not have done so with the same masculine grace as Guy Keating.

Her heart fluttered at this intimate sight of him. He was by no means the tallest of gentlemen, only perhaps five or six inches above her own height, but there was such an air of compact energy about him that he seemed to take up more space.

That first glimpse of him came back to mind, in the Pump Room, her eyes drawn to him almost of their own accord. He had been leaning down to speak to two elderly ladies whom she now knew were his mother's aunts, an expression of acute tenderness on his face. That look alone had disarmed her. When he'd picked up one lady's shawl and wrapped it lovingly around her shoulders, Emily had thought she would weep for the sweetness of the sight.

Later that week at the Assembly he had walked up to her at her brother's side, having begged an introduction. *To her.*

Emily still marvelled at it. She watched him now pulling at his other boot, his dark hair curling around his head, his blue eyes shadowed by dark lashes any woman would covet. Why this good man had sought her out for attention, she still could not countenance. Nor could she explain why he had offered for her, when for three London Seasons no other man had fixed his interest on her.

She'd feared he must be mad or playing some cruel trick, but her brother assured her Guy Keating was top o' the trees, come into a handsome property, as game as he could go.

She'd also asked her brother why such a man would be interested in her, for it seemed so mystifying that he should be, when no other man had been.

Robert had said, 'Wager you ten to one his mama and those old crones of hers gave him a wigging for not setting up his nursery. His brother never did, y'know. Never fell in parson's mousetrap, never got an heir. One or two by-blows, but that is of no consequence. Shot himself, y'know. Lost at hazard. Lucky for Keating. Inherited the title.'

She had not asked her brother to speculate further, but, once begun, Robert tended to chatter on in his affected way of speaking. He added that the new Viscount had still been wearing black during the last Season. Robert suspected Keating, with his elderly charges in tow, had come to Bath to find a wife.

Still, there had been other eligible young ladies in Bath; why had Keating fixed his interest upon her?

It had been every bit as mysterious when Keating told her that her father refused his suit. Keating was so perfectly respectable. He was a viscount, after all.

Perhaps her father had been exacting revenge, because she had ruined his deranged scheme to trap the wealthy brother of a marquess into marrying her. She suspected her father had also set the town's unpleasant rakes upon her as well, showing her what sort of men were left to her, since she'd refused his plans. What other explanation could there be for the false flatterers to suddenly court her and pay her their absurd compliments? Such men preferred women with some looks or fortune, so it could have been nothing else but a trick.

Keating had been her only respectable suitor.

She must have been mad to agree to this Scottish elopement with him! But, what if she had not dared to sneak off? She might never have had another chance to marry a decent man.

So now she stood next to an unmade bed, dressed only in her shift, watching him remove his coat, waistcoat and shirt.

She hoped she was not gaping like the silliest of maids. She had tried so diligently to be correct. She wanted noth-

ing more than to do everything correctly, though she had
only the vaguest of notions of what was to come.

He stood, his chest bare, and it was all she could do
not to stare at the wide expanse of skin. Each muscle
looked as if it had been sculpted by some Greek master
long ago. Her heart raced again as it had done when he'd
removed her corset, touching her with only the thin fabric
of her shift between her skin and his fingertips.

Was she to do something at this moment? She was
conscious of a desire to place her hands on that wide
chest, to feel the muscles for herself, but she dared not
appear too forward. He looked away at that moment, and
she took the opportunity to glance at his trousers, bold
enough to eagerly anticipate what a man really looked
like.

He glanced back at her, a half-smile on his face. He
reached his hand to caress her cheek, and a surprising bolt
of sensation shot to her female parts. Her face grew hot,
and she was suddenly very impatient for this matter to
progress.

'Shall we…shall we lie on the bed?' he asked, his voice
low and raspy.

She nodded, too fearful of appearing incorrect to ask
why he did not ask her to remove her shift nor he remove
his trousers.

She climbed on to the bed, its linens cool through the
thin muslin of her shift. He settled next to her and her
heart raced again. He covered them both with the blanket
and, after a pause in which she had no idea what to do,
he removed the remainder of his clothing. Somewhat relieved she would not yet have to gaze upon a man's anat-
omy, she took that as her cue to remove her stockings and
her shift, for the first time in her life naked in bed.

He stiffened for a moment when she tossed those undergarments to the floor. 'I forgot to extinguish the candles,' he said, hurriedly slipping out of bed.

She trembled as she watched his bare form walk across the room. He looked quite like a Roman statue she'd glimpsed once at a wealthy London townhouse.

The light from the fireplace did not prove bright enough to show more than a shadow of the front of him when he returned. He crawled back under the covers and faced her in the darkness, his handsome features only dimly visible.

Would he be able to see how full of anxiety she was at this moment? She dared not appear too forward, as carnal as her sister had undoubtedly been, but it would certainly displease him if she shrank away.

. He took a deep breath and reached for her, pulling her towards him so that her bare skin touched his. She felt the parts of him she had not been able to discern press against her own intimate parts. He was softer than she would have imagined. His hands stroked her back, creating an unexpected thrill of pleasure matched only by the sensation of her breasts against his chest.

His hands continued to explore her in what seemed to her a resolute way, but, then, she'd had no experience with which to compare. His body broke away from hers while his hands stroked her breasts. The sensations he created were almost frightening. Were these the emotions that had caused her sister's downfall?

'I have no wish to…to hurt you,' he murmured haltingly.

'I am certain you will not,' she replied.

She knew that the first time was painful, but that was all she knew. It was difficult to imagine pain when her whole body had never felt so suddenly alive.

'I must try to ease it for you,' he said with a strong tone of duty.

His hand slid from her breast to her abdomen, her belly, to between her legs. She gasped, momentarily clamping her legs together. She quickly forced herself to relax.

He fingered that secret place of hers. Was it wicked for him to do so? She certainly had been taught by nurse-maids and governesses that she must not touch it unless absolutely necessary. The sensations created were almost unbearably intense. Not painful, really, but not at all comfortable.

His fingers became slippery, and she worried for a moment that her courses had started. She could not bear that particular humiliation. It seemed not to deter him.

Without warning his fingers entered her and she could not help gasping in surprise.

'I must,' he said.

She had no idea such actions were possible. Surely it was not as wicked as it felt! Her husband was not a wicked man, was he? To her surprise, her hips seemed to convulse without her willing them. She tried to remain as still as possible for fear moving might offend him. Maidens were supposed to hesitate at this moment, were they not?

His fingers created a strange, almost pleasureful pressure inside her. It made it quite difficult to think. Suddenly he pulled them out.

'I will enter you,' he said, sounding very solemn.

He gently urged her on her back and rose above her, the entire length of his body above hers held up by the strength of his arms. Slowly his muscles eased and he lowered himself, his legs between hers.

The part of him that had been so soft was now mysteriously hard and so much larger than it had been. Surely it was too large for her. He pushed against her and slowly, gently, the tip entered. It was difficult for her not to rise to meet his stroke.

He lunged and pain shot through her. She could not help but cry out. He immediately ceased.

'It is all right,' she managed, not wishing him to think herself truly injured.

The pain, in fact, could not compare with the other sensations, burning ones, insistent ones, ones that seemed to beg him to continue. It was a great relief when he did so, pushing in and out of her, faster and faster.

He suddenly gave a deep guttural cry and tensed. As he collapsed on top of her, her body still pulsated with such an intensity she thought she might shatter. Unbidden, tears sprang to her eyes.

He eased himself off her, and she felt like her body had been strewn into broken shards. That part of her where he'd entered hurt, but the rest of her ached. She wanted to rage at him, but was unsure why. He had done what men were supposed to do, had he not? Was she supposed to feel the way she did, wanting him to repeat the act, but wanting more to never feel such carnality again?

Her eyes had long adjusted to the dim light, and she gazed at his face, the arch of his dark brows, the way his lower lip was thicker than his upper. It was a handsome face, but the face of a stranger.

His brows knit together, and his blue eyes looked piercingly at her. 'I am sorry,' he said.

One tear rolled down her cheek.

Chapter Two

Each rut and furrow in the long road back to Bath jarred Emily's already aching heart. She managed to feign composure, although she imagined jagged pieces of her heart dropping like bread crumbs all the way back to Scotland.

Her husband, with amiable formality, made polite conversation. Asking after her comfort. Desiring to assist her. Apologising for the tediousness of the journey. She thought she would go mad with it.

Such a journey together in a snug carriage might have become a treasured interlude, a bridal trip as pleasant as a Parisian sojourn or a Venetian gondola ride. Instead, gloom permeated the atmosphere, and Keating's solicitude did nothing to banish it.

The carriage dipped in what must have been a very deep rut.

'Are you all right, my dear?' Keating asked. 'I dare say the roads are in a fair way to impassable.'

'I am not harmed in the least, sir,' she replied. Not harmed by the road, perhaps. With her husband, it was more difficult to say.

His words were all that was proper, but he seemed as distant as Buenos Aires or even the Sandwich Isles. Places reached in dreams. She might as well be alone. She had been alone the past two nights when her husband thoughtfully arranged separate rooms. 'For your comfort,' he'd said.

Her comfort, indeed. It simply gave him an excuse to avoid repeating the act that consummated their marriage.

Men were supposed to desire that act. She must have done something wrong, however, something so objectionable he could not bear to bed her again.

Between the bumps in the road, she tried to devise some manner of discovering what she'd done to displease him. She could not think of the correct words to form the question and thus remained silent on the subject. It put her to the blush to even contemplate speaking to him about what they had done. And what if speaking of it would be considered too forward? What if performing the act with her had been distasteful to him? How could she bear it?

Eventually the golden buildings of Bath came into view, shimmering in the sunlight of the crisp autumn day. They passed the King's Circus, proceeding up Brock Street. Her insides twisted into knots as their carriage pulled up to a building on Thomas Street where Keating leased a set of rooms.

'We have arrived,' he said in a tone she thought nothing less than ominous.

He spoke a few words to the coachman and picked up their travelling bags, carrying them into the building himself. They walked silently down a hallway where Keating set down their baggage and rapped on a door. An ancient man, thin as a stick and dressed in a nearly threadbare coat, stuck his head out.

'My lord.' The man spoke as if Keating had merely

spent a morning at the Pump Room instead of several days' absence. He gave a dignified bow and batted not an eyelash at Emily, half-obscured behind the Viscount.

'Bleasby.' Keating's one-word greeting managed to convey genuine fondness, even amusement at the butler's ability to remain composed. He stepped aside and brought Emily forward. 'I have brought my…my wife, Bleasby. Lady Keating.' Her husband presented her without actually having to look at her. 'Bleasby is our trusted butler, my dear.'

Bleasby maintained the hauteur of a high man in the servants' quarters in light of what must have been a very big surprise. He barely flickered an eyelid.

'Delighted to meet you, Bleasby,' Emily said.

The old man executed an arthritic bow. 'Very good, my lady.'

Bleasby reached for the baggage, but Keating had already retrieved it. 'No. No. Do not attempt moving these.' He placed them inside the doorway. 'I will attend to them directly. Is my mother in?'

'In the parlour with the ladies,' Bleasby answered.

'Ah,' he said with a cryptic nod. He turned to Emily. 'My dear, I suspect it would be better for me to seek a private audience with my mother and aunts. I hope you do not mind.'

What she did mind was being called 'my dear,' as if he could not trouble himself to recall her name.

'I am sure you are right,' she said.

Would his mother despise her for agreeing to the impropriety of an elopement? Would she think Emily had put him up to the mischief? She could not recall ever seeing the now Dowager Lady Keating. The aunts had not looked formidable, however, at least from a distance.

'I shall be but a moment.' He took two long-legged

strides before pressing his fingers to his temple and turning back. 'Bleasby, convey Lady Keating to…to the library and see to some refreshment.'

Bleasby limped, staggering a little with each step. Emily found herself wishing to give him her arm to lean upon, but the library was just around a corner. The small room had shelves, but no books to speak of and no fire in the grate. Managing to retain his dignity in spite of his infirmities, Bleasby limped out, closing the door behind him.

Emily stood in the centre of the room. She'd not even removed her hat and gloves. She could barely form a coherent thought. Her throat tightened and tears sprang to her eyes, blurring her vision.

No, she scolded herself. She would not become a watering pot like her sister Jessame, who wept over the slightest difficulty. Jessame had shed buckets at her wedding, a modest affair in St George's Church at the end of her first Season. Jessame's husband had been perfectly respectable, though a good dozen years her senior. If their father had ever thought to milk that gentleman's fortune, he'd been sadly mistaken. Jessame's Viscount had whisked her away from the family with creditable success. Emily had had barely more than a letter or two from her sister since.

She dug into her reticule for her handkerchief and dabbed at her eyes with its corner. If only she could be more like her other sister, Madeleine, who'd been daring enough to land on her feet after being banished from the household and passed off to everyone as dead. Madeleine had lived in sin with a man, borne a child out of wedlock, and still managed to marry well.

But what did it gain Emily to think of Madeleine marrying Devlin Steele? She'd once had the fantasy he would marry her, but discovering her sister alive and sharing his house had put an end to that. In truth, her parents' reprehensible behaviour had killed that illusion.

They had let her believe Madeleine dead for three years, when, in fact, they'd simply given her to Lord Farley, a man twice her age and a scoundrel.

How could Emily remain under her parents' roof after learning that evil? How could she resist the escape Lord Keating offered when he pressed his suit?

Her husband entered the room, looking a little grim. His interview must not have gone well.

'Come,' he said.

She followed him, but paused before they entered the parlour. 'Shall I remove my coat and hat?'

He had the grace to appear abashed. 'By all means.'

To her surprise, he assisted her. His hands only lightly brushed her shoulder when he helped her off with her spencer, but an echo of his touch lingered as he escorted her in to the parlour.

The parlour was another small room, but rendered cheerful by a flickering fire and personal items placed about the room. A chair held a piece of mending in progress. A copy of *La Belle Assemblée* lay open on a table.

Less cheerful, three ladies stood awaiting her entrance as if expecting a dragon to appear.

Keating brought her to them, first to a regal-looking woman with dark hair shot through with silver and the same startling blue eyes as her son.

'Mother, may I present to you my wife, the former Emily Duprey.'

Emily found not a hint of friendliness in those eyes. 'Ma'am,' she said softly. 'I am pleased to meet you.'

Lady Keating did not speak, but accepted the hand Emily extended to her.

Keating continued to the elderly ladies standing next to his mother. One, as if made of only bone and skin, leaned heavily on a cane. The other appeared sturdier, but was hump-shouldered and bent over.

'Let me present my mother's aunts,' Keating said. 'Lady Pipham and Miss Nuthall.'

Miss Nuthall glared at her, but Lady Pipham regarded her with a shy smile.

Emily extended her hand to each of them, shaking gently, a little in fear of breaking them. 'I am honoured.'

The arthritic butler at that moment entered, carrying a tea tray, the cups rattling like window panes in a storm. Emily held her breath as he made his precarious way, sure the pot, cups and small plate of ginger cakes would topple on to the floor. Keating took it from his hands and placed it upon the table. The butler bowed himself out of the room.

'Shall we sit,' said the Dowager Lady Keating. She dipped gracefully on to a satin-covered armchair. The elderly ladies found chairs for themselves, but sat with more effort.

Lady Keating added with a note of sarcasm, 'I suspect you need refreshment after your *long* journey.'

'You are very kind,' said Emily.

To her relief, Keating sat next to her on a sofa. She did not know if his support was genuine, but she welcomed it. The news of their marriage had obviously not been met with happy wishes.

Lady Keating poured. 'You understand this news of your…elopement comes as a great shock to us. Guy was not reared to perpetrate such folly. Indeed, he gave us no idea of this plan.'

'I am sorry it distresses you,' Emily said. 'It was not our intention to do so.'

'It is not quite the thing, you know,' added Miss Nuthall. 'A Gretna Green wedding is not quite the thing. It is not done in our family.'

Lady Pipham murmured, 'There was cousin Letitia…'

'Never mind *her*,' said Miss Nuthall repressively.

Keating rubbed his brow. Emily wished he would speak, because she did not know quite what to say. None of her exact attention to behaviour in polite society quite covered this situation. Lady Keating handed her the cup of tea and she sipped, relieved at having something else to do.

'Our housekeeper is preparing a room,' Lady Keating said. 'The chamber adjoining Guy's. It shall be ready directly.'

Had Lord Keating—Guy—given instructions to put her in a separate room? It was the way of married people in society, she knew. She was uncertain if she were pleased or disappointed that he'd not insisted she share his room.

'I hope this will not inconvenience you,' she said politely.

'My daughter will have no room.' Lady Keating folded her hands in her lap, but her fingers pressed into the skin.

'Oh!' exclaimed Emily. 'I am sorry—'

'No need,' said Keating quickly. 'Cecily is at school and has no need of a room here.' He paused. 'As you well know, Mother.'

Emily had not even known Keating had a sister. She opened her mouth to remark again upon this, but stopped herself. It would not improve matters to admit she knew so little about her husband. She took another sip of tea.

'Dear Cessy,' murmured Lady Pipham.

'Tell me, Miss Duprey—' began Lady Keating.

Her son interrupted her. 'She is my wife, Mother.'

'Oh, yes.' She smiled, but mirthlessly.

'Perhaps you could call me Emily, if that would be more comfortable for you.' Emily truly sympathised with Lady Keating. It must be difficult to give up one's title and status without warning, and to a stranger as well.

'Emily.' The Dowager pronounced her name with asperity. 'Do your parents know of this…this escapade of yours?'

Emily felt her face flush. 'No, ma'am.'

'I am a little acquainted with your mother,' said Lady Keating with disapproval. 'And my husband spoke of your father on occasion.'

Oh, dear. The discreditable Baron and Baroness Duprey were obviously not a desirable connection, but Emily was well aware of that fact. Her parents were a blight upon herself as well.

Keating stood. 'I will check on your room.'

Half an hour later Guy settled his wife into the bedchamber prepared for her. He could barely speak, he was so ashamed of his mother's shockingly poor manners. Even Aunt Dorrie had been disagreeable. He knew the news of his elopement would upset them, but he'd no idea they would behave so abominably. He marched back to the parlour.

His mother looked up from reading her magazine. 'Is your *wife* quite comfortable in Cessy's room?'

'My…wife is due any room I wish to rent for her,' he snapped.

'Then perhaps she will take over all these rooms, and we shall be on the street.' His mother's voice caught on a strangled sob. 'How could you do this, Guy? Marry into such a family and court such scandal? The Dupreys are not good *ton* at all. He's a gamester, you know, and she is said to drink.'

'The daughter had pretty manners, though,' murmured Lady Pipham.

Guy walked over to his frail great-aunt and placed a kiss on the cap covering her thinning white hair. 'Thank you, Aunt Pip.'

He stood next to Aunt Pip's chair, regarding Aunt Dorrie and his mother. These three ladies had always doted upon him and his sister Cessy. His mother had never made any secret of her hope for a fantastic match for him, teasing him to offer for young ladies whose papas would never have given him the time of day. The sad state of the family finances could easily be guessed by anyone who had encountered the perennially unlucky and now deceased Lord Keating and his elder son.

Emily Duprey had been a godsend, though he doubted God would approve of his methods of snaring her any more than his mother and great-aunts would. Or he himself.

'Emily is a respectable girl, Mother,' Guy said. 'No scandal attaches to her, and I'll wager you will not complain when her money pays your bills.'

'Money? Hmmph!' His mother glared at him. 'The family is headed for River Tick.'

'The family may be done up, but Emily has an inheritance,' he continued. 'If anything, our marriage prevents her father from throwing away her fortune on his gaming.'

Aunt Dorrie stared at him with a horrified expression. 'Can you mean you eloped with that girl for her money? It is the outside of enough.'

The dignified, but impoverished and impractical Miss Nuthall was indeed correct to a fault about his motive for marrying Emily Duprey. By God, the ladies knew their finances were in a sad way, even if they did not know the true extent of their difficulties. Why would they fault him for marrying his way out of it? Was this not preferable to his father and brother's empty promises of fortune at some faro bank?

His grip tightened on the arm of Aunt Pip's chair. 'My reasons for marrying Emily Duprey are none of your concern, and I will thank you to accord her every courtesy in this house.'

Aunt Pip bent her head. Aunt Dorrie and his mother glared at him.

'We have no choice, do we?' his mother whispered.

'No,' he agreed. 'You do not. I must also tell you that I took the liberty of asking Kirby to attend to Emily.'

His mother straightened in her chair. 'You gave my maid to that girl?'

Guy gritted his teeth before speaking. 'I borrowed her. And you would have done better by offering my wife her services yourself. You have been sadly remiss in hospitality, Mother.'

His mother did not even have the grace to look ashamed.

Guy forced himself to take a breath and to regain some composure lest he say more to his mother than was prudent. He knew she had always been unrealistic in her aspirations for her children. He could forgive her wishing he'd made a better match.

Still, she ought to have been kinder to Emily. There was no excuse for her rudeness. Her open disapproval made the whole business worse.

If his mother insisted upon keeping her head in the clouds as she had done during her marriage and the succession of her eldest son, it was none of Guy's problem. Rupert had been as big a wastrel as their father, but their mother thought the sun rose and set upon his sallow complexion and bloodshot eyes. To be fair, she could never think ill of any of her children, nor begrudge them any of their heart's desires. Why, she'd insisted upon sending Cessy to that dashed expensive school. Until his marriage, Guy had been racking his brains as to how to pay the fees.

Emily walked back in to the parlour, where there remained a tense silence. Guy's stomach clenched as it always did when he saw her. Would his guilt over marrying her ever dissipate?

She addressed his mother. 'Lady Keating, thank you so much for the services of your maid. She was most helpful.'

His mother barely looked up. 'You are welcome, I am sure.'

Emily turned to Guy. 'I wonder if I might speak to you a moment, sir?' She looked as if the tension in this household had indeed taken a toll.

'Of course,' he said, conscious that her discomfort ultimately lay at his door.

He stepped out into the hall with her. 'What is it, my dear?'

She winced a little. 'I…I think I should call upon my parents. It is not yet the dinner hour, and I might still find them at home. I feel it my duty to inform them of…of my marriage.'

He nodded. 'I will go with you.' Another unpleasantness to endure this day. Might as well get it done with.

She looked faintly surprised. 'Do you wish to come with me?'

He tried to smile at her. 'It would be shabby indeed if I allowed you to go alone.'

A ghost of a smile flitted across her face. 'I thank you. I need only don my coat and hat.'

She fled back to her room and Guy found his own coat and beaver hat.

Minutes later they were on the street. Her parents' rooms were close by, but in a more fashionable building. As they walked in the fine autumn afternoon, Guy could think of nothing to say to her, except to warn her of cracks in the pavement or bid her take care as they crossed the street.

When they reached the door of the house, Emily hesitated. He squeezed her arm, and she gave him a grateful look.

Guy sounded the knocker and a footman opened the door. From a doorway, a stately butler appeared.

'Miss Duprey,' the butler said in a monotone.

'Sutton,' she returned. 'Are my parents in?'

'Indeed,' intoned Sutton with barely a glance towards Guy. 'Your mother is in the back parlour.'

'Would you ask my father to join us there?'

Sutton flicked his fingers at the footman, who had been more open in his curiosity. The footman bowed and rushed off as the butler disappeared into another room.

Emily took a deep breath. 'Well,' she said. She cleared her throat and led him to the back parlour.

She knocked on the door before entering. Lady Duprey reclined upon a sofa. She looked up and adjusted the fine shawl that had slipped from her shoulders. 'Oh, Emily, it is you. I thought perhaps I had a caller.' She noticed Guy and sat up, patting her curls, still untouched by grey. She remained a very handsome woman, though she must be well near her fiftieth year.

'I see we do have a caller.' Lady Duprey's eyes kindled with interest as she extended her hand to Guy.

'Mama, may I present to you Viscount Keating,' Emily said.

Guy took the lady's hand, returning her limpid grasp and smelling sherry on the lady's breath. 'I am pleased to meet you, Lady Duprey.' What kind of mother was this, that she greeted a stranger with more interest than a daughter who had been absent for several days?

'Mama, I have been away, you know.'

Lady Duprey's gaze reluctantly wandered from Guy to her daughter. 'Yes…' She appeared lost in thought for a spell. 'Did you leave us a note? I cannot recall what it said.'

'I did,' Emily answered, as if this were the most normal conversation in the world. 'I told you I would be away for a while. Now I am back.'

Lady Duprey appeared to lose interest in this conversation. She turned her attention back to Guy. 'Won't you sit down, Lord Keating?' She patted the space next to her.

The door opened and Lord Duprey rushed in. 'What the deuce is so important, I ask you, that I must be interrupted? I have better things to occupy my time.' He saw Guy. 'Oh, Keating. What the devil are you doing here?'

'Papa…' Emily spoke in a wavering voice.

By God, perhaps this marriage had been right after all, Guy thought. Anything would be better than living with these unnatural parents who had not even heeded that their daughter had been gone almost a fortnight.

Guy interrupted Emily. 'Lord Duprey, Lady Duprey, we have come to announce our marriage. Your daughter and I were wed not more than five days ago.'

'What?' exclaimed Lady Duprey.

Lord Duprey gave a bark of a laugh.

'Yes, Mama, I am married,' Emily said. 'To…to Lord Keating. We will place an announcement in the papers in due time. I came to tell you of this and to arrange for my possessions to be sent to Thomas Street.'

'Well, we must drink to this, mustn't we?' said Lady Duprey eagerly. 'Pull the bell and desire Sutton to bring something fitting.'

Emily meekly did her bidding, but Guy fumed that his wife was made to arrange her own family celebration.

A bottle of French champagne was produced and poured. After the butler left the room, Lord Duprey lifted his glass. 'Here's to another daughter launched without me spending a groat. I must say, I thought this one too plain to catch a man without exerting myself. My luck has been running capital well lately.'

Emily turned bright red, and it was only with effort Guy managed not to plant his new father-in-law a facer. Baron Duprey tossed down the contents of his glass, while his wife poured herself another.

'I must be off,' Duprey said. 'Pressing engagement, you know.'

Guy stepped into his path to the door. 'One moment, sir. When may I call upon you to discuss business?'

Lord Duprey laughed. 'Business, you say? What the devil. You may call tomorrow, if you have a mind to. Not too early.'

Guy watched in stunned silence as Baron Duprey rushed out of the room without having said one word of a personal nature to his daughter.

Emily was certain her cheeks must be beet red. She was so mortified at her parents' behaviour, she could not bear to look up from the Aubusson carpet for fear of what expression she might see on Keating's face. What must he think of them? It was humiliating.

'If you will excuse me,' she said to her mother and Keating, who still gaped at the doorway through which her father had fled. 'I believe I shall attend to the removal of my things.'

She hurried to the room she'd occupied while her parents were in Bath, it seeming as foreign to her as the room in Thomas Street. Neither felt like home.

Once, perhaps, Malvern had felt like home, with its sunlit bedchambers and cheerful nursery. The family estate had seen many carefree childhood days, but even its walls seemed tainted now.

Besides, Malvern was rented for the time being and given that she could not expect her father to cease his gaming, it would probably remain rented, the revenue used to keep her family afloat.

She stood in the middle of the room, not sure what to do first.

'Excuse me, miss.' Lady Duprey's maid hovered at her door, her young niece with her. 'Is it true, miss?' Shelty asked. 'Is it true you are married to that gentleman?'

News travelled very fast among servants.

'Yes, it is true, Shelty.' Emily replied. 'He is Lord Keating. And I am afraid I must beg your assistance in packing up my possessions.'

'Hester, do whatever Miss Duprey—oh, I mean, her ladyship requests.' The older woman pushed her niece into the room. The girl, about sixteen years of age, had come to Bath from Chelsea where her father, a cobbler, owned a small shop and had been blessed with five daughters. Two of the others had gone into service. Hester was the last to be placed.

'My lady, would you be needing a maid in your gentleman's house?' Shelty looked at her hopefully. 'I would be beholden if you would take Hester here. It has become a mite difficult for her here.'

'Difficult?'

Shelty looked abashed. 'Well, you know, she is a pretty thing, and I'm afraid your father has taken notice of her.'

How much worse could her family get? Emily closed her eyes, remembering her sister Madeleine. Much worse.

'Of course she can come.' Emily smiled at the girl. 'Can we find a portmanteau to pack up some clothes for a day or two? And a trunk for the rest?'

Emily opened the drawer of her bureau and unrolled one of her spare corsets. Out fell a cloth purse. She breathed a sigh of relief. She'd no doubt her father had searched her room for her grandmother's pearls and emerald ring, but her guess had been right that he would not disturb her undergarments. She put the purse into the portmanteau. She rooted around in the drawer until she found the envelope containing the money she'd hidden from him.

Half an hour later she returned to the parlour. When she told Keating she would be bringing her maid with her, he'd looked rather grim, but perhaps that was due to being forced into her mother's company for such a spell.

When they made to leave, Lady Duprey extended her hand to Keating again. 'Do come to call any time, dear boy,' she purred. 'Welcome to the family.'

Keating mumbled something Emily could not make out. He turned to her. 'I'll give the butler the direction to deliver your trunk.'

After he'd left the room, Emily planted a dutiful kiss upon her mother's cheek. 'Goodbye, Mama,' she said, but her mother had poured herself the last of the champagne and had returned to perusing the magazine on the table beside her.

The young maid stood waiting with a portmanteau,

looking much more eager to embrace her new life than Emily felt.

'I am forever beholden to you, my lady,' the girl said in a shy voice. 'I will do anything you wish, I promise.'

Emily gave her a reassuring smile. 'Thank you for your willingness to change houses, Hester. I am in need of a maid.'

She glanced around the place. At least there was nothing to regret in leaving behind this old, so very empty part of her life.

As she and Keating strolled down the pavement towards Thomas Street, the maid trailing them, he threaded her arm through his.

Emily thought she might weep for the kindness of the gesture.

Chapter Three

Nothing imaginable could have put Guy so much in charity with his wife than this visit to her parents had done. Why, he could almost conceive himself a champion for whisking her away from that bleak atmosphere. The behaviour of his mother and great-aunts paled in comparison to Baron and Baroness Duprey, and surely, his mother, Aunt Pip and Aunt Dorrie would warm up to Emily in time. There was nothing to dislike in her.

Guy's heart actually felt buoyant. He managed to exert enough diplomacy to make their dinner go on comfortably. Aunt Pip, bless her heart, even ventured to ask Emily a few polite questions. And Emily, as ever, behaved in a perfectly proper fashion, saying nothing incorrect. He could not precisely remember anything she'd said, but he was certain of its faultlessness.

It had been an exhausting day, and Emily could not be blamed for retiring to her room early. His mother and aunts shortly thereafter bid their goodnights.

Guy remained in the parlour, pouring his third glass of brandy by the light of the fireplace. He'd extinguished the candles out of a habit of economy. Soon such miserly ways would be unnecessary, however.

He experienced only a twinge of guilt for being glad Emily's fortune was nearly in his hands. He would pay her back every penny, he vowed he would, once the estate became profitable again. In the meantime, she would never again suffer the slights of attention he'd witnessed at her parents' house. He might have no affection for her, but he would care for her, as was his duty.

Guy drained his glass of its contents and rose to his feet. His wife might be asleep by now, warm between her blankets, smelling as only a woman could.

Perhaps he ought to contemplate performing his husbandly duty. He'd not attempted a repeat of that first night, knowing he'd hurt her.

Come to think of it, though, she'd not complained. She'd not acted as if the marriage act was abhorrent to her. Perhaps he could be very gentle with her.

All concerns about his ability to perform on his marriage night had disappeared after he'd forced himself to go through the motions. Ultimately he'd experienced all the pleasure a man could expect. Perhaps he had been too long absent from a woman's bed, but that was not it. He'd remained celibate for longer periods. Perhaps it had been his wife's rather sweet response to him, so frightened, yet compliant, even willing.

Still, it seemed devilish shabby of him to enjoy himself with a woman he'd tricked into marriage in order to plunder her fortune. Reprehensible.

Such thoughts had prevented him from approaching her again in those uncomfortable inns. Tonight, however, he felt a decided tenderness towards her. He had rescued her from that dismal family. That had been good of him, and he owed it to her to give her what all women coveted. A child.

He lit one small candle from the dwindling fire and,

keeping a hand on the wall to steady himself, walked down the hallway to his bedchamber. Once inside, he placed the candle on a side table and pulled off his boots. He untied his neckcloth and flung it aside. Shrugging out of his coat and waistcoat, he stared at the door connecting his room with his wife's.

It was his duty, he repeated to himself, though the stirrings of arousal suggested baser motivations. With a light knock of warning, he opened the door. The bed linens rustled and she sat up, a blur of white muslin in the dim light of his little candle shining through the doorway.

'My lord?' she said. The sound of her voice, husky from sleep, and the thought of her dressed only in a nightdress further stirred his senses.

How did a husband ask his wife if he might bed her? He smiled reassuringly, though she could not possibly see the expression on his face. 'Do you wish my company?'

She remained still, like a ghost about to dissolve into the air. 'If it pleases you,' she finally said.

The blood already coursed through his veins. 'It pleases me.'

She drew back the covers and slid over, making room for him. His loins ached as he made his way to the bed. Removing his shirt and breeches, he climbed in beside her. Her hair was bound in a braid and he longed to release it, but dared not, lest it offend her sensibilities. He pulled her towards him, savouring the feel of her feminine curves from beneath her nightdress, but wanting, needing to feel more. He drew the thin nightdress over her head and dropped it to the floor.

His hands explored her breasts, gently at first. She gasped, but did not move away. Encouraged, he stroked with more intensity until her nipples peaked under his fingers. His breath quickened.

The candle in his room guttered and went out. Darkness wrapped around them like a blanket, heightening the sensation of her skin beneath his touch. Her scent, lavender and something indefinable, filled his nostrils, and the cadence of her breathing sounded in his ears.

Desire shot through him. He wanted her pliant beneath him. He wanted to take her quick and rough and ease the aching need inside him.

But he resisted, determined to make the experience pleasant for her as well. She'd been so tight when he'd entered her that first time, but warm and wet and firm around him. He wanted this again. Needed it, but he would take care not to hurt her.

He let his hand slide down her abdomen. She arched beneath his touch, the change in position slight, but enough to encourage him. He moved his hand between her legs. She was already sweetly slick, and he'd be damned if he'd wait too much longer.

But she deserved some pleasure from this experience as well as he. He gently stroked between her legs. She made a tiny noise, and her breath came faster, the sound intensifying his arousal.

He could wait no longer. He mounted her, and her legs spread open almost as if to welcome him. He forced himself to enter her slowly, carefully, but no sooner had he done so than all control fled. A primitive rhythm overtook him, and he moved to it, feeling her hips rise to meet him at the perfect beat. Faster. Harder.

He felt a flutter from her body, like sweet tiny fingers squeezing him from inside her. He could bear no more. His release erupted in a spasm of pleasure even more intense than he'd hoped.

He collapsed on top of her, all energy spent, all muscles relaxed into liquid. Conscious suddenly of how heavy he must be, he slid off of her, but held her in his arms, as soft as if he cuddled a kitten.

All would work out well, he was certain. He would not regret this marriage. He could almost feel hopeful about it. They faced each other, so close her breath cooled his passion-heated face. He stroked her cheek and rested his fingers beneath her chin, closing the distance between them, tasting her lips and pulling her flush against him. She sighed and relaxed in his arms.

Yes, their marriage would be a good one, he was certain.

With that final thought, he plunged deeply into sleep.

Emily woke to the sound of rain rattling against the window pane. The light from the window barely illuminated the room and it had taken her a few seconds to realise dawn had come.

She rolled over to survey the man still sleeping next to her, his hair so dark against the white linens, his face relaxed and boyish. The bedcovers were tangled between his legs and all of his glorious body was exposed to her view. She felt wicked looking at it, but was unable to help herself. He was a truly beautiful man, all lean muscle, shoulders broad enough to carry her burdens.

She felt near to bursting with joy. Who would have thought marriage could bring such pleasure? It had been all she could do to remain still and quiet during his love-making. Her body had seemed to move without her saying so, and she almost cried out when that explosion of delight erupted inside her. She'd almost behaved like a wanton woman.

Smiling, she dared to touch one lock of his hair.

His eyes opened, their intense blue startling her. He

stared blankly at her, then comprehension seemed to come to him, and one corner of his mouth turned up.

'Good morning,' he said.

'Good morning,' she replied. What more was there to say? Surely ladies did not thank their husbands for making love to them. Or did they?

He reached out and touched her cheek. For a moment she thought he might make love to her again, and her heart skittered in anticipation, but instead he rose and groped for his breeches, slipping them on with his back to her.

He picked up her nightdress and handed it to her. 'Your maid may knock at any moment.'

A maid could be sent away, though, could she not? Emily dared not suggest this, however. She did not wish to risk disrupting the magic of the previous night. She sat up in the bed and donned her nightdress.

As he put his muscular arms through the sleeves of his shirt, she asked, 'Is there anything you wish me to do today?'

He looked at her. 'I can think of nothing. I will ask my mother to acquaint you with the workings of this household, though there is not much to learn on that score. I hope to provide better for you soon.'

His mother would derive little enjoyment out of that task, she was certain, but it would please him if she could find some way to ease the tensions her presence brought to the household. She wanted so very much to please him.

'Perhaps there is some service I might do for your mother,' she said.

'That is too good of you.' He again touched her cheek, his expression softening. 'My mother will soon learn to appreciate you, I promise. She was merely taken by surprise.'

The feel of his fingers on her face nearly drove out all

rational thought. 'I do understand. I will endeavour to put her mind at ease.'

He leaned down and kissed her, and she thought her spirit might soar through the heavens in pure ecstasy. She could barely keep from plunging her fingers into his hair and opening her mouth to taste more of him.

He broke off. 'I will call upon your father today.'

She could not imagine why he would wish to do so.

He regarded her with a serious expression. 'Emily, I promise to do right by you. The sooner I get control of your fortune, the better. I would not have your father plunder it.'

'My fortune?'

His face stiffened. 'The money your aunt left you.'

'My aunt?' She wrinkled her brow. 'But that is hardly a fortune, Guy. I have it here in the drawer.'

She hurried to the bureau and removed the leather envelope, handing it to him. He opened it and pulled out the five ten-pound banknotes.

He gave her a questioning look, bordering on alarm. 'What is this?'

Emily felt a rock forming in her stomach. 'It is my inheritance.'

Guy fingered the banknotes, staring at them as if they were some mysterious Chinese currency. Fifty pounds? No, this could not be the sum of her inheritance. She must be mistaken. There had to be more, there had to be.

His fingers trembled and he crushed them, the paper crackling. 'This is all of it?' His neck was so tense he could barely talk.

Her brows knit in confusion. 'Yes, all. I would not withhold it from you.'

Only fifty pounds? Guy's insides twisted into coils. Panic threatened to cut off his breath.

'You may keep the money, of course,' she added, her eyes wary.

He smoothed the notes and put them back in the envelope. He handed it to her, took it back again, and finally thrust it at her. 'Keep it,' he snapped. 'I must get dressed.'

What he needed more than anything right now was to get away from her before he lost total control of his temper. She must be mistaken. There must be more money, or what would become of them all?

Leaving her incredulous, standing with the envelope in her hands, he spun on his heel and rushed into his bedchamber, slamming the door behind him.

Guy's caped topcoat and beaver hat were soaked from the rain, as he paced outside the building where the Dupreys lived. He'd spent much of the morning walking the streets of Bath, heedless of the weather. The sense of foreboding was strong, as strong as before a battle when one went through the motions of eating and sleeping, knowing the next day life might be snatched away.

It was finally past noon, though the clouds obscured any confirmation of sun high in the sky. Holding his breath, he sounded the knocker.

The butler opened the door, took his coat and hat, and ushered him into the same parlour where he'd been the day before. He cooled his heels there a good half an hour before Baron Duprey sauntered in. The man chuckled, interrupting Guy's anxious pacing in front of the fireplace.

'Well, Keating, I always took you for a man of sense. Knew your father, who hadn't a groat of the stuff, but word's been you're cut from different cloth.'

Guy could only stare at him.

The Baron went on. 'Can't imagine what maggot got

in your brain to marry that daughter of mine. Thought I'd never be rid of her.'

Guy took a step towards him. 'Do not speak of my wife in that manner.'

Duprey laughed. 'Next you will persuade me you have a *regard* for her.'

Guy's right hand closed into a fist. He'd relish the opportunity to vent his disordered emotions on this poor excuse for a man.

Still chuckling, Duprey sat on one of the chairs and fingered the sleeve of his coat. 'Now what business must you conduct with me? What is so important you disturb my peace at this early hour?'

A porcelain clock on the mantel chimed one o'clock.

'My wife's assets are no longer yours to control,' Guy said bluntly. 'I came to arrange their transfer to me.'

The Baron pressed folded hands against his chin and gave Guy a blank stare. 'Assets?'

'Do not humbug me, sir,' Guy persisted. 'You have been bantering it all about town that you have control of your daughter's fortune. I demand you turn it over to me. If we need a solicitor to draw up papers, I shall arrange it.'

A smile slowly creased Duprey's face. 'Ah, the clouds clear.' He chuckled again. 'This is a famous one.'

'Pray include me in your jest, sir,' Guy fumed.

The older man's eyes brimmed with a malevolent mirth. 'Quite an inventive story, do you not agree? It kept my creditors at bay, I assure you. How fortunate I no longer require the ruse, since you make further use of the tale impossible. Won a big sum off young Jasperson, fool that he is.'

Guy's heart beat erratically. 'Explain yourself, if you please.'

'I did explain myself,' said the Baron pleasantly. 'I concocted that story about Emily's inheritance in order to extend my credit. I was in Dun territory, my lad. What else would you have me do?'

Guy felt blood drain from his face.

'The tale contained but a speck of truth,' Duprey went on. 'All the best tales do, you know. The girl did inherit. About one hundred pounds. I managed to get my fingers on half of it before she snatched it away. Never could find the rest and I looked for it, indeed I did. Everyone knew Lady Upford cocked up her toes, so could I help it if they believed she'd dropped a huge sum instead of that damned pittance? Left the bulk of it to some scientific society, for which I shall never forgive her.'

A pittance, not a fortune? Nothing but a ruse? Like a simpleton, Guy had fallen for Duprey's story. It did not console him one bit that a myriad of other fools had done the same.

'And don't be looking for a dowry,' said Duprey, waving his finger at Guy. 'That went last Season after she wrecked my plans to marry her off to Heronvale's brother. What a honey pot that would have been.' The man sighed. 'I despaired of being rid of her, I tell you. Who could have guessed a fool like you would marry a dull piece like her? Ha!'

Guy marched over to the man's chair and grabbed him by the lapels of his coat. 'Do not ever speak of my wife in that manner.' He lifted Duprey from his seat and thrust him down again, heading for the door.

'Do not tell me yours was a love match,' the Baron called after him.

Guy heard the man's laughter all the way out of the building and down to the street.

What the devil was he to do? No fortune. No damned

fortune. No money at all. Just one more charge upon his finances.

Damn his idiocy. He'd bought the tale of a fortune, lapping it up as the milk of his salvation. Not only had Duprey boasted of it, others had passed it on. There had been no rumour of it being false. Ordinarily he would have waited for some verification, but Cyprian Sloane, that notorious fortune hunter, had begun to turn his charm on Emily, and Guy had feared he'd be cut out if he did not seize his opportunity now.

He'd gambled on the rumours being true. Did his folly know no bounds? He'd gambled. And lost.

Guy strode back to Thomas Street and entered the house still in a towering rage. He shoved his coat and hat into Bleasby's frail hands and headed to the library, slamming the door behind him.

What the devil was he to do now?

He searched the cabinet in the room for a bottle, finding some old port. He poured himself a glass and downed it in one gulp. He poured another glass.

From the corner of his eye he saw a movement and swung around.

There his wife sat, in a chair by the window, a book in her hand. He had the insane thought that she must have been desperate to read whatever was in this room. Three books about farming methods he'd rescued from rot at Annerley. One dusty volume of sermons that had been left on the shelf when they'd leased the place.

Her eyes widened. Indeed, he must look like a wild man. He felt like a man who had lost his senses.

'What is amiss?' she asked, her voice coming out hoarse and nearly inaudible.

He laughed and downed another full glass of port. He

poured a third. 'What is amiss? I have been to see your
father. That is what is amiss.'

Two spots of red appeared on her cheeks. 'What did he
say to upset you?'

'He said that you are penniless.'

Her brows knit.

He had no patience for her confusion. 'Do not tell me
you were not aware he was passing you off as an heiress.'

She paled. 'I was not aware of it.'

He gulped down more port. 'Well, neither was I.'

She stood. 'My father said I was an heiress?'

'He led the world to believe you were. A big inheritance from your aunt, Lady Upford.'

'It was not a big inheritance,' she said.

He laughed again and finished the port. 'Yes. Now I
know.'

She stared at him, her bland face showing only a glimmer of confusion. Did it make it better or worse that she'd
not known of her father's tale about her? Perhaps it would
have been some meagre comfort to think she'd deceived
him as much as he'd deceived her.

Her distress convinced him. She was innocent. The vil-
lains in this sordid mess were her damnable knave of a
father—and her husband. God help him, he resented her
anyway, hated that blank expression on her face, despised
the fact that he was saddled with her for life. If not for
her, he could search for a genuine heiress. Marry his way
out of this fix.

How would he now rebuild Annerley? How would he
return its fields to planting, its tenants to prosperity instead
of wasting away for lack of food and decent shelter? How
would he provide for his mother? Would his elderly aunts
end their days in a poorhouse, cold and hungry? What
harm would befall his little sister, so blissfully unaware

of their troubles? How would he pay for her school? Find her a husband? The list was endless.

Waterloo had seemed like a walk in the park compared to the devastation he'd discovered when he returned home. Annerley House was a crumbling ruin. His brother had put a bullet through his own head, leaving a bloody mess and a mountain of debts. It had taken Guy months to sort through the disorder of the family finances. His father's man of business had long abandoned the family as a lost cause, and his brother had continued in his father's footsteps, raiding the capital and leaving nothing more than entailed property. Crumbling, rotting, fallow entailed property.

Emily's fortune was supposed to settle the debts and turn Annerley around. The land would be prosperous again. All he needed was time.

Now what would he do? What would he *do*? She'd let him down, and now he had one more person to worry about. Two, if he considered her maid. He supposed the maid was also his responsibility. By God, he'd pensioned off his father's valet and done without, but now he had an extra maid to support.

He glared at his wife, his penniless wife, aware of the injustice of his anger, but who else was there to vent his temper upon?

Her expression changed, her eyes widening and her mouth dropping open, then closing into a thin, grim line. Her eyes narrowed, and her voice came out low and filled with suppressed emotion. 'You married me to gain a fortune.'

Guy's level of anxiety was so high he snapped back at her. 'Of course I did. I needed the funds.'

She continued, her fingers clutching the book, her body

trembling. 'And what of your story of asking my father's permission to court me and he refusing?'

He was feeling perverse enough to tell the truth. Hang his vow to protect her from it. 'I never asked your father. I wish to God I had.'

'You lied to me?' Her voice shook.

He met her eyes. 'Yes.'

Then she did something he would never have anticipated. She threw the book at him, the action such a shock he barely had time to raise his arm to deflect it.

'That is for lying to me!' Her eyes flashed, and her face flushed with passion. Inexplicably, he felt a flash of carnal desire as unexpected as the book flying across the room.

'Why did you need this fortune of mine?' she cried. He'd not known her voice could have such volume, nor as much emotion.

'I haven't a feather to fly with, my dear,' he said.

'Do not call me that!'

He blinked. Her words struck him with nearly the same violence as the missile she'd thrown.

She paced back and forth in front of him, her arms folded across her chest. 'Where did you meet my father?' she demanded. 'Where did you hear these tales of my fortune?'

He'd once seen a mechanical doll, one that moved after a key was turned in its back. She was like such a doll coming to life, suddenly filled with genuine animation. He almost forgot to answer her question. 'At a card game.'

She twisted around as if to look for something else to throw at him.

'I cannot believe it!' she cried with a voice low and harsh and echoing his own rage. 'You are like him.'

'Like who?' he couldn't help but ask.

'Like *him*.' Her eyes shot daggers at him. 'You are a liar and a gamester, and I cannot believe I have married a man like my father. I thought I had escaped him!'

Her words stung as sharply as if she'd slapped him in the face. He stooped down and picked up the book, *Modern Concepts in Agriculture, 1732,* hardly modern, but a book he thought might be useful should he ever again have crops to plant.

Words leapt to the tip of his tongue. He would tell her he was nothing like her father. He'd done it all to save his family and estate and all the people who depended upon him.

What was the use? He had lied to her. Manipulated her. Tried to take her money from her. He was too painfully like her father.

She brushed past him with a swish of skirts, leaving the room like a Fury of ancient Greek mythology. It felt like she sucked the air from the room as she left.

Guy sank into a chair and put his head in his hands. He could not spare a thought about what he had done to her. He needed to think his way out of this morass.

What else could he do to save them? He had to try to reverse his ill luck in some manner.

Nothing came immediately to mind. If one could no longer marry for money, where was one to win a fortune?

The answer reluctantly dawned, but he could only feel like a condemned man awakening to the day of execution.

He would become a gamester, haunting gentlemen's clubs and gaming hells for the next big game. Just as she accused him, he would wager all their futures on a turn of the cards, exactly like his father and brother before him.

Exactly like her father as well.

Chapter Four

A week later, Emily walked into the Upper Assembly room on the arm of her husband, her first public appearance as his wife. She would have gladly forsaken the opportunity, but his mother pined for entertainment, and he had relented. Emily could hardly refuse her husband's request she accompany them.

Only two tiers of seating had been set up on the sides of the large room, and perhaps a hundred guests filled it. Not a bad showing for early October, but not even approaching the numbers at the height of the Bath Season. She glanced nervously around.

Her mother sat on the opposite side of the room next to the ageing Lord Cranton, whom Emily knew to be her latest flirtation. She leaned over the gentleman, giving him an ample view of her generous bosom. He laughed and whispered something in her ear. Emily touched her cheek, hot with embarrassment. Even more mortifying, her mother-in-law and husband were also gazing in Lady Duprey's direction. Her mother-in-law gave a disapproving huff.

Emily supposed she would have to greet her mother for propriety's sake. She dearly hoped her mother would be civil and return her greeting. Much depended upon how many glasses of wine her mother had consumed at dinner. On the other hand, if her father was present this evening, she hoped to avoid him altogether. He was bound to be in the card room, where her husband would certainly be headed.

Like a true gamester, her husband had been out every night since their arrival in Bath, coming home with the first glow of dawn. She knew because she was often still tossing and turning when he came in and could hear him moving about. Sometimes his step was light. A winning night, no doubt. Sometimes he moved like his feet were bound with irons. A losing streak. Only when the sounds from his room ceased could she sleep.

A dozen or so people looked towards the new Lord and Lady Keating, the ladies whispering behind their fans. Emily knew her marriage to Guy had been announced in the papers, because she'd read it there, but she and her husband had seen little of each other. They had conversed less, although he seemed inclined to put up a good front in the presence of his mother and the aunts.

'You have made us the latest *on dit*, Guy,' Lady Keating said in a petulant voice. 'I confess, I thought it might be worse. I don't suppose anyone will cut us, not that it would be of any consequence. Half of them are from the navy or the army, for goodness' sake. I declare, Bath has been overrun by military men.'

'You forget I was once a military man. Retired soldiers have to live somewhere,' Guy said.

She sniffed. 'Well, they are fair to ruining Bath. In any event, we ought to be at Annerley this time of year.'

'You know we cannot be at Annerley,' he said.

Emily wondered at the reason they could not go to the family property for the winter months. Was it rented like

Malvern? She would not be surprised, but she would not
ask. She had decided to converse as little as possible with
the man she married. Otherwise, she feared losing her
temper again.

'Let me find you some seats,' he said.

Emily noted that he spoke more to his mother than he
did to her, so perhaps he felt the same as she. He was
angry with her for having no money, even though her
father had been the real villain in this perfidy. Not Emily.
She had not deceived Guy Keating. He had deceived her.

Was there ever a man who could be trusted? Even Lord
Devlin had deceived her, making her think he would offer
for her when he was living with her sister and in love
with her. At least he'd done right by Madeleine. Their
marriage had been announced months ago.

She sighed. She'd never truly believed Devlin meant to
marry her anyway. But she'd thought Guy Keating to be
different. Why? Simply because he'd shown such kindness to his great-aunts? It seemed an absurd notion now,
to believe that one glimpse of his kindness meant he'd be
kind to her.

Guy seated them near friends of his mother's and very
properly introduced her as his wife. Emily endured the
ladies' appraising looks, knowing they were dying to ask
why this attractive man had married the very plain Emily
Duprey, daughter of the shocking Baron and Baroness.
Never mind. As was her custom, she would behave so
properly no one would have a thing to say about her.

She chatted politely to Lady Keating's friends, and
within moments, her husband excused himself, promising
to return in time for tea. Emily supposed he'd been eager
to escape to his cards. He'd certainly not felt compelled
to ask her to dance, though eight couples were at this
moment forming the first set.

Her mother-in-law, having her friends to converse with, required nothing of her, so Emily occupied herself by watching the dancers perform their figures. The ladies' dresses swirled prettily, like flower petals in a breeze. She found her toes itching to tap time to the music. She kept still, however, and tried to appear perfectly content.

Her mother glanced her way and gave her a half-hearted wave. Emily acknowledged the greeting with a nod of her head. She quickly continued to scan the room, lest she see her mother beckon her to walk over. Her eyes lit on an impeccably dressed gentleman, tall and elegant.

Mr Cyprian Sloane.

He caught her looking in his direction, and she could almost feel his steel grey eyes travelling over her in that manner that always made her think he knew what she looked like without her clothes. His full lips stretched into a knowing smile.

Oh, dear. He probably thought she'd been staring at him, but she never stared at gentlemen.

Not that Sloane was a gentleman precisely. By birth, perhaps, but he had the most shocking reputation as a rakehell. Ladies, from much younger than his thirty-odd years to much older, were said to throw themselves at him every bit as much as Caroline Lamb had at Lord Byron.

To Emily's total dismay, Mr Sloane excused himself from the people he was with and crossed the room. He could not be coming to speak to her. He could not.

He walked directly to her. 'Good evening, ladies.'

His white-toothed smile encompassed the whole group and brought their chatter to a sudden halt. Emily saw more than one set of raised eyebrows when he turned exclusively to her.

'I understand I must wish you happy, Emily…Lady Keating.' He spoke her Christian name as if she'd given him permission. She most assuredly had not. He extended his hand. What could she do but raise her own hand to him? He lifted it to his lips.

Her cheeks burned. 'Thank you.'

He held her hand a moment too long and she was forced to pull it from his grasp. He continued to discomfit her with the intensity of his gaze.

'If your…husband has not otherwise engaged you, I wonder if I might have the pleasure of the next dance.' His smooth voice paused significantly on the word *husband*.

Emily wished he would simply go away, but she could think of no excuse to refuse his request. Besides, she longed to dance. 'Very well.'

He bowed and walked away, leaving her to endure the knowing looks of her mother-in-law's cronies. The attention of Bath's most notorious womaniser did her reputation no good at all.

Emily could never quite comprehend why Sloane had bothered to pay his addresses to someone as plain as she, but, in the weeks before her elopement, he'd begun to notice her. She'd been so relieved when Guy began courting her. She'd fancied Guy had plucked her from the salivating jaws of a veritable wolf.

That was nonsense, of course. She knew that now. Guy had been far more dangerous. She'd fallen for Viscount Keating—no, for his kindness. She'd fallen for his kindness. But he'd turned out every bit as false as Cyprian Sloane.

Her gaze lifted to the crystal chandelier above the dancers, and she pretended to blink from the brightness of the flickering candles. Suddenly all was as clear as those twinkling crystals. Sloane must have heard her father's tale about her being an heiress. That was why he'd given her the scant attention he had.

But she was married now. Why attend to her still?

When the musicians tuned up for the next set, Sloane appeared at her side and threaded her arm through his to lead her to the dance floor. Emily could hear the murmurings of her mother-in-law's friends wafting behind her.

Sloane faced her in the set, his intense grey eyes riveted on her face. 'Well, Emily, my dear, you have desolated me entirely.'

My dear. What maggot entered these men's brains to assume she'd believe herself *dear* to them?

'I do not understand you, sir.'

They needed to complete the figure before he could speak to her again.

One corner of his well-defined mouth turned up. 'You have eloped with Keating and quite broke my heart.'

The steps parted them and they had to thread through the other couples before coming close again.

Emily narrowed her eyes. 'Do not speak nonsense to me.'

His brows shot up in surprise, but he retained the amusement in his countenance.

For the remainder of the set Emily endured more pretty words, more falsities. She pretended she did not hear them, but instead let herself keep step to the music. At the end of the dance, he bowed and she curtsied. He escorted her back to her seat.

To her astonishment, Guy stood there, a grim expression on his face.

'I return your lovely bride to you,' Sloane said to him with a wicked smirk.

Guy merely inclined his head, but when the man sauntered away, he gave her a stern look. She'd clearly dis-
pleased him by dancing with Sloane, but where had he
been when the music started?

'You are finished with cards so soon?' she asked in a
casual tone, determined to get her barb in first.

He did not appear to notice. 'It is time for tea,' he said,
turning from her to his mother. 'Shall I escort you both
to the tea room?'

As a good husband ought, he fetched tea for her and
sat next to her at a table shared by his mother and two of
her friends.

As the older women engrossed themselves in their own
gossip with words such as *that man* and *shocking* audible,
Emily was left in Guy's company.

He gave her a sombre look. 'I do not wish to criticise
you, my dear—' those words again '—but Cyprian Sloane
is not precisely the sort of company to keep.'

'Indeed?' she responded, having difficulty maintaining
her precise standard of composure. 'And, pray tell, how
am I to fend him off without creating a scene and calling
even more attention to myself?'

A flash of surprise lit his eyes. 'I concede your point.'

She took a satisfying sip of tea, disguising it as an ordinary one.

The look he gave her next seemed almost…caring.
'I…I would not wish your reputation to suffer. Sloane's
partiality cannot bring any good.'

He reached over and for a moment she thought he
might touch her, but he did not.

'I shall not behave with impropriety, I promise you.'
She kept her voice low. 'But I cannot prevent him from
seeking me out and I cannot stop those who wish to comment on it.' Her insides were churning, but she was not

sure if it were because he sat so close that she could feel
his breath on her face, or because he dared comment on
her behaviour. After all, he had rushed off to wager sums
at whist, leaving her to fend for herself.

'True.' His ready agreement unnerved her more than if
he'd given her a good scold.

It was his turn to sip his tea and for her to wonder what
thoughts ran through his head. It was inconceivable he
took Sloane's attentions seriously. She had never been the
sort sought after by rakes. Or any other type of gentleman,
for that matter.

He turned to his mother. 'Mother, would you enjoy
some cards this evening, or do you prefer to watch the
dancing?'

'I had hoped to play cards, I must confess,' Lady Keating replied. 'Are there other ladies in the card room?'

'Several ladies,' he said. He leaned towards Emily.
'Perhaps if you came in the card room with me, Mr Sloane
would not disturb you further.'

In spite of herself, her heart fluttered.

'You can partner my mother,' he added.

Ah, he did not desire her company after all. Emily lifted
her cup to her lips again. After a fortifying sip, she said,
'If your mother wishes it, I should be happy to partner
her.'

Very shortly after, Emily found herself seated across
from her mother-in-law at a whist table shared by an elderly gentleman and his wife, who were acquainted with
the Keatings. Unfortunately, she was positioned so that
her husband was in her view, seated in a corner with other
black-coated men who hunched over their cards with
grave, resolute expressions on their faces.

She'd seen an identical expression on her father's face.

He was in the room this very moment. She'd seen him when she entered, but, to her relief, he was too engrossed in his play to notice her.

Emily picked up the cards to deal. As soon as the deck was in her hands, habit took over. The cards rippled rhythmically as she shuffled. She could almost deal the cards without looking. Such were skills honed in a household obsessed by card-playing. She, her sisters and brother had been weaned on whist and piquet and quadrille. When her father could find no one else to play cards, he sought out his children. It was the only time he sought them out. In those days Emily would play whist until night left her yawning and rubbing her eyes, if it meant having her father's regard. Like a good father's daughter, she'd prided herself on playing better than her sisters and brother. If she'd thought it would win her father's respect, she'd been mistaken. When she won against him, he became furious.

The dealing done, Emily picked up her hand and spread the cards in a fan. A shiver ran up her spine. She felt the spades, diamonds, clubs and hearts call to her, as if beckoning her back into her father's influence.

Lady Keating and the other couple appeared not to notice. They seemed rather to find great enjoyment from the game. Lady Keating turned out to be merely competent as a player, and their opponents not as skilled. Emily held herself back from getting pulled totally into the game. Instead, she let her gaze drift to where her husband sat. He was an effective distraction.

She marvelled at the sheer symmetry of his face, the fineness of his chiselled features, the softness of his lips. She could swear the blue of his eyes glowed like sapphires in the room's candlelight. He concentrated on his cards, sitting very still in his chair, while the other men shifted at times, even occasionally rising to their feet when taking a trick.

So her husband was as cool a player at cards as he was at marriage. She shrugged. She did not care, did she?

She allowed herself to be lured back into the card game.

Cyprian Sloane leaned lazily against the door-frame of the card room, an amused expression on his face. So Keating had persuaded the so very plain and all-too-correct Emily Duprey to elope to Gretna Green? How daring.

He gave a mirthless laugh. With parents like the Baron and Baroness Duprey, a daughter might do anything to get away, even a woman as lacking in spirit as Miss Duprey.

When several gentlemen, including Keating, had turned their attention to Emily Duprey, Sloane had joined the competition. Now he could not help feel that Keating had won and he had lost.

Too bad he hadn't thought of asking her to run away with him. Not that he'd have contemplated taking her to Scotland like Keating did. Rather out of character for Keating to be so on the ball. Sloane had misjudged him.

He glanced at Keating, deep into his cards. That was a surprise as well, but he ought to have known. Bad blood always won out. Keating looked to be cut from the same cloth as his father and brother after all and would probably complete the family's journey to the River Tick.

An idea struck Sloane. Maybe Keating had believed Duprey's hum of a story about his daughter inheriting a fortune. Poor fellow, if he had. Would serve him right for winning the girl.

Sloane gave an imperceptible shrug. Virgins were more trouble than they were worth anyway. Besides, taking a maid's virginity was below even his low standards of conduct.

There were plenty of other women in the world. His eyes swept the card room. None of them, unfortunately, were in Bath.

He cast one more regretful look towards the new Lady Keating, turned around, and left.

Chapter Five

Guy sat at the desk in the library, rubbing his cold hands. He'd not bothered to light a fire, though it seemed a small, useless economy against the enormity of their debts. In a moment he'd be throwing a shawl over his shoulders like Aunt Pip.

He counted his money a third time. Last night's winnings had been modest, but then he'd been off his game shockingly. His wife had been the distraction, no doubt. True, she'd made no demands upon him during their visit to the Assembly Rooms, but he was not accustomed to having his attention divided. Dancing attendance upon a wife took much away from concentration on the cards.

He rubbed his face and stood.

Let him not fool himself. He'd scarcely given his wife a moment of his time at the Assembly. He was looking for excuses to explain the hands he'd lost, the money he'd pushed over to the winners.

The Bath crowd would certainly talk more of his card playing and lack of solicitude towards his new wife than gossip about her dancing with that rakehell, Cyprian Sloane. The man's presence vexed him, however, and he was not sure why. Perhaps because Sloane courted trouble. Other people's.

Guy ought not to be so concerned. His wife was too respectable to interest Sloane for more than a moment. Still, Guy disliked him paying any attention to her. What was the fellow about? Originally Sloane might have been after her fortune—her purported fortune—but that possibility vanished when Guy married her.

Perhaps he ought to commend himself for being the one to trick her into marriage. If Sloane had done the deed and discovered her penniless, what would his response have been?

Guy paced over to the window.

Could Sloane treat her much worse that he himself had done? He had neglected her at their first public outing. She did not deserve such treatment. None of the trouble he was in had been her fault.

Even so, he could not help resenting her. This anger did him no credit at all, but, devil take it, marrying her had made his financial situation worse. He could not even bed her now, could not risk repeating that one moment of pleasure with her, not as long as their future was so bleak. He did not dare produce an heir into this life of penury. What sort of irresponsible act would that be?

He placed his forehead against the cool pane of glass, but it did nothing to lessen the emotions boiling inside him like a cauldron of some noxious brew.

His resentment went deeper than her lack of fortune. His meagre glimmers of hope aside, he could only resent her complete lack of spontaneity, of life.

He ran a hand raggedly through his hair. He almost wished she would rail at him again. Throw another book at him. Damn him to the devil. At least there would be some excitement between them.

Any chance of making this a true marriage had disappeared when he told her he'd lied to her. He doubted she could forgive him for what he'd done to her by marrying her, for what life would be like for her if he could not reclaim their fortune.

Shivering with the chill, Guy gazed into the street.

More rain.

No relief to be gained by a brisk walk in this weather, he thought. Even the Royal Crescent would look dismal.

Like his future.

From beyond the library door he heard his great-aunts' shrill voices and other sounds of the household stirring. Poor dears. He supposed they were becoming a bit hard of hearing. He ought to join them for breakfast. He had some responsibility to keep up everyone's spirits.

And to smooth the tensions his wife's presence caused. Aunt Pip seemed inclined to be friendly to her, but Aunt Pip was no match for his mother and Aunt Dorrie. They seemed determined to continue to make Emily's life even more miserable than he had done.

Walking back to his desk, he plopped himself in the chair and placed his winnings back in the leather pouch. At least he'd come by enough blunt to buy some winter supplies for the tenants of Annerley and to pay for Cecily's fancy school. Along with the pouch, he placed the politely worded letter from the headmistress back in the drawer.

Still, these winnings were only meagre patches in a dam that was bound to burst. Postponing the inevitable, unless he could raise more blunt. There was no doubt he needed to find games played for higher stakes.

He must go to London. In London betting ran deep and huge sums were won and lost every day. In London he might win enough money at one seating to set them up for life.

In London, of course, plenty of skilled gamesters would be equally willing to take his last ha'penny. Still, what else could he do? Quietly let Annerley go to rot and its people with it?

Guy slammed the desk drawer and turned the key in the lock. His heart pounded in anxiety, for what he was about to propose to his mother and her aunts—and his wife. London could mean salvation or it could hasten the end. What a choice.

He entered the dining room, where Aunt Pip and Aunt Dorrie sat at the table, sipping their chocolate.

'Good morning,' he said, trying to put some cheer into his voice. He gave each of them a quick kiss on the cheek. 'I hope you ladies slept well.'

'That bed is an abomination,' grumbled Aunt Dorrie. 'It's a wonder I get any sleep at all.'

'Oh, I'm sure you get some, Dorrie, dear,' Aunt Pip said in her soft voice. 'I do hear your snoring from my chamber.'

'I do not…' began Dorrie in a huff.

Guy laughed. 'Well, I am certain you both look well rested, at least—' He cut himself short.

He'd not noticed Emily at the sideboard, filling a plate. 'Good morning, my dear,' he said stiffly.

She placed the plate down in front of Aunt Dorrie, giving him the barest glance. 'Good morning.' She turned to Aunt Pip. 'Lady Pipham, what shall I place upon your plate?'

Aunt Pip gave her a little smile. 'Oh, an egg, I suppose. And toast… No, a biscuit and ham.'

Guy walked over to his wife at the sideboard, reaching for his own plate. 'Bleasby usually serves them.'

She did not look up from her task. 'He woke with a dreadful cold this morning. I sent him back to bed.'

'And he went?' Guy said with surprise. 'It is not at all like him to shirk his duties.'

'I ordered him.'

She took the plate to Aunt Pip and waited at the table until he'd made his selections and sat down.

'Would you like some tea?' she asked, reaching for the pot.

He nodded. 'Thank you.'

Her demeanour remained perfectly composed. How did she accomplish that? he wondered. He feared all his worry would show on his face unless he battled constantly to conceal it. Another drain on his nerves.

She poured his tea and without a further word returned to the sideboard to place two pieces of toast on her plate. She sat down on a chair opposite his aunts and delicately spread raspberry jam on each slice.

'That is not much breakfast,' he said.

She darted a glance at him. 'It is what I like.'

He did not know what else to say to her. He watched her lift the piece of toast to her mouth and take a tiny bite. No relishing gulp of food for the self-contained new Lady Keating. A drop of jam clung to her bottom lip and her pink tongue darted out to lick it off. He remembered how her tongue had felt against his own, how she had tasted. He had to look away.

Aunt Pip and Aunt Dorrie intently chewed their food, offering no help in filling what seemed to Guy to be an oppressive silence. It was his responsibility to make the conversation, but what of? He could not speak his thoughts about tongues and tastings. He would not divulge that he meant them to go to London without his mother present. He cast about in his mind for something to say.

'I suppose I should check on Bleasby,' he finally came up with, though he ought to have thought of saying so when she'd mentioned Bleasby's illness.

'That would be good of you,' was all she responded.

His mother's entrance saved him from having to invent something else to say. He stood.

'What a dreary day.' His mother swept into the room. 'I declare I shall have nothing at all to do.'

'The rain makes my joints ache,' Aunt Dorrie said.

'It will not last, I'm sure,' assured Aunt Pip.

'Good morning, Guy,' his mother said, lifting her cheek, which he dutifully kissed.

Her complaints about the weather continued as she fixed her plate and sat down. He noted she'd neither spoken to nor even glanced at her daughter-in-law. Damn her. It made him ashamed.

'Mother, did you enjoy your cards last night?' Perhaps reminding her of Emily's willingness to partner her would help.

'Oh, indeed. I won some money.'

'How much?' His voice came out a little too eager. He hoped the ladies did not notice.

'A guinea and five shillings.'

Not precisely a fortune. 'Your share of the pot, or Emily's, as well?'

Emily stood to pour his mother a cup of chocolate. His mother did not look up at her. 'She gave the winnings to me.'

Emily sat down again and took a bite of her toast.

Guy stared at her. 'That was a generous deed, Emily.' His mother most assuredly did not deserve it.

She glanced up, looking surprised. 'It was a trifle,' she said.

Guy took another sip of tea lest he vent his temper on

his mother. She deserved a scold, but it was best done privately. As soon as he could get her alone he would speak with her about her treatment of his wife. Again.

But since they were all present and a change of subject would have its advantages, Guy decided to seize the moment.

He cleared his throat. 'I thought we might spend some time in London. Perhaps stay through the winter.'

His mother clapped her hands in glee. 'London! How delightful!'

'London air is bad for my lungs,' said Aunt Dorrie.

'Whatever you think is best, Guy,' Aunt Pip said.

His wife glanced up at him, but said nothing.

'Would it suit you, my dear?' he pressed.

She paused before answering in her bland way, 'I'm sure it will be very pleasant.'

He supposed he ought to be grateful that she was so accommodating, but, dash it all, he'd liked it better when she'd thrown the book at him.

'Won't be pleasant,' grumbled Aunt Dorrie. 'I'm sure to get an inflammation of the lungs.'

His mother rose to her feet and danced over to him, giving him a big hug. 'Oh, it will be a delight. Thank you, Guy. There will be some other important people in town as well, I'm sure. Some entertainment, at last.'

Another matter to speak with his mother about. It would not do for her to spend his money as fast as he could win it. He'd have to speak with her about economising. Again.

He glanced at his wife, who quickly averted her eyes. It would ease his conscience if he thought her as delighted as his mother to travel to London. It would ease his conscience if he knew anything he did pleased her.

He stabbed his slice of ham with his fork and let his mother's exuberant chatter wash over him.

* * *

Emily washed down the last crust of her toast with a sip of tea.

London.

Did she not have a considerate husband, asking her if a decision he'd already made suited her? Not that she had any illusion that a husband gave a wife any say in matters. Her father's luck or lack of it had always dictated where they would go and what they would do. Her mother went along, managing to find her own enjoyment. Perhaps that was what Emily would do as well, find her own enjoyment, though she could not imagine herself seeking out the sort of entertainment her mother craved.

She'd spent years ensuring that her behaviour did not entice the sort of men who danced attendance upon her mother, men like Cyprian Sloane.

She swallowed another mouthful of tea. She was certain Sloane's attention to her the previous night has been some sort of jest. Perhaps some other gentleman had put him up to it. 'Bet you a quid you won't get her to dance with you.' She could imagine it.

At least Sloane had sought out her company, whatever the reason. It was more than her husband had done. But she would not think of her husband. She would think of London.

Was she pleased to return to London? It could hardly be worse than Bath, and perhaps their London accommodations would give her less reason to be in her mother-in-law's way. Or her husband's way, for that matter.

Her maid would like the change, Emily was sure, as it placed her so near her parents. For Emily, the distance away from her mother and father was an advantage.

She wondered if her brother would still be in London. After his brief visit to Bath, he'd said he was returning there. Robert had never been very pleasant company for

Emily, loving cards as much as their father did even if he lacked the wit to be as conniving. Still, she would not mind seeing him.

She felt her eyes sting with tears and quickly poured herself another cup of tea. She must be lonely indeed if she pined for her brother's company.

'I thought we might leave in a week, if that would suit you.'

It took her a moment to realise her husband had spoken to her. 'If Bleasby feels well enough to travel by then.'

Her husband murmured, 'Yes, of course. I had quite forgotten.'

Did he think she'd chastised him? Good. His servants were his responsibility, after all.

'What about Bleasby?' her mother-in-law asked, still chewing her food.

Emily let the others answer. Her mother-in-law would like it so much better to listen to them explain, even though it had been she who had noticed Bleasby's cough and ordered him to rest.

Peering through her lashes at her husband, she pressed her lips together. What was the real reason he wished to go to London? Was he fleeing creditors? That had always been her father's reason for a change of location. Perhaps she ought to again offer him her vast inheritance of fifty pounds.

No, she said firmly to herself. As long as he did not require her to turn over the money, she would use it to help herself.

But help herself do what?

She sighed inwardly. Life had seemed so uncompli-cated when she'd simply gone along with whatever her parents decided. She'd always known her father liked his cards excessively and that her mother was a frivolous creature, but she'd always thought she could trust them to see her well married.

All that changed when she discovered her sister Madeleine was alive.

She'd been a fool to trust her parents with her future, and she'd be no less a fool to trust Guy Keating. He was as willing to deceive her as her mother and father had been.

The only person she could depend upon was herself. She alone must determine her future.

Looking as if she were merely lifting her cup to her lips, Emily secretly gave herself a hearty toast to her new resolve.

A few days later Emily called upon her mother. She'd not bothered to mention her intention to do so to her husband, and she knew the ladies of the household would have little interest in her whereabouts. Indeed, she herself had little interest in making the call, but it seemed the dutiful thing to do. Though her parents had not noticed her absence when she'd eloped, it still behooved her to let them know she was bound for London.

The day was brisk and still damp from the nearly constant rain. Rain may have prevented some activities, but it had not stopped her husband from leaving the apartments every night. Did he truly go out only to play cards? Or perhaps did he also meet a mistress? She shivered at the thought. What a humiliation that would be for a new wife, but he certainly had ceased taking care of his manly needs in his wife's bed.

Telling herself she did not care what her husband did, Emily walked up to her parents' door and sounded the knocker.

In a moment, the footman answered. 'G'd afternoon, Miss Emily,' he said.

She did not bother to correct him. 'Good afternoon, Samuel.' She pulled off her hat and gloves, and he assisted her with her pelisse. 'Is my mother at home?'

'Indeed she is. She's in the parlour.' He placed her items on the hall chair.

It was the fashionable hour for afternoon calls, but she hoped to find her mother alone. 'Does she have other visitors?'

He frowned. 'A gentleman, Mr Sutton said, miss, but he did not give me the gentleman's name.'

Just her luck. She was probably interrupting one of her mother's assignations. Perhaps with Lord Cranton. She had no wish to walk in on them. 'Perhaps you should announce me.'

He bowed and went to the task, returning in a moment. 'Lady Duprey says you may come up directly.'

She thanked him and proceeded up the stairs, trying to be optimistic. If her mother had company, perhaps her visit would be a short one. As she neared the parlour she heard a man's voice and her mother's trilling laughter.

As she stepped inside the room, her mother twisted around on the Grecian sofa. The gentleman stood.

Cyprian Sloane.

'Emily, my sweet,' her mother gushed, extending her hand. 'Look who has come to call.'

With the briefest of hesitation Emily walked over to her mother and clasped her outstretched hand. 'Hello, Mama.' She nodded. 'Mr Sloane.'

He bowed, his lips stretching into his most charming smile. 'Lady Keating.'

Emily sat primly in a chair, facing her mother.

Her mother giggled. 'Yes, can you countenance it, Cyprian? I am old enough to have a married daughter! It is too bad.' She fussed with the lace on her dress. 'Of course, I was married very young.'

Yes, Emily thought, her mother would most probably pretend to be a good ten years younger than her age, and neglect to inform the gentleman that she had an older married daughter as well, and a son nearing age thirty. As well as another daughter, younger than Emily.

'Indeed you must have been, ma'am,' he said agreeably. He turned to Emily and gave her that kind of appraising look that made her so uncomfortable.

'I hope you are well, Mama,' Emily said, trying to ignore him.

'Oh, famously well, darling.' She gave Sloane a flirtatious flutter of her eyelashes, before turning back to her daughter. 'Emily, be a dear and have Sutton bring our guest some refreshment. I believe your father has some very nice sherry put away.'

She crossed the room to the bell cord and a moment later met Sutton in the doorway to give her mother's instructions.

'I must not stay so long, my lady,' Sloane said, his glance sliding to Emily as she returned to her chair. 'My errand was with your husband, after all, and I would not intrude upon your visit with your daughter.'

Her mother flung out her hand as if to stop any attempt to flee. 'Oh, nonsense. You must have a glass of sherry with us. I insist upon it.' She made room for him to sit next to her on the sofa.

He laughed. 'I never could resist the entreaty of a beautiful lady.' He sat down.

Emily gave an inward groan.

After Sutton delivered and poured the sherry, Emily asserted herself to break into the bantering between her mother and Sloane. 'Mother, we are bound for London in two days' time. I came to inform you.'

'London!' her mother exclaimed. 'Oh, I envy you. How naughty of you to leave me when I am in such need of diversion.'

As if her mother had given her daughter's presence in Bath a moment's thought. Since Emily's marriage, her mother had not once called upon her.

'I believe my husband's affairs require it.' One way of describing a flight from creditors.

'Oh, that is right,' chirped her mother, acting as if she'd forgotten all about her daughter's marriage. 'Where is that handsome husband of yours?'

Sloane's eyebrows rose in anticipation of her answer.

'He has much to do to get ready.' Another half-truth, though her husband had been very busy cramming in as much card playing and who-knew-what-else as he could.

'Bath will be much duller without your presence, Lady Keating,' Sloane said, his voice silky.

Her mother tapped his thigh with her fingers. 'Oh, we shall contrive to stir up some excitement, will we not?'

He laughed, carefully placing her hand back upon her own person. 'Lady Duprey, you must not say such things. Your daughter will get the wrong notion of my visit.'

Emily's lips thinned.

Sloane inclined his head towards her. 'See, she looks at me very disapprovingly.'

Was he mocking her? Emily could not tell. In any event, he made her difficult interview with her mother much worse.

'I must not stay, Mama.' She stood and placed her nearly full glass on the table next to her mother's empty one. 'There are many preparations to be made.'

Emily had assumed the task of arranging the household's transfer to London. It kept her busy and relieved her mother-in-law of a tedious chore, though she expected no thanks from that quarter.

'Wait,' her mother said, again flinging out a hand. 'You may perform a task for me.'

She sat again. 'Certainly, Mama. What is it?' Likely something troublesome, and something she would rather not do.

'Take a trunk back to London for me.' Her mother used a tone of voice as if talking to a servant. For some odd reason, it irritated Emily that Sloane witnessed it.

'A trunk?'

'Yes.' Her mother nodded. 'A trunk of old dresses. I do not know why Shelty packed them. They are hopelessly out of fashion. All from last year.'

Emily stole a look at Sloane. He caught her, and a smile slid across his face.

She quickly looked back to her mother. 'Perhaps Shelty expected you to give them to her.' It was the custom, after all. A way for Shelty to make a little money on the side by selling them.

'She has no need of them, I assure you,' her mother shot back. 'Besides, they might be altered. Who knows what fashions will be the rage next year?'

Emily had a fair idea of how many boxes and trunks the Keatings needed to transport to London. 'I am not sure if—'

'You must take them,' her mother wailed. 'I am tripping over that trunk every time I take a step. I threatened to make Kirby store it in her own room.'

Emily sighed. She knew better than to oppose whatever her mother wanted. There would be no peace if she did not acquiesce.

'Very well,' she said in sinking tones. 'Have Sutton send it over not later than the day after tomorrow.'

'Will you tell him before you leave?' her mother pleaded.

She sighed again. 'Certainly.' Rising from her chair, she said, 'I really must leave.'

'Oh, if you must.' Smiling, her mother gave a sideways glance to Sloane, who also rose.

'And, dear lady, I must depart as well.' He took her hand and blew a kiss over it. 'I have left my card for Lord Duprey.' He turned to Emily, an amused expression in his eyes. 'May I escort you home, Lady Keating?'

'It...it is not necessary, I assure you, sir,' she stammered.

He smiled like a cat who'd got into the cream. 'It would be my pleasure.'

The walk back to Thomas Street seemed inordinately long to Emily, though Sloane behaved like a gentleman and spoke to her in the most proper of ways. They finally reached her door.

'Well, thank you, sir,' she said with nothing more than politeness.

'As I anticipated—' he grinned '—it was my pleasure.'

She opened the door and entered, feeling like she'd narrowly escaped getting tangled in a snare. Before she closed the door, he said, 'My regards to your husband.'

She hurried inside.

Sloane paused a moment before proceeding on his way. He smiled to himself. The new Lady Keating. It was amusing to rattle her, to see what cracks he could make in that armour of perfect primness.

Well, it was of no consequence. Now that she was off to London he must give up that mild amusement. How grim. Bath society had been thin enough that she had once been an attraction.

As he strolled down towards Union Street, he wondered if Baron Duprey would make good his gambling debt, the sole reason Sloane had made this call. He suspected not. Shocking when a gentleman shirked a debt of honour. If one wanted to sink low in society's eyes it was much more enjoyable to be known as a rakehell. That sort of dishonour earned a man some respect.

Chapter Six

When Emily stepped into the hall of the Keating London townhouse, she was unprepared for such a fashionable residence. Tucked into the corner of Essex Court, it was a few doors from the grand Spencer House, tiny in comparison, but perfectly large enough to accommodate them all in some style.

The journey had been tedious. Poor Miss Nuthall had complained of every bump and jolt, which Lady Pipham immediately countered as trifling. Lady Keating had much to remark upon about the countryside, about who might be in London and what entertainments they might find there. Her remarks were not directed to her daughter-in-law, however. Emily spent most of the trip looking out of the window. She'd found herself wishing she were outside the carriage, riding on horseback, like her husband, though she was merely a passable horsewoman.

The housekeeper and a footman rushed to greet them all, receiving a barrage of instructions from the elder Lady Keating while assisting in the removal of hats, gloves and outer garments. Guy had remained in the street, watching for the coach carrying the baggage, the ladies' maids, and a still sniffling and coughing Bleasby.

Emily examined the surroundings. The hall was bright with white flagstone floors and marble staircase, pale grey walls, plaster mouldings with gilt trim. A white marble statue of some Greek god gave the entrance its focal point.

A beautiful entranceway, like the interior of a small Greek temple, but perhaps a bit old fashioned. It wanted colour, she thought.

Lady Keating gave the footman, whom she called Rogers, three different instructions at once, and the man bowed and hurried out of the door to do one of them. The housekeeper became disengaged from her ladyship for the moment, and Emily took the opportunity to introduce herself.

'Good afternoon,' she said to the somewhat flustered woman. 'I am Lady Keating, Lord Keating's wife.'

The woman clapped her hands to her cheeks. 'Goodness,' she said, belatedly remembering to curtsy. 'We did hear his young lordship had married. I am Mrs Wilson. I did not realise who you were, ma'am. I beg pardon.'

What had the housekeeper expected? A more beautiful lady? Or had she merely thought the new Lady Keating would be introduced by the Dowager? That, of course, had not happened.

Emily extended her hand. 'I am very pleased to meet you, Mrs Wilson.'

Mrs Wilson clasped it briefly and curtsied again. 'Do you have any instructions, ma'am? I had planned for dinner at seven, because her ladyship always likes it that way. I hope it is to your liking. Do you wish to approve the menu first?'

Emily was lady of the house. She had quite forgotten. Apparently her mother-in-law had forgotten, too, since that lady was busy directing everything and everybody, though merely adding to the confusion.

She smiled at the housekeeper. 'I'm sure whatever Lady Keating likes will be quite acceptable to me. She is so used to making the decisions, is she not?'

Mrs Wilson looked relieved. 'Yes, my lady. She's been mistress of the house a long time, but I cannot say she likes making the decisions.'

Guy strode in. 'The baggage has arrived.' He saw the housekeeper, who curtsied once again. 'Good day, Mrs Wilson. Would you be so good as to supervise?'

Bleasby was ushered in on the arms of the maids, protesting all the while he did not need their help and should not enter the front door, but he was clearly in no position to direct the bags, boxes, trunks and portmanteaux. Guy firmly insisted he retire for the rest of the day, also directing Mrs Wilson to have Bleasby served hot broth and whatever else he might request.

The Dowager Lady Keating and the aunts climbed the staircase to the first floor, Lady Keating tossing instructions to Mrs Wilson to bring some refreshment.

'Yes, ma'am,' the housekeeper called back. She turned to Emily with a panicked look.

Emily took her aside. 'Ask the footman—Rogers, is that his name?—to take care of the baggage, then have the cook prepare Lady Keating's refreshment. It will take Mr Bleasby a bit to settle in. You may discover his needs later.'

Mrs Wilson smiled gratefully and started to rush away. She stopped, turning back to Emily. 'The bedrooms are prepared as Mr Guy...I mean Lord Keating's letter instructed. Do you require anything else, my lady?'

She had required nothing at all to this point. 'No, indeed. I am well satisfied.'

'Thank you, ma'am.' Mrs Wilson curtsied and hurried away.

The hall suddenly quieted. Emily stood at its centre, none too certain where to go.

Her husband spoke from behind her. 'Thank you, my dear.'

He startled her and she forgot to be annoyed at his typical salutation. 'For what, sir?'

The corner of his mouth turned up in a half-smile. 'For bringing some order to the chaos.'

She tried to think of what she had done. Nothing of consequence.

They were alone and they stood for a moment without speaking.

He finally said, 'Would you care to retire to the drawing room? Or do you wish to refresh yourself in your bed-chamber?'

She knew where neither of those rooms could be found. 'Wherever you wish.'

He stepped towards her. 'My apologies for the commotion. It was hardly a fit introduction to your home.'

Her home? It did not feel as if she would ever belong here. 'There is no need to apologise.'

He made no effort to look at her, but said, 'Perhaps tomorrow you can properly meet the servants.'

It seemed to her as if he were merely being polite, saying words he was expected to say.

'I hope you had a pleasant journey,' he added.

She clamped down a desire to tell him exactly how unpleasant it was. 'Very pleasant,' she said instead.

His eyes still slightly averted, he offered his arm. With a hesitation she accepted it. He escorted her up the stairs. 'Do you join my mother in the drawing room, then?'

Emily did not think she could endure a moment more of her mother-in-law's company. Not after that interminable coach ride.

'Do you mind very much if I refresh myself in my bedchamber first?'

'Not at all, my dear,' he said. 'I will show you where it is.'

She forced a smile. Of course it made no difference to him what she did. 'Thank you.'

He left her very quickly at the bedchamber door, before she could ask where to find the drawing room. This was not some sprawling country house, she thought. She doubted she would have to wander too far.

Hester, her maid, was already in the room, busy unpacking her trunk. The girl looked up, face flushed with excitement. 'Good afternoon, my lady,' she said. 'I cannot believe I am back in London.'

At least someone besides her mother-in-law was happy about the change in locations. 'I expect you will be eager for a visit to Chelsea to see your mama.'

'Oh, yes, ma'am.' The girl grinned.

'Then we shall have to contrive a day off for you as soon as possible.'

Hester's eyes grew larger. 'Oh, thank you, ma'am. My aunt—Miss Kirby, I mean—said I was not to ask you and I wasn't meaning to. Not at all.'

Emily gave her a reassuring smile. 'Indeed, you did not ask me. I offered.'

Hester grinned. 'You are so kind.' She darted around the trunk to put clothes in the tall mahogany chest of drawers against the wall. Another pleasant room, Emily noticed. Except the carpet was worn of its nap in places, and the curtains looked frayed.

The footman appeared in the doorway with a trunk hoisted on his shoulder. 'Where shall I put this, my lady?'

It was her mother's trunk.

She looked about the room. 'Perhaps we can tuck it in the corner out of the way.'

'There's a small dressing room over here where it might fit.' Hester skipped over to a door and opened it.

On the other side was not a dressing room, but another bedchamber. No lamp burned there, but a large trunk and portmanteau stood in the centre of the room. Her husband's, undoubtedly. No one was tending to his unpacking.

She'd not had time to consider, but should he not have a valet? Bleasby helped him on occasion in Bath, and she'd not thought to question it, except to fear the family expected too much of the elderly servant. Here in London, however, it seemed odd indeed for a gentleman to be without a valet.

The footman noisily shifted the trunk.

'Gracious,' said Hester. 'It is the other door.' She danced around to a door on the opposite wall that indeed opened to reveal a small dressing room.

'That will be an excellent place for the trunk,' Emily agreed. The footman placed it in the little room.

Hester quickly pushed it to the best corner of the dressing room. Emily envied her maid's energy and enthusiasm. She was glad to have rescued the girl from her father's household. Indeed, now she could not fathom how to cope without sweet Hester. The maid was so grateful to her, it was almost like having someone on one's side.

Indeed, it was difficult at times to keep the energetic maid busy.

Emily glanced into her husband's room. 'Hester, I suspect Bleasby would have unpacked Lord Keating's belongings had he been well. Would you mind doing so? It should not be too difficult.'

'Yes, my lady. I would be happy to do so.' Hester

grinned again and said with a sigh, 'His lordship is a very nice gentleman.'

At least his lordship did not grope young maids or try to get them into bed as her father did. That was one thing to her husband's credit.

'Yes,' she replied. 'He is a nice gentleman.'

Emily sat at the mirrored dressing table and fussed with her hair, tucking away tendrils that had come loose during the journey. She'd wait until the dinner hour to change her dress, though a change of clothing was a tempting excuse to delay her appearance in the drawing room, but soon she rose and made her way to the first floor. Her husband was ascending the stairs at the same time.

'Ah, there you are, my dear. Shall we go in together?' he said.

My dear, again. She almost lost patience. 'I had thought you already there.'

'I decided to see how Bleasby goes on.' He waited for her.

How kind of him. Sometimes she hated being reminded of his kindnesses. It made her feel like weeping. 'How does he fare?'

He offered his arm, another kind gesture. 'He is quite fagged, but no more than that, I think.'

It felt almost companionable.

They turned to the first room on that floor and he opened the door, stepping aside to let her pass.

Her mother-in-law rose at their entrance, but looked beyond her daughter-in-law. 'Guy, dearest, where have you been? You have not yet told me how your journey was.' She presented her cheek for him to kiss and gave him no chance to respond. 'Ours was uneventful.'

'I'm a mass of bruises, I'm sure,' said Miss Nuthall. 'That hired vehicle was not well sprung at all.'

'I thought it most comfortable,' murmured Lady Pipham.

Guy left Emily's side to greet his aunts. 'I am sorry it gave you pain.'

'It did not give *me* pain,' Lady Pipham said.

Miss Nuthall tossed her sister a scathing glance. 'I cannot see how anyone could tolerate being jostled about like mail-coach baggage. Why could we not ride in one of the Keating carriages?'

Guy darted a quick look at Emily. 'They are at Annerley, Aunt Dorrie.'

Emily watched her husband more closely. Why look guilty about carriages? The coaches were very likely to be let to the tenants. Why not just say so?

He tucked his aunt's shawl more snugly around her, and fondly patted her back. Another kind gesture.

He looked back at her again and this time she quickly averted her eyes. 'Did you have a difficult ride as well, my dear?'

She wanted to blurt out, 'My name is Emily!' but she would not. Neither would she complain of his mother's poor manners towards her. If he cared, there was plenty of opportunity for him to witness it.

She made herself assume a pleasant expression. 'I had not noticed any undue discomfort, but, of course, I am perhaps less delicate than your aunt.'

Lady Pipham nodded vigorously, and the hint of an approving look crossed Miss Nuthall's face. Her mother-in-law took no notice at all.

Her husband placed a chair near the fire and invited her to sit. He turned to Lady Keating. 'Mother, I'm sure Emily would appreciate you introducing her to the servants. There is much for her to learn of the household.'

His mother pursed her lips. 'Guy, I declare, I am too exhausted to contemplate such a task.'

'Tomorrow will do,' he responded in a tight voice.

'I would be most grateful for anything you might teach me, Lady Keating,' Emily said. 'But I do not wish to trouble you.'

No matter Lady Keating's behaviour towards her, she vowed no one would accuse her of being an improper daughter-in-law.

Lady Keating, however, turned her back.

'Mother!' her husband cried sharply. 'My wife was speaking to you.'

The sharp tone of his voice took Emily by surprise.

The Dowager turned back and spoke in a clipped fashion. 'I will show you the house tomorrow and introduce you to the servants.'

'Thank you,' Emily said.

Lady Keating began talking of other things, matters which did not concern Emily, who took some time to recover her equilibrium. She glanced around the room, warmed by a small fire in the carved marble fireplace. More colourful than the hall had been, its walls were pale green trimmed with rectangular white moulding. The furniture was also in the classical style, sofas and chairs in the same pale green as the walls.

There was a very subtle air of neglect in the house, Emily thought, though the scent of beeswax suggested someone had recently dusted and polished. Perhaps the house had been unused for a time. She could not recall any of the Keatings present in town during her last two Seasons, but it was more than that. This décor belonged to her grandmother's time. It was as if no one had cared enough to tend to it since the last century had passed.

In Malvern, where she'd grown up, her mother always

kept up with the latest styles, no matter how big the expense or the debt. But that was a mere illusion of caring for a house.

Emily gazed at her husband, mother-in-law and his aunts. They formed a circle where they sat, a circle that kept her on the outside.

The footman arrived, bringing the refreshments, and Emily busied herself pouring for the others.

After the ladies retired to their rooms to await the dinner hour, Guy remained in the parlour alone. He searched a cabinet, pleased that Mrs Wilson had been thorough enough to stock it with port, the bottle still smelling of the wine cellar from which it had been unearthed. He poured himself a glass and plopped down in a chair by the fire. He would give his mother a few moments, but then he would have more words with her.

The gulf between himself and his wife was difficult enough, but her presence was a reality none of them could—or should—ignore, as easy as it seemed. His mother must be made to understand that her disregard of her daughter-in-law was not to be tolerated.

He downed the contents of his glass. His guilt at trapping Emily into marrying him was not eased by her perfect manners, her quiet way of doing whatever was required. With a few kind words, she'd already made a conquest of Mrs Wilson. And goodness knows what would have happened to Bleasby if she had not noticed his illness. He felt certain his mother would rush to report any sharp words from Emily, but none existed. Each day brought new evidence of what a fine woman he had married, how much more she deserved than a man who must make his fortune with cards and neglect her in the process.

Guy stood. The very reserve he admired in her dealings

with his mother rankled him at the same time. It left him at sea as to how to make amends to her, how to go about begging her forgiveness.

A few minutes later he knocked at the door to his mother's room, announcing himself. She bade him enter.

She lay upon her bed in a dressing gown and cap, but sat up as he walked to her side. 'I had not recalled what a small room this was. Kirby was barely able to find places for my clothing.'

He glanced around. It was more snug than she was used to, but perfectly adequate. 'What would you have me do about it, Mother?' he asked in a flat voice.

She waved her hand dramatically. 'Oh, there is nothing to be done.' She flung herself back on the pillows and gestured for him to sit in a nearby chair. 'She has quite taken over.'

He chose to remain standing. 'Now you know that is unfair. I made the decision. She, by the way, has asked for nothing.' He gave her a direct look. 'Emily is the new Viscountess Keating, and she is due all the advantages to the title.'

His mother closed her eyes, as if that would prevent her from hearing what he had to say.

He came closer and took her hand in his. She opened her eyes again. 'Mother, Emily is an agreeable creature. I urge you to treat her with more consideration.'

She sighed, clasping his hand tightly. 'I do apologise, Guy. But I simply do not like her.'

He pulled away from her fingers. 'And why is that? What is there to dislike in her?'

Her brows knit and she pursed her lips. He waited for her response. It did not come.

He leaned down and kissed her on the head. 'See, there is nothing to dislike in her. Do try, Mother. Introduce her to the servants tomorrow. Be gracious. Take her with you when you make morning calls, when you wish to go to entertainments Aunt Dorrie and Aunt Pip will not attend. She will be useful to you in that way, will she not?'

His mother met his entreating gaze. She gave a grim smile and patted his hand. 'I will try to be civil.'

He kissed her again, on the cheek this time. 'There's my girl,' he said. 'I'll leave you to rest now.'

But dinner was no more comfortable than it had been in Bath. As soon as he was able, Guy excused himself and left the house, intent on a visit to White's in search of a good card game and to get wind of where the most money was to be won.

Chapter Seven

All too soon days in London became routine. Emily smoothly assumed the management of the household. Her mother-in-law did not fancy the tedium of such mundane tasks as approving menus, overseeing expenditures and dealing with servant problems. The Dowager much preferred spending her time in more social pursuits, to which Emily was often expected to accompany her. Their visits were always very cordial, but such afternoons and evenings did nothing to raise Emily's spirits.

In one low moment, Emily had written to her brother at his rooms in the Albany, to inform him she was in town and to beg him to call on her. She had not heard from him. It was nonsensical to believe that Robert, of all people, could banish the blue-devils that so often plagued her, but she still longed for his companionship.

She did not seek companionship from her husband. He absented himself each evening, presumably to pursue his love affair with diamonds, spades, hearts and clubs. On the rare occasions he escorted his mother and wife to evening parties, he always left promptly after delivering them home, disappearing into the night like a stone thrown into an inky pond. Emily typically woke when he returned in the wee hours of morning, still listening carefully to the sound of his footsteps to tell her if he had won or lost. It became increasingly difficult to tell.

She dared not think what other nightly pursuits he might engage in, but it stood to reason he frequented the same gaming hells her father knew, places where one's fortune rose and fell upon the roll of dice or the turning of a card, and where there would be female company offering celebration for the wins and consolation for the losses.

The loudest sounds Emily heard from her husband's room were the clink of coins when dawn barely peeked into the windows. When her father had returned from his late-night gaming, he, like as not, would stumble in, mumbling to himself or yelling for a footman to assist him on the stairs. At least her husband avoided getting so foxed he could not walk. His footsteps were always steady.

Any day now Emily expected to see sure signs of a losing streak. Creditors should appear at the door. Her husband's even temper would then crackle like Vauxhall fireworks, and he would take to hiding in his rooms. How familiar that would be. Soon they would dash off to a country house party, or, perhaps, back to Bath. Anywhere the payment of gambling debts might be avoided.

There were no such signs, however. No creditors hounding them. No outbursts of temper. In fact, her husband was always painstakingly agreeable. Nor were there signs of great winnings. No lavish spending, no extravagant entertaining, no gifts purchased that shortly thereafter must be returned.

It was all so difficult to understand.

This night was to be one of the exceptional evenings when her husband would escort his mother and herself to a *musicale* and card party. Lady Keating was quite as mad for card playing as her son, and it well suited her to have her daughter-in-law as her whist partner. With Emily as her partner, she seldom lost.

Her mother-in-law had chattered all the week about the new gown she was to wear that evening. Emily had accompanied her when she'd ordered the dress from the mantua maker. She had been unable to convince Lady Keating to economise.

Emily did not know the exact nature of their present finances. Her husband always approved whatever household expense she brought to his attention, but she had a horror of the debt that would certainly come. She refused to spend any of her husband's money on herself, preferring to mend her old dresses rather than purchase new ones. It turned out Hester had a talent with the needle and an ability to slightly alter a garment so it appeared a bit less like one from two Seasons ago.

When it was time to depart for the *musicale*, Emily descended the staircase wearing a pale lavender gown she'd worn often, but with new lace trim. She carried her black cloak over her arm.

Guy waited in the hall, rocking on his heels, looking splendid in his snow-white knee breeches and dark black coat. She wished he were not so handsome. She wished he would not take her breath away at times like this.

As always, the smile he gave her seemed tinged with regret. 'Ah, you are ready, I see.'

At least he had not called her *my dear*.

'Yes.' She half-wished she had fished for a compliment. Even false flattery might feel more pleasing than none at all.

His mother arrived at the top of the stair, and both

Emily and her husband were saved the awkwardness of having nothing to say to each other.

Lady Keating put on her gloves as she descended. 'Guy, I hope you have a carriage ready. We are late.'

'It is waiting,' he replied.

He assisted his mother into her cloak. Bleasby, who had been standing aside, stepped forward to assist Emily.

'Thank you, Bleasby,' she said.

He bowed in his dignified, if arthritic way. Though apparently recovered from his recent illness, he'd slowed down considerably. He ought to be pensioned off, set up in a nice snug cottage on the family estate, perhaps.

'Shall we go, my dear,' her husband said, waiting by the door.

Bleasby limped over to open it, and Emily hurried to follow her husband and mother-in-law out to the waiting carriage.

They rode the short distance to the townhouse on Hanover Square, and were announced into a room where the chairs were lined in rows. The musicians were set up at the front of the room: a piano, viola, cello and two violins. Lady Keating exuded good spirits, greeting her friends, remarking on the lovely arrangements of flowers throughout the room. Emily stood quietly at her husband's side. The musicians began to tune their instruments, and Lady Keating rushed to find seats. Guy followed his mother through the line of chairs. Emily trailed behind him.

Soon strains of Haydn and Mozart filled the air. Emily closed her eyes and let the beautiful music wash over her. She almost felt as if she were floating on the melodies played by the strings, rising and falling with the notes, like a feather tossed on the wind.

The programme concluded with one of her favourites, *'Quasi una fantasia,'* a Beethoven sonata, once scandalous, now so fashionable its sheet music could be found in all the best parlours. The piano sound began peacefully, threading itself into and around her heart. It continued, growing, surging, like a storm about to erupt, a storm of emotion, pure and raw. She gave herself over to it, let it whip at her like a gale, until she felt the emotion clutch at her, taking her breath away.

When the ending came, she sat stunned, unable to move. Those around her rustled to get out of their seats.

'Are you feeling unwell, my dear?' her husband asked, placing his hand on her arm.

She glanced at him in some surprise, having forgotten even his presence during the turmoil of the music. 'No, I…I was merely listening.'

He let his hand remain for a moment, staring at her.

'I am quite well,' she said, embarrassed that her reaction to the music might show.

'Come, Guy,' her mother-in-law broke in. 'The card party is about to begin.'

There were several rooms set up with card tables. They wandered through them, looking for a place to sit. Being one of the last to make their way out of the music room, most guests had already chosen partners.

'See, we are late,' Lady Keating fussed. 'We shall not find anywhere to sit.'

A silver-haired gentleman approached her. 'Good evening, Verna, dear. What a pleasure.'

Lady Keating burst into smiles. 'Sir Reginald! I have not seen you in an age!' The gentleman took her hand and lavishly kissed it. She giggled like a girl, and turned to her son. 'Guy, do you recall Sir Reginald? He was one of your father's particular friends. My son, sir!'

'Ah, yes, Keating.' Sir Reginald shook Guy's hand. 'Spitting image of your father, I declare.'

Too much like the father, Emily thought, recalling her brother's assertion that the deceased Lord Keating had been every bit as bad a gambler as their father.

Guy presented Emily to Sir Reginald, and she shook his hand graciously.

'Come, let us make a foursome!' the gentleman said, ushering them to an empty table in the corner. 'Verna, be my partner, will you? A pleasure. A pleasure.'

Lady Keating pulled back. 'I want my daughter-in-law to be my partner,' she said, avoiding the use of Emily's name as did her son.

'No, no,' Sir Reginald cried. 'Not done. Not done at all. We cannot have two gentleman playing against two ladies.'

'But I like to be her partner,' Lady Keating persisted. 'We always win.'

Sir Reginald dramatically clutched at his heart. 'You wound me.'

Lady Keating giggled again.

'If you wish,' the gentleman continued, 'you may partner your son, and I will hook up with his lady. I assure you any son of old Justus will be a formidable opponent of mine.'

Lady Keating wrinkled her brow, considering this.

'I will be happy to partner you, Mother,' Guy said.

She acquiesced and they settled down to play.

Only a few hands showed Emily that Sir Reginald was a skilled player, and her husband as well, but then she'd expected him to be. She and Sir Reginald easily won the first game. Guy and his mother took the second, but only due to Honours points. Lady Keating, the weakest at the table, seemed also to be the sole person who cared about the outcome.

Until the third game. Guy had intensified his attention

to the cards, as any true gamester would do. Winning was always an object. Emily understood this perfectly. The gamester in her rose to the challenge.

'By jove, you are quite a player,' Sir Reginald declared to her as the last round of the third game was played. They'd won again, but it had been very close. 'I swear you would give any gentleman of my acquaintance a run for his money.'

Emily glanced at her husband, who was gathering up the cards. Perhaps if she played cards at those places he went at night, she would beat him as she'd done her father. If Sir Reginald were correct, she might even win the kind of fortune for which her husband married her. What she wouldn't give to win enough to tell them all to go to the devil.

Guy dealt the next hand and Emily stared at her cards. Her heart beat faster. If she could easily win at these *ton*nish card parties, why not with serious gamesters? Did not her father always say fortunes could be won at cards? But she would not give her winnings to her husband to gamble away. She would keep them for herself.

Could independence be purchased if the fortune won was large enough? Such a feat would require even more secrets than her husband kept from her, she'd wager.

Emily nearly trembled with the boldness of the plan forming itself in her head. Trying very hard to hide her growing excitement, she carefully restrained her card play to allow her mother-in-law the final win.

Supper was announced and they all retired to another room. Guy solicitously filled her plate, but she ate with very little appetite.

Her husband made the effort to converse with her. 'Do you enjoy whist, my dear?'

What ought she to say? That she thought it might be her salvation? 'Well enough,' she said.

He soon abandoned engaging her in conversation, getting drawn in to his mother and Sir Reginald's talk of old times.

After they'd finished their repast and wandered into the parlour, now free of card tables, Emily glanced across the room and saw a young man standing stiff in his form-fitting evening attire.

Her brother. So he was in town, the wretch. He had not bothered to answer her letter. Without a word to her husband, whose ear was bent to listen to Sir Reginald, she hurried across the room.

Her brother, seeing her approach, glanced to each side as if seeking an escape.

'Robert,' Emily said, almost out of breath. 'I am so glad to see you. Why did you not respond to my letter? I asked you to call on me.'

He flinched. 'Very busy, Emily. Meant to call. Really.'

Her brother much resembled her in colouring, but he presented a flashy appearance, fancying himself among the dandy set. This evening his collar points nearly touched his ears and his neckcloth was a labyrinth of intricate knotting.

She grabbed his arm, and he gave a quiet shriek at having his coatsleeve wrinkled. She led him aside, to a more private spot. 'Robert, I would very much like for you to call upon me. I insist upon it.'

He tried to pull away, but she gripped the fabric of his coat in her fingers. 'Have a care. My coat, Emily.'

She merely glared at him and squeezed more tightly.

'Let go,' he pleaded. 'Won't run. Promise.'

In addition to dress, Robert also affected what he considered a dandyish way to speak. In phrases. The habit annoyed Emily to distraction.

She released him, but stood in his way, blocking any sudden impulse he might have to run.

He eyed her sheepishly, patting his carefully curled hair and fingering his neckcloth. 'Must wish you happy, I suppose. Married Keating. Good fellow.'

'You ought to have warned me about him being a gamester,' she whispered.

His eyes widened. 'But he ain't a gamester. I mean… never was.'

'You've gammoned me, but no need to discuss that now,' she said.

He released a relieved breath, as if he'd escaped some dire catastrophe, like her pulling the chain of his watch and ripping his fob pocket.

'But you must call upon me, Robert. Tomorrow, if you can.'

'Tomorrow?' His voice rose uncertainly. 'Might be busy.'

'Tomorrow,' she insisted. 'Promise me.'

He shuffled his feet. 'Don't get in a pet. Will do it.'

Only then did she step back. 'Thank you.' She turned to leave him, but hesitated. When she swung back to him, he flinched again. 'You promise?' was all she said.

'Yes. Yes,' he grumbled.

Emily crossed the room to where her husband and mother-in-law stood. Two other ladies, friends of Lady Keating, had joined them with Sir Reginald. They had probably not even noticed her absence.

Guy spent the next morning in the library puzzling out how much of his winnings to reserve for debts, how much for daily expenses, how much to risk at the tables that evening. It was a daily balancing act that seemed more like constructing a house of cards than safeguarding the future. One careless step and the whole would tumble down around him.

As he'd hoped, he managed to gain ground by coming to London. He'd barely ventured from White's, where play was deep the year round, but still kept his ears open for more lucrative settings. He'd not always won. There were some nights his losses were deep, but slowly he'd gained enough reserves to play for higher stakes. He should do so soon.

He glanced at the figures he'd written on the paper in front of him. Not bad, but the icy, insinuating fear of losing everything was constant. So was the intoxication of winning. He'd felt that same intoxication even at the tame card party with his mother and Emily.

Emily was a good player, as Sir Reginald had said. For that one hand Guy had been locked in combat with her to win—the game of cards, that is. He'd enjoyed sharing that excitement with her, though, typically, he could not tell if she cared to win or not. She had the perfect face for cards, giving nothing away.

He gave a grunt of frustration.

He placed a packet of his winnings in his pocket and returned the rest to the desk drawer to lock away. He was off to the bank and to the post, to send another sum back to Annerley.

He walked past the front drawing room. Emily was seated by the window, peeking through the curtains.

His wife.

She looked pretty with the sun illuminating her features and shooting gold through her brown hair. Had he ever told her she was pretty?

She'd looked pretty the previous evening in the

lavender dress she'd worn several times before. She'd done something new with it. He did not know what. He ought to have told her she looked well in it, but his mother arrived in what was obviously an expensive new dress. Emily should have had a new dress to wear. He ought to have given her money for a dress.

He might tell her now, how pretty she looked by the window, her face aglow. Maybe she would smile. He longed to see her smile as she had the morning after they'd made love, before all went wrong between them.

She glanced to the doorway. For a moment, her expression was almost animated, but had he imagined that? When she saw him, the veil dropped over her eyes.

He forgot his intended compliment in his disappointment. He tried to smile. 'Good morning, my dear. Or is it afternoon by now?'

'A bit after,' she said, her voice without expression.

He paused, but then decided to enter the room. She clearly was not eager for his company. 'My mother and aunts are not with you?' he asked, then kicked himself. This was nothing like what he'd intended to say.

With perfect equanimity she responded, 'They prefer the small sitting room. There are fewer draughts, Miss Nuthall says.'

He smiled again, more genuinely. 'Yes, she would say that, wouldn't she?' He picked up a chair and moved it close to where she sat. 'You are not cold by the window, my dear?'

She continued to look at him, but without apparent emotion. She finally spoke. 'I am perfectly comfortable.'

'Ah,' he said.

More silence, as usual between them. He hated the silence.

'You are well, I hope,' he tried again.

'Yes,' she said.

The silence returned.

His head always flooded with all manner of things he ought to say to her, beginning with, 'I'm sorry.' Her composed expression stopped him. He was a bundle of emotions with her, but she seemed to have no emotion at all. He halfway wished, as before, she would rail at him, throw more books at him, torment him with what he had done to her. It was what he deserved. It was what he would like. He said nothing.

She glanced back to the window, fingering the fringe on the curtains. 'My brother is supposed to call. I am watching for him.'

'Indeed?' At least she'd spoken to him. She rarely added to a conversation. 'How nice for you.'

He'd met Emily's brother a time or two. A frivolous young man. A poor card player. When Guy decided to marry Emily, he'd reasoned Robert Duprey would be no threat to the scheme. He was not the sort of brother to chase after a carriage headed to Gretna Green.

She fixed her gaze out of the window again, and the silence returned.

'Emily?' He spoke her name so softly he was not sure he'd even done so.

She turned to him, slowly, it seemed. 'Yes?'

He faltered. 'I…I hope all is well with you here. That is…I hope you are enjoying London.'

Good God, he might be addressing a guest in his house instead of his wife. Why was it so difficult for him to talk to her?

'I assure you,' she said, her voice composed, 'all is well.'

Guy met her nondescript eyes, which did not waver. If eyes were supposed to be windows to the soul, hers were shuttered, curtains drawn. He doubted he would be able to open them to the light. With an inward sigh, he stood, his body suddenly heavy with fatigue. 'Enjoy your visit with your brother,' he said and walked out the door.

Emily remained at the drawing-room window, her husband's brief visit putting a pall on her excitement. He'd seemed so sad. A part of her had yearned to comfort him, but not for gambling losses, for that surely must be what troubled him. What else would bother him? Marrying a woman and regretting it?

Her mother-in-law appeared at the door. 'Do you accompany me? I have several calls to make.'

'I fear I cannot, ma'am,' she responded. 'I must stay here.'

Lady Keating gave her a sour look and left in a swish of skirts, never asking one question about Emily's plans.

Emily waited, trying to pass time by catching up on some mending for Miss Nuthall. She glanced at the clock on the mantel. Nearly four o'clock. Robert would not come. She needed him so, and he would fail her.

She'd been mad to think Robert could be trusted to help her. He was as consumed by his own interests as were all men. Why did she think she could bully Robert into helping her as she'd always done when they were children? He was a man now. A very foolish man, but a man none the less.

With a sigh of resignation, she stitched the rent in Miss Nuthall's lace cap. An approaching carriage sounded in the street below, and she nearly decided not to bother to look.

Her brother drew up in a stylish curricle. He had come! She fairly flew from the room. By the time Bleasby had admitted him into the hall, she had already fetched her bonnet, gloves and warmest pelisse.

Her brother barely lifted the hat from his head when she descended the stairs. 'Robert, take me for a turn in the park.'

'The park?' His hat remained in mid-air. 'Dash it, Emily. Cold out there.'

'Nonsense,' she replied, donning her pelisse with Bleasby's assistance. 'It will be refreshing.'

She pulled him out the door, assuring Bleasby she would be home in plenty of time for dinner.

Grumbling the whole while, Robert flicked the ribbons and the horses pulled away from the house. Emily's chest was a-flutter with excitement, as if this were truly the moment of her escape.

They reached the end of the block, and she saw her husband turning the corner on foot. She hurriedly looked away, pretending not to see him. She did not wish to think of him.

'Dash it, Emily. Why do we have to drive in the park?' her brother complained, using a rare complete sentence. 'It's cold.'

'I wished to speak with you in private,' she said, tucking a rug around her feet.

'Me?' He gaped at her, neglecting to attend the horses.

A hackney driver shouted, and he barely had enough time to pull on the ribbons and avoid a collision.

'Don't talk now,' he grumbled. 'Driving. Not a Four-in-Hand fellow, y'know.'

After a couple more close calls, they turned into Hyde Park where the pace was more sedate and the paths nearly empty.

'What the devil, Emily?' he said, which she took for permission to speak.

'I want you to take me to a gaming hell.' No sense in mincing words, not with her brother.

He nearly dropped the reins. 'G-g-gaming hell?'

She nodded vigorously.

'Hoaxing me,' he said.

'No, indeed. I am very serious.' Her heart beat rapidly. To speak her plans out loud made them seem very real. 'I need money, and the only way I can get it is to play cards.'

'Bamming me,' he said. 'Can ask Keating for money.'

She drew in a breath. 'No, I cannot. Besides he gambles away the money, but never mind that. I'll explain, but you must promise to tell no one.'

'Very well,' he said in a resigned voice. 'Won't like it one bit, though.'

She began by telling him of the rumour their father had spread around Bath and how Guy had believed it and married her, expecting a fortune. Best to start there instead of telling him their sister Madeleine was alive, no thanks to their parents. Madeleine had never made her existence public, so Emily felt she could not. Neither did Emily remind her brother again that he'd been the one to assure her Guy Keating was not a gamester like the previous Lord Keatings. What a Banbury tale that had been. Fussing at him now would serve no purpose. She desired his help.

'So I wish to win enough money to live alone,' she concluded.

'Jove, Emily,' Robert exclaimed. 'He ain't beating you?'

She waved her hand dismissively. 'No, he does not beat me. He's perfectly civil. It is just—'

'Nothing to it, then,' he said.

'There is something to it. He…he does not wish to be

married to me, you see. It is unbearable.' Her voice cracked.

Robert cleared his throat. 'Dash it, don't bawl like Jessame. Won't abide it.'

She drew in another deep breath. 'I want to have money enough to set up my own household. Nothing fancy. A cottage somewhere.'

'Can't do it,' he said firmly. 'Married now.'

'Oh, I know. Anything I won would be his, by rights, but I plan to run away where he'd never find me.' She expected her husband would not even trouble himself to look for her.

She'd been round and round about this in her head. It was her duty to give him an heir, true, but he'd not approached her bed since that first night in Bath, when he'd thought she would bring him a fortune. She must conclude he had no wish to bed her now, heir or not. For all she knew he might have another woman to fulfil those manly needs.

But she could not bear to think of that.

'Won't fadge,' Robert said.

'It will so,' she countered. 'I have fifty pounds from our aunt's inheritance. I can stake that money on cards. I want you to take me to a place where ladies can gamble. Where I can win huge sums.'

He neglected the horses, but the beasts trudged ahead anyway. 'Botheration, Emily. Don't play the cards much any more. Lost a bundle. Stay away from those places.'

'Take me to one just one time, so I might be introduced. You don't have to play. After that, I will go on my own.'

'Can't go on your own, Emily,' he said. 'Ain't proper. Bound to see you. Tell your husband. Talk all about town.'

'I have no intention of going as myself,' Emily said. 'I will go in disguise.'

Robert dropped the ribbons and nearly lost his seat retrieving them.

Chapter Eight

Guy finished dressing for dinner, assuring Bleasby, whose assistance was often more taxing than doing without, that he had no further need of the butler's services and would indeed follow him downstairs directly. Bleasby finally ceased fussing over his master's coat and his neckcloth and left the room. Guy followed a pace or two behind.

A quick footstep sounded on the stairs, and Guy heard Emily's voice. 'Good evening, Bleasby,' she said brightly. 'I told you I would return in time for dinner.'

'Indeed, ma'am,' Bleasby answered.

She turned the corner at the top of the stairs, hurrying to her room, her face aglow with colour, a smile on her lips. The smile stopped Guy in his tracks.

'Oh,' she said, seeing him. Her smile fled.

He tried to disguise the plummeting of his spirits. 'I see you enjoyed your visit with your brother.'

Her cheeks turned a darker pink, the effect unintentional but most becoming. 'We…we took a ride in the park.'

Guy felt a stab of envy, which ought to have been some relief from the guilt he felt about her, but it wasn't. Her face had come alive for a fleeting second. Until she spied him.

What did he expect? Her brother had given her enjoyment. Her husband gave her nothing.

'The air did you good.' Guy's voice emerged stiff.

'Yes,' she said.

The familiar silence returned.

'I must hurry to dress for dinner,' she said.

'Of course.' He stepped past her, but turned before heading to the stairs. 'Emily?'

She paused at her doorway. 'Yes?'

'I am glad you enjoyed yourself.'

She stared at him, unspeaking, then entered her room.

That night Emily again could not sleep, her mind flooded with schemes. She'd extracted a promise from her brother to introduce her to a private gaming club where ladies could play. He would take her there a week to this day, an evening when no other obligations would impede her.

She'd dosed off finally, only to wake when she heard her husband open his bedchamber door. Wide awake again, she could not help but listen to him moving about the room, more restless this evening than other times. He'd probably lost.

His footsteps came towards the door connecting their rooms, and her heart nearly stopped. She held her breath. Surely he would not come in her room. To what purpose?

Memories of the two nights he'd spent with her came flooding back. How he'd gently undressed her on their marriage night. How his hands had felt on her skin that night in Bath. The thrill of him entering her. The sensations that erupted.

His footsteps retreated and soon all was quiet in his

room. She bit her lip to keep it from trembling. She'd promised herself never to think of the nights she'd spent with him. *Never.* He'd thought her wealthy then. He did not want her now.

How like a gamester, when holding aces and kings all full of bonhomie, but if the hand contained twos and threes, suddenly consumed by self-pity.

She would show him she was more than a widow hand, the hand dealt but left on the table for no one to play. She would be in the game at last and she would win.

The widow hand would win.

After breakfast she called Hester to her room. If her scheme was to work, she needed to call in the young maid's debt to her. Hoping her credit with Hester was high enough to ensure the girl's assistance and discretion, she described her plan.

Hester listened with widening eyes. 'But, my lady,' Hester interrupted her. 'Why ever would you want to do this? Won't it make his lordship angry if he discovers what you are doing?'

'He must not discover it, of course,' Emily said, trying to think of a reason the maid would accept. 'He…he needs money, you see.' True enough. 'And I wish to help him.'

'Aye.' Hester nodded. 'I've heard the others speak of his lordship needing money.'

Emily was a bit taken aback by Hester's statement, but she supposed the servants knew very well of her husband's gambling. 'Yes, and I wish to help him. I am skilled at cards, but he has refused to let me play at the places where good money may be won.'

'Lady Keating thinks you are a very good player,' agreed Hester.

Lady Keating had made that known? What a surprise.

'So I am. I know I will be successful, but Lord Keating must never know what I am doing. No one must know. I need a disguise, and that is where I beg your assistance.'

'Mine? I know nothing of gambling.'

'No, I need you to craft me a disguise,' Emily said. 'You are good with a needle.'

The girl beamed at the compliment. 'I thank you, ma'am, but you said you must be ready in a week. I cannot make you a disguise in a week. I do not know how to make a disguise.'

Emily opened the door to the small dressing room. She opened her mother's trunk. 'You shall do very well. We will alter my mother's dresses, and craft a mask and hat to obscure my face. I have it all worked out in my head.'

Her mother's clothes were nothing like what Emily wore. They pulled out rich silks in a rainbow of vibrant colours, gold, red, green, blue—not a muted tone among them.

Hester fingered the fine material, 'Oooh. They are beautiful!'

Emily pulled up a small chair and draped several dresses across her lap. The fabrics were lovely, but she could never wear so many frills. Her mother loved frills.

'Do you think you can work with these?' she asked the maid, still exclaiming over each new discovery in the trunk.

'Oh, my lady,' Hester responded dreamily, 'I don't know about making a disguise, but I can make these dresses into the prettiest in all London.'

A week later, Emily stood in front of the full-length mirror in her room. Her mother-in-law had retired in a miff when learning Emily would not be home to play cards with her and the aunts. Lady Pip and Miss Nuthall had said their goodnights shortly after. Her husband had gone out hours before. There was no one to concern themselves about her preparations.

She and Hester had selected an emerald green dress from her mother's trunk. Hester had removed much of the lace and ribbon on the bodice and narrowed the skirt. The result was a plain but elegant drape of satin, though the neckline was daringly low. With the extra material, the girl had created a hat, an elegant cap of satin and silk that included netting to pull over her face.

The mask, however, was Hester's real masterpiece. A buff-coloured silk, almost flesh in tone, it seemed moulded to the top half of Emily's face, leaving holes for her eyes. Hester had so cunningly crafted the mask it was barely noticeable, but managed all the same to obscure her identity.

In the trunk Emily had discovered a box of face powders and tints that her mother had either discarded or forgotten. Emily used them to rouge her cheeks and tint her lips and eyelashes, though she did so with a much lighter touch than her mother would have done.

She had also found an envelope of paste jewellery, more likely misplaced in the trunk. She chose an emerald-like pendant, surrounded by false diamonds.

Emily stared transfixed at her image in the mirror. She saw a stranger, an exotic, mysterious woman, nothing like herself. Surely no one would know who she really was, if she did not.

'You may call me Lady Widow,' she practised, using her mother's voice and holding her head up proudly as her top-lofty aunt had always done. It came more naturally to her than she would have supposed. 'Is there any gentleman kind enough to partner me in a game of whist?'

Yes, she sounded nothing like herself.

There was a soft knock on her door. Hester jumped to answer it, opening the door a mere crack. Rogers, the footman, had come to announce Mr Duprey's arrival.

Emily's heart leapt into her throat. She carefully removed the cap and mask and reached for her black cloak.

'Good luck, my lady,' Hester said, helping her into the garment.

'Oh, Hester,' Emily exclaimed, 'I shall need luck.'

She carefully tucked the hat and mask in an inside pocket, and impulsively gave the girl a quick hug.

Hester skipped over to open the bedchamber door. Emily hesitated. It was not too late to abandon this wild scheme. She could send her brother away—he would be delighted, she was sure—and continue her days as the new Lady Keating, wife to Guy Keating, in name only.

She set her jaw firmly, squeezed her hands into fists and strode purposefully through the doorway and down the stairs to where Robert waited, twirling his hat in his hand and bobbing from foot to foot.

Bleasby stood nearby, looking as if he might topple over from fatigue.

'I'm ready, Robert,' she said unnecessarily.

He responded with a look of gloom.

As Bleasby opened the door for them to depart, Emily whispered, 'Go to bed, Bleasby. That is an order. You will not be needed this night. Have Rogers attend the door.'

A grateful but guilty look passed his face. 'As you wish, my lady.'

Robert assisted Emily into a waiting hackney coach. Like another lucky card drawn off the top of the pack, Hester had a brother who drove a hackney coach and who, for a hefty fee, agreed to transport Emily on her nightly jaunts. Her brother's worries about her welfare were thus appeased, for the burly young man had also agreed to look out for her.

The cards had fallen so neatly into place, Emily had to believe in the rightness of her course of action. It was not a mistake to take her future into her own hands. Card hands, that was.

The hackney made its way down St James's Street. Emily thrust a pocket mirror at her brother and aimed it to where she could see to don her mask and turban.

'Zounds, Emily,' Robert said when she'd completed her disguise. 'Don't look like yourself.'

She flashed him a smile. 'Exactly so. And I am not Emily, you must remember. I am Lady Widow.'

'Ghastly name,' he said. 'Makes no sense.'

The name made sense to her, however.

They pulled up to a sedate-looking house on Bennett Street and Emily was relieved it looked like a respectable residence. Robert helped her out of the coach and escorted her to the door opened by a giant of a man dressed in livery. Robert nodded familiarly to the man, and they were admitted without question.

Inside, the house was ablaze with light, and the murmur of voices could be heard from rooms above stairs. They passed by a gentleman who greeted Robert by name and who ogled Emily with open curiosity. Robert quickly led her into the large gaming parlour. Its walls were bright yellow with carved white moulding, so bright she almost had to blink, as if in strong sunlight. She glanced up at the ceiling and quickly glanced back. The ceiling depicted a Bacchanal scene, with many unclothed figures whose activity she dared not examine too closely.

Card tables were set up in the centre. Along the walls were hazard tables and faro banks, with gaily dressed women to run them. There were mostly gentlemen playing at the tables, but a few women players dotted the room.

A lady circulated among the card players. Not a lady, actually. Her bright red dress was cut so low, her generous breasts seemed ready to topple out at any moment. It made Emily's look like a Quaker's. Her lips and cheeks were almost as bright as her dress and her hair, also red, was a shade Emily was certain did not exist in nature. As the woman threaded her way through the tables, she rested her hands on the gentlemen's shoulders or patted their cheeks.

Surely she was a madam, Emily thought, in the baser use of the term. She could not help but stare, fascinated, as one stared at the oddities displayed at Bartholomew Fair. The creature in red glanced in their direction, flashed a white-toothed smile at Robert, and headed directly for them. Emily, still clutching Robert's arm, felt him fidget.

She nearly panicked. As the madam came nearer and nearer, Emily suddenly remembered seeing a stairway to an upper floor. What sorts of rooms were up there? Rooms for gentlemen to pass time with women such as this one? She gazed around the room. There were other women patrons playing cards, but no one she'd ever been introduced to. She'd landed in the world of the *demi-monde*. What was she doing in this place?

The riffle of cards and clink of coin brought her back to her senses. She was here to win money, as were the more respectably dressed ladies who dotted the room, playing cards or throwing dice. She would not flee back to Essex Court now.

She stiffened her back. The creature in red descended on Robert, taking both of his cheeks in her hands and kissing him full on the lips. Emily nearly dropped her jaw.

'Robert, darling,' she said. 'Where have you been? We have missed you.'

Robert blushed as deep a red as the woman's dress. 'Been busy.'

Emily contrived to look composed. It was somewhat of a challenge.

The woman eyed her. 'Who have you brought with you, *chéri*? A paramour?'

'Good God, no,' exclaimed Robert. 'She's my—'

Emily pinched his wrist. Hard. 'I am a mere friend, I fear,' she said, remembering in time to affect her mother's voice.

'That's the thing.' Robert pulled away and rubbed his wrist. 'Friend. Wants to play. Secret. Masked, you know. Call her Lady Widow.'

The woman extended her hand to Emily. 'I quite understand. I am Madame Bisou.' She laughed. 'Like your name, a description. "Little kiss", no?'

Madame Bisou's French accent was undoubtedly as affected as Emily's own speech.

She returned the handshake with a wide smile. 'I see you do understand.'

Madame Bisou turned back to her brother. 'Robert, *chéri*, if I do not know your…friend's name, how am I to know she will play an honest game? How will my loyal guests be assured she will pay her debts?'

'Uh,' said Robert. 'Vouch for her. Upon my honour.'

Emily flashed Madame Bisou another smile. 'I do not intend to lose.'

The woman laughed. She threaded her arm through Robert's and pressed the profusion of her bosom into his chest. 'I like her, *chéri*.'

Emily averted her gaze. Raising her voice, she said, 'I

would like to play whist, *madame*, if some gentleman present would be kind enough to partner me.'

Several gentlemen looked up. They stared at her with a boldness that would get them banned forever from Almack's.

One gentleman stepped forward, grasping her hand to actually kiss it. 'It would be my pleasure, ma'am.' He kept hold of her hand and caressed it with his thumb.

It was Sir Reginald, her recent card partner and Keating family friend.

Emily's heart banged against her chest. He would recognise her. Surely he would recognise her.

She laughed, as her mother would have done at such attention. 'I am called Lady Widow, sir. And you are?'

'Sir Reginald Roscomb at your service, Lady Widow.' He kissed her hand again, and she could swear she felt his tongue through the lace-mittened gloves she wore. 'You must call me Reggie.'

Trying not to appear as discomfited as she felt, she laughed again, but pulled her hand away. 'Such familiarity, sir? Don't be shocking.'

Another gentleman approached from behind. He spoke in a smooth, silky voice. 'My lady, you will surely lose, if Sir Reginald is your partner. You must partner me.'

'Oh?' she said, arching one brow and turning towards this new voice.

Her knees almost gave way from under her. Cyprian Sloane gazed down at her, his smoky grey eyes drinking in every inch of her with more blatant appreciation than when he'd eyed her in the Assembly room at Bath. Surely *he* would recognise her.

He bowed. 'Mr Cyprian Sloane.'

Her head felt full of cotton wool and all the air seemed

to leave the room. But no recognition dawned in Sloane's sleepy eyes. Had she fooled even him?

She curtsied, leaning over ever so slightly to show her low neckline to best effect. The gentleman's gaze riveted to that very spot.

When she rose, she forced herself to form a most charming smile. 'Mr Sloane. You may call me Lady Widow.'

'I would be delighted,' he said smoothly. 'But which of us do you choose to be your…partner? The older man…or the younger? I assure you, ma'am, I play a more stimulating game than Sir Reginald and will have more stamina when matters become…more heated.'

'Stuff!' interjected Sir Reginald.

Even with her limited experience, Emily caught the *double entendre* in Sloane's words. He, of all gentlemen, thought of her in that…that bedroom way? It was inconceivable. And Sir Reginald, old enough to be her father, did he too want to bed her?

It could not be so. She ought to be scandalised at this behaviour, repelled, but, oddly enough, she mostly felt a very satisfying feminine thrill.

These men desired her. What a novelty.

In a moment three others came to press her to select them. She tittered and giggled as her mother might have done, flirting with each of them. Robert, standing at the edge of her new admirers, wore a horrified expression. She caught his eye and made a face.

'Gentlemen, gentlemen,' she admonished, turning back to her flock. 'I intend to play all night. And if the cards are very good to me, I promise to return. You may all have a chance to play with me.'

While she spoke, the double meaning of her words dawned on her, every bit as shocking as Sloane's had been. She laughed at herself. What fun it was to say and do what one pleased.

All this masculine admiration, however, was not fattening her pockets. She had come to play cards.

She raised her arms to silence her new admirers. 'I will have Sir Reginald as my first gentleman,' she said, giving him a meaningful look that brought a huff of pride to his face.

She knew Sir Reginald to be a skilled player. She would not risk the little money she had partnering someone who had no card sense. Perhaps when she'd had an opportunity to observe the players, she would discover the best player, then she would know who her next partner would be.

She turned to Sloane. 'You may be my opponent, Mr Sloane. Do you fancy engaging in a contest with me?'

A seductive smile grew slowly across his face. 'I would fancy engaging you in any manner,' he said.

Oh, this was capital fun!

She searched her other admirers and picked a gentleman who had said he was with the East India Company, surmising he might have plenty of money to lose. 'Would you like to play as well, sir?' she asked.

'My pleasure,' the man replied.

Sloane assisted her into her chair, brushing his hand across her bare shoulders. Sir Reginald took his place opposite her.

As Sir Reginald dealt the cards, she spied Madame Bisou whispering in Robert's ear. A moment later, Robert left the room with her, disappearing in a blur of red as her skirts swished out the door. Emily felt her cheeks heat and hoped the gentlemen at her table did not notice. Her brother?

With all the artistry of a coquette, she charmed the gentlemen of her table to limit the stakes to suit her, ensuring her fifty pounds would be sufficient. She hoped in the future to have less need of limits. Their agreement was unanimous and immediate. They would do anything she desired. It was a heady feeling, indeed.

Winning came more easily than she'd dreamed, but she suspected Sloane and the East India man were conspiring to be kind to her. It wounded her pride to think they assumed she was not their equal at cards. Or perhaps they merely wished to court her favour. Sir Reginald, not to be outdone by the younger men, plied her with lavish compliments. So much so, she feared flushing with embarrassment.

In any event, her pile of counter pieces grew higher.

'La, gentlemen,' she exclaimed, 'you bring me such luck I dare renege on my promise to give others a chance.'

Protests sounded from all directions. She eventually allowed three other gentlemen to sit at her table, but the only contest seemed to be who could build her stack higher.

Sloane contrived to escort her in to supper and to seat her at a table in a secluded corner.

'You intrigue me, my lady,' he murmured to her, handing her a glass of champagne.

She sipped, and the bubbles seemed to sparkle inside her. 'I, sir?' She fluttered her lashes.

'I want to know who you are. Why you must hide such beauty under a mask.'

Such beauty? Now that was flummery, indeed. Still, her chest fluttered, and she felt the colour rise in her cheeks.

She took another sip. 'It is very simple, my lord. I wish to play cards and I prefer not to be spoken of for doing so.'

He peered at her from above his glass. 'So you are known in town?'

She gave him a sly smile. 'Isn't everyone?'

At that moment Robert walked up. 'Found you, Em—mmm—my lady.' His neckcloth was a dishevelled mess, and the perfect curls of his hair had been thoroughly disordered. 'Must leave. Getting late, y'know.'

'Not so soon,' protested Sloane. 'We were just becoming…acquainted.'

Emily pretended to sigh. In a bold move, she touched Sloane's cheek as Madame Bisou had done. 'Another time, perhaps,' she murmured. 'I should enjoy another round of whist with you.'

He lifted his glass. 'To another round, Lady Widow.'

She rose from the chair. Cyprian Sloane rose as well, capturing her hand and kissing it. Three more gentlemen, including Sir Reginald, kissed her hand before she made it to the door. Madame Bisou, waiting in the hall, gave Robert a full-on-the-lips kiss. Emily swore the woman's tongue was in his mouth before it ended. Surprisingly she felt a wave of sensation, remembering exactly how her husband's tongue had tasted.

Her husband.

Would her husband even care if another gentleman kissed her the way Madame Bisou kissed Robert? Any number of the gentlemen she met this night might kiss her that way if she allowed it. Emily ought to have been shocked at thinking such a thing, but somehow, as Lady Widow, she found it rather intoxicating.

When they were in the hackney, Emily pulled off her hat and mask.

Robert exclaimed, 'Zounds, Emily. Acting like a high-flyer. Not proper.'

'Look what pot calls the kettle black,' she countered. 'What were you and Madame Bisou engaging in while I was merely playing cards?'

She could almost feel him blush. 'Don't want to say, Em. Cost a bundle, though.'

She patted his arm. 'Do not fret about me. I am there to play cards, nothing else.'

'Not a proper place, Em,' he said.

'Oh, do not be a gudgeon. I won, Robert,' she cried, shaking him with her excitement. 'I more than tripled my money!'

He curled up to escape her revelry.

She ignored him. 'Will you come with me again? I think I can slip out tomorrow evening after the others are asleep.'

'Won't do it,' he said.

She pursed her lips and glared at him. What did it matter? She didn't need him. She would go alone.

When the hack left her off at Essex Court, she made the arrangements with the driver to pick her up the following night at the place they had agreed upon. She would sneak down the servants' staircase and cross the mews.

Emily leaned in the coach window. 'Thank you, Robert,' she said.

'Don't like it, Emily,' he responded, his voice gloomy.

The coach pulled away.

Rogers must have been watching for her, because he opened the door as soon as she walked up to it. She made her way up the stairs as quietly as she could. When she reached her bedchamber, the door to her husband's room opened.

She jumped. 'Oh!'

'I thought I heard you come in,' he said.

He was dressed in his shirtsleeves, the white of his shirt

glowing in the near darkness of the hallway, lit only by one small candle.

She gathered her cloak more tightly around her to hide her dress, glad it was too dark for him to see her face clearly.

'Yes,' she said. 'It is dreadfully late, I know, but—'

He rested one arm against the door-frame, high, so that his shirtsleeve slid down, revealing his bare skin. 'You went out with your brother?'

'Yes. To a…a card party.' *Please don't ask where*, she silently pleaded. Foolish of her not to have a ready story prepared, but who would have guessed anyone would be curious enough to ask?

'Did you enjoy yourself?' he said.

'Yes.' She felt weak with relief that he, this time as always, did not care where she had been.

He stood there staring at her. All the courage with which she'd faced the evening fled. No more giddy excitement. No heady sensation of feminine attraction. At this moment, she felt more like the Haymarket ware her brother accused her of being.

His voice crossed her gloom. 'I'm glad,' was all he said. 'Goodnight.'

He disappeared into his room. Emily expelled a long breath, but the glee at the night's success had suddenly left her.

Cyprian Sloane left the house on Bennett Street and stepped into the chill of the night air. No matter. He fancied a walk to his hotel.

Swinging his swordstick, he made his way to St James's Street, feeling more alive than he had in months, and all due to the mysterious Lady Widow.

Boredom had brought him to London, where the lure

of the gaming hells promised more excitement than Bath. What entertainment had been in Bath? Dull card games without a shred of excitement? The priggish Emily Keating? He needed more than the diversion of putting a milk-and-water miss to the blush.

London offered better sport. By Jove, hadn't he found it at Madame Bisou's? He'd expected at least a decent card game, maybe a toss in the blankets with one of her girls, but then *she* walked in.

Lady Widow. Arrogant and seductive and full of mystery. Desired by every man in the room. He'd be damned if he didn't become the first to peel off that mask of hers and to keep going until he peeled off the rest of her clothes as well. He'd wager on it.

Life was grand. He laughed out loud, startling the watchman sitting in his box. 'Good evening, man!' he called, thumping on the box with his stick.

The man grumbled a reply.

With another laugh, Cyprian set off again, whistling 'The Lass on Richmond Hill'.

Chapter Nine

Two weeks later at half past midnight, Guy sat near the bow window at White's, nursing a brandy. The card room was thin of players, a good excuse to relax with a drink before letting the cards perform their own manner of intoxication.

He would much rather have remained at home. He'd escorted his mother and Emily to the theatre this night and had not relished going back out after they both retired. If he did not play, however, he would not win. So here he was.

He swirled the brandy in his glass, idly watching how its spiral reflected in the light of a nearby lamp. It would have been pleasant to sit in front of a fire in his own parlour, sipping his own brandy, going off to bed at a decent hour. More pleasant than facing a stuffy card room with men whose luck and skill might exceed his own.

Even more pleasant would be to knock on his wife's bedchamber door. Enjoy the fruits of married life, but that was too soon to contemplate.

Maybe some day he could contrive a way to woo his wife, renew that intimacy they'd only begun to explore.

If he hadn't bungled everything, that is. If he could ever risk creating an heir.

He set the brandy to spinning again, eyes fixed upon its play, like a man in a trance. It would be very pleasant to mend that particular breach with his wife. In daylight so much distance loomed between them, but perhaps through that physical act of marriage they could forge a real union with each other.

Her response to his attempts at lovemaking had been sweet, really. Touching. Hopeful.

But hope could be sucked away in an instant. Sometimes it seemed to him that catastrophe loomed in every corner of the realm, perhaps in the whole world. Corn prices kept rising, riots were reported out in the countryside. People were starving. Whenever he walked down the street desperate men begged for pennies, the same men who had fought beside him on the Peninsula and at Waterloo. No winning at cards would ever be enough to stem this tide of poverty.

He raised the glass to his mouth, tasting the amber liquid, savouring the warmth it created as he swallowed.

Cards were a respite, he had to admit. When he was deep in play, he never thought of the world's catastrophes. Nor of his wife, his family, Annerley. He only thought of winning and losing. If he won a hand, he wanted to see how much more he could win. If he lost, he wanted to play until he reversed his luck.

It was a constant struggle to make his head control his play. To force himself to quit when ahead, to walk away when he lost. So far, he had won the struggle and had won more money than he had lost. He could credit himself with coming a long way towards saving Annerley and his family's future.

But he had not quite completed the battle. At the next seating, would he keep his head?

'Why, Keating!' a man's voice boomed from behind him. 'That is you, by Jupiter. I thought so.'

Sir Reginald clapped him on the shoulder and plopped his portly frame in the opposite chair.

'How do you do, Sir Reginald?' Guy said. 'Rare to see you here.'

'Yes. Yes.' Sir Reginald signalled for a drink. 'I don't fancy White's much at this hour. More tempting enticements in town.'

'Indeed?' said Guy, without true interest.

'Yes, indeed.' Sir Reginald nodded thanks to the footman who set a drink on the table. 'Just came in to collect on a small debt. I'm off to Madame Bisou's.' He took a sip. 'Come with me, lad.'

'Madame Bisou's?' he repeated automatically.

'Delightful place, I assure you.' Sir Reginald gave a jovial laugh. 'Games are honest. Women, pretty and clean, if you fancy a bit of sport.'

Honest games?

That caught his attention. He had considered venturing out to one of the gaming establishments that abounded on and around St James's Street. He'd been afraid to risk it.

Sir Reginald sipped his drink. 'Capital sport there, I tell you.' He leaned forward, speaking to Guy in hushed tones. 'There is a woman there I fancy very much. She is perfection. A piece of quality baggage. I'm about to offer her *carte blanche*. Called in a few vowels here to fatten my offer.'

Guy tried to sound amused. 'She sounds like a veritable Venus. What makes you think this Madame Bisou would let her go?'

'No. No. No.' Sir Reginald held up his hand. 'This

one's not in the business. No, indeed. She's a patron. Comes to play cards, she says.' He leaned closer. 'She is magnificent, Keating. Figure is perfection. And she wears this mask, you see—'

'To cover some imperfection, no doubt,' Guy interjected.

Sir Reginald looked wounded. 'I am sure there is not one part of her that is flawed. She just don't want anyone to know who she is, that's the ticket. All I need is one more run of luck and I shall have enough blunt to win her. Young blokes won't have a chance. There's a wager going, don't y'know, on who beds the lady first. I intend to win it.'

Guy smiled inwardly. Just one more run of luck? Just another big win? Sir Reginald repeated words that were constantly swimming around Guy's mind. One more round of luck and maybe Guy would win the lady, too, only the lady would be his wife.

He glanced back to the drink in his hand. If Sir Reginald's masked lady was the object of such a wager, she was probably out of the man's reach. Perhaps Emily was out of Guy's reach, as well. He'd certainly done nothing to win her.

'Come with me, Keating,' insisted the older man. 'One look at her and you will see what I mean.'

Guy glanced towards the game room. He'd not likely win his fortune there tonight. 'Games are honest, you say?'

'Depend upon it,' Sir Reginald said.

'Is the play deep?'

'Deep as you like,' assured Sir Reginald.

He shrugged. 'Very well. As you said, things are too tame here. Perhaps I should try my luck elsewhere.'

'Excellent. Excellent.' Sir Reginald rose, clapping him on the shoulder again. 'Let's be off.'

Emily rushed in to Madame Bisou's, later than usual. She'd waited until she was sure Lady Keating was asleep and her husband had departed. She hoped the card room would not be too full for her to play.

'Evenin', ma'am,' the footman said.

'Good evening, Cummings.' She was familiar to him now, a regular customer. She handed him her cloak and rushed up the stairs.

Cyprian Sloane was walking in the opposite direction. He gave her one of his most charming smiles. 'Why, Lady Widow, I nearly gave up on you. I was about to depart.'

She laughed at him. 'Mr Sloane, do not say you come here only to see me.'

He stood in her way, much too close. 'Very well,' he purred. 'I will not say it, for all that it is true.'

Sloane had become one of Lady Widow's most faithful admirers, singling her out, contriving to share supper with her alone on more than one occasion. It was flattering, even amusing, to watch his rakish technique, how he drew her in and tried to cast her under his spell. For two nights he'd seemed to ignore her completely. What an excellent ploy that had been. Without even realising it, she'd found herself wanting to seek him out.

This was a mere cat-and-mouse game they played, she knew. She doubted his intent to be any more serious than her own. Although he might relish a brief liaison, she definitely would not, as she told him when he asked her to accompany him to the upper floor. Several times.

'If I might pass, sir?' Emily kept her voice light.

He did not move.

'I must go, sir,' she said, irritated at him. 'I came to play cards. That is my passion, you know.'

He favoured her with the smile again. 'Are you sure you would not fancy other passions? Come above stairs with me. I will show you more excitement than a hand full of trumps.'

She spoke more firmly. 'Indeed not, sir.'

He leaned on the banister, but still took up too much space for her to get by. 'Why not?' he asked. 'Do you have some husband somewhere whose anger you fear? I assure you I am a match for any husband.'

'I will not tell you.' She made her voice light again. Matters went easier with him when she treated everything as a joke. 'So don't tease me, Mr Sloane.'

Again he leaned closer, his breath hot against her tender skin. 'Call me Cyprian. I long to hear my name on your lips.'

She placed her hands on his chest and pushed him away. The game had gone far enough for one night.

'Mr Sloane,' she said sternly, 'it would not be proper to address you so familiarly.'

He gave her a pained look, one she suspected was designed to melt a woman's resolve. 'You wound me mortally, my lady.'

'Gammon,' she said.

He grinned and stepped aside so she could go in the card room. 'Another time, perhaps?'

She tossed him an exasperated glance and hurried in to see who might play whist with her. Madame Bisou rushed up to her immediately.

'Lady Widow,' the woman said in her false French accent. 'Have you brought your…friend Robert with you?'

What did the woman see in her fribble of a brother? 'Not tonight, *madame*.'

The madam, dressed in a truly awful shade of purple, pushed her mouth into a moue and quickly lost interest in Lady Widow.

Several gentlemen leapt to their feet upon seeing her and begged her to play at their tables. It never ceased to amaze her. They treated her as if she were the most desirable creature in London. It was the mask, of course. It lent mystery. It also was curiously liberating. She could say and do as she pleased and no one knew who she was. No one could reproach her.

Thus far, Emily had confined her play to whist, no matter how strenuously she was urged to throw dice or turn cards at faro. Those were fools' games, too dependent on luck, a goddess her father and husband might revere, but she did not. Luck alone was too fickle. Skill gave her a winning edge.

Ironically, Madame Bisou's house gave her little opportunity to exercise her skill. Her counters might stack higher and higher in front of her, but the gentlemen who begged her company mostly contrived to let her win. She could tell. She'd watched their play at other tables, taking no time at all to recognise the serious players.

The women had no interest at all in playing whist with her. On the contrary, they often tossed her jealous looks when men clustered around her, acting like buffoons. These men played cards like buffoons as well, with the intent of currying her favour. Did they think she could not tell?

She supposed she ought not to complain, for her fortune grew steadily. The gamester in her protested, however.

A place was made for her at one of the tables, and she sat down with the son of a Duke, the East India man, and a much decorated naval captain. Men who had been deep in cards when she first walked in, now straightened in their seats, asked after her comfort, begged to get her a glass of wine. Lady Widow laughed at their solicitousness.

'Let us play cards, gentlemen,' she said.

The Duke's son dealt. She saw Sloane enter the room. He had not decided to leave after all. After her rebuff, would he finagle a chance to play at her table or was this a night to ignore her? It would be amusing to find out.

The hands went quickly and Emily's stack rose higher, as usual. In a fortnight, her fifty pounds had quickly ballooned into more than two thousand. How much she needed to live as an independent woman, she did not know, but it would require many more nights at Madame Bisou's. She did not mind. Life had become rather exciting.

Even if the card games lacked excitement. After several unchallenging games, other gentlemen begged her to change tables. Her stack grew higher. When Madame Bisou announced that supper was served, Emily was almost relieved. In spite of the exhilaration of Lady Widow's success, with any challenge lacking, she was beginning to get bored.

The East India man was the first to beg her company at supper. A glance at Cyprian Sloane showed he was not at all pleased. Emily grinned to herself. It was so easy to make a man jealous. She gave Sloane a saucy glance as she allowed the East India man to walk her to the door.

Sir Reginald appeared in the doorway, a huge grin erupting on his beefy face when he spied her. He strode towards her, another gentleman behind him.

With a face flushed red, Sir Reginald grasped her hand and kissed it. 'Lady Widow, you are a feast for my eyes.'

Emily laughed. 'I thought you had forgotten all about me, sir.'

'Never. Never. You are constantly in my thoughts.' He gave her a meaningful smile and squeezed her hand.

She pulled it away. 'You tease me, of course.'

'I was never more serious,' he said, 'But I've brought someone I wanted to meet you.' He stepped aside.

Emily froze.

Her husband stood before her. He would recognise her. He must. No one else who knew her had recognised her, but surely her husband would! A loud buzzing sounded in her ears. Everything faded from her sight except her husband, handsome as always, still in the evening attire he'd worn escorting her to the theatre.

Sir Reginald gestured him come forward. 'May I present Lord Keating to you, dear lady.'

He bowed to her. 'My pleasure, Lady Widow.'

When he rose from his bow, he looked straight in her face, shrouded as it was by her mask and the netting of her hat.

This is the moment, she thought. *He will know me.* Her knees turned weak. She thought she might faint.

But no recognition flickered in his sapphire blue eyes. Guy Keating, the man she married, looked at Lady Widow the same way every man in this room had done. With definite masculine appreciation.

'My very great pleasure.' He took her hand and raised it to his lips as Sir Reginald had done.

'Lord Keating, is it?' she managed to say.

He still did not recognise her. He smiled at her, that smile of unspoken invitation. She'd come to expect such smiles at Madame Bisou's. But not from her husband.

But he thought her to be Lady Widow, did he not? Lady Widow, who dressed in daring fashions. Lady Widow, who tinted her lips and cheeks. Lady Widow, who'd become the toast of one bawdy gaming hell. Her husband smiled at Lady Widow. Not Emily. Not his wife.

'You are going in to supper?' The gleam remained in his eye. 'Perhaps Sir Reginald and I might join you?'

The East India man huffed in disapproval. Emily ignored it, feeling an anger building in her so fiercely, she thought she might plant her husband a facer, pop his cork, draw some claret.

How dare he look at Lady Widow in this…this leering sort of way, when in his own home, he did not look at her at all? Is this what he was about when he went out at night? Was he jauntering through the London hells, searching for just such a creature as Lady Widow? A woman he might dally with? Goodness knows, he had no wish to dally with his wife.

Her throat constricted and a bitter taste filled her mouth. Why could he not look at Emily in that manner? Why could he not look at *her*? The jelly her insides had become now solidified into sharp-edged steel.

If her husband so desired Lady Widow, Lady Widow would lead him a merry dance. She would entice him and tease him. She would become everything he fancied. She would lead him to the brink and then she would push him over so hard, he would be knocked out of his senses. And when Lady Widow left him, he would know exactly what he had lost.

She leaned towards him to make sure he appreciated the low cut of the gold silk gown Hester had transformed. She lifted her hand and ran her finger slowly down his arm. He responded. His eyes darkened. Colour infused his face. His posture changed.

She smiled. 'Your company, sir, would give me great pleasure.'

Taking his arm, she pressed her bosom into his side as

she'd seen Madame Bisou do to Robert. He escorted her to the supper room, leaving Sir Reginald and the East India man to trail behind like two baby ducklings. Sloane glared at her from across the room.

Guy's gaze feasted upon the woman seated across from him in the supper room, his blood coursing through his veins. She had certainly roused his senses.

When he'd seen her stride gracefully across the room, her chin had been elevated regally. Her hips swayed gently. She'd moved with the knowledge that every man in that room wanted her in bed with him.

God help him, Guy was no exception. No wonder Sir Reginald was besotted. Guy was somewhat shocked that he'd reacted so physically. Every sense in his body was aroused. Every one.

Why her? He had certainly encountered other beautiful women on occasion. What was it about this one that stirred him so?

He had an uncanny notion he ought to know her, but that was nonsense. Surely he would remember. Lady Widow, masked or unmasked, could not be a female to forget. Still, the feeling of familiarity nagged at him.

She flirted openly with him, batting her eyelashes, touching his arm, pressing her knee against his. He was not immune. No, she'd whipped him into a vortex of sexual desire the likes of which he had not known since before he'd reached his majority.

When a droplet of wine rested on her lip and she slowly licked it off with her pink tongue, he was struck again with the feeling he'd seen this before, and reacted as strongly. At least the notion distracted him from his sudden raw sexual need.

'Why have you come to Madame Bisou's, Lord Keating?' she asked, music in her voice. 'To sample her lovely girls?'

He swallowed some wine. 'To play cards.'

'Indeed?' Her eyes widened from under her mask. 'That is why I attend as well. To play.' She paused and gave him a saucy look. 'Play cards, that is.' She was a seductress all right.

She swept her gaze over the other gentlemen at the table, lighting upon Sir Reginald, who puffed up like a rooster about to crow. 'The gentlemen here are not very good players, I fear.' Her eyes, looking golden like her dress, glittered with amusement. 'I seem to win almost every game I play. Perhaps you wish to partner me? You will win, too.'

He took another sip of wine, a bit wary of the effect she had on him. 'If you wish it.'

Her smile widened, and she shifted her attention to one of the other gentleman sitting with them, asking him something about trade with India.

A few minutes later, she declared supper over, and all the gentlemen rose in unison. Lucky Sir Reginald had the pleasure of escorting her back to the card room. Guy took up the rear.

He regarded her more dispassionately, an easier task with her back turned, even though that view of her was delightful as well. She flirted with him quite blatantly. Did he wish for a dalliance? Lord knew, he ached for release. Lady Widow was more temptation than his imagination could have conjured up, and he'd not lain with a woman since that night with his wife.

His wife. Emily, alone at home in bed. Always alone. And her husband could do nothing to bring enjoyment into her life, as her brother had so briefly done. Never her husband.

Lady Widow turned around, as if checking to be sure he followed her, smiling when she saw he did. Damn him, he could easily be hooked.

He blew out the breath he'd not been aware of holding. He had no intention of being unfaithful to his wife, no matter how much temptation a masked lady might be. Even if she could never discover it, his conscience would never allow him. He'd betrayed his wife enough.

Lady Widow led him to a table, directing him to be her partner and designating Sir Reginald and another man as their opponents. They all scurried to do her bidding, like bees buzzing around their queen.

She pointedly favoured Guy with her coy glances and flirtatious banter throughout the game. As she'd predicted, Sir Reginald and the other gentleman played like simpletons, putting down high trumps when low ones would do or leading with suits they knew she'd held. Lady Widow squealed becomingly at every trick she won. She grinned when the losing team pushed their counters to her side.

Guy gave Sir Reginald an amused glance. He'd watched Sir Reginald partner Emily in whist and knew the man to be a crack player. The love-struck old fool was merely tossing away money. Sir Reginald was a nodcock for letting his funds dribble through his fingers. He'd be better off playing at a high-stakes table and winning the fortune he said would entice the lady. The man could do it. He and Emily had been formidable opponents.

Sir Reginald and Emily.

Guy's head snapped up. He stared at Lady Widow as she regarded the hand she'd just been dealt. She tapped the cards against her fingertips, then snapped the cards into place exactly like a practised gamester.

Exactly like Emily. Guy's heart thudded in his chest. Could it be?

She looked up. He quickly averted his gaze for the moment, arranging his own hand. As the round commenced, he watched her carefully. When the cards were in play, her face held no expression. No smile, no frown, no clue to what she really thought or felt.

How many times had he seen that same lack of expression? Certainly in that game of whist more than a fortnight ago. He'd not thought about it, but, then, he'd glimpsed the same lack of expression every day when he said good morning at the breakfast sideboard.

By God, she was Emily. Lady Widow was Emily.

'Your turn, Keating,' Sir Reginald said.

He quickly put down a trump, winning the hand.

The game was theirs. Lady Widow's face lit with delight. 'Oh, thank you, Lord Keating! We have won again!' Smiling, she leaned over the table and scooped up the counters, giving all the gentlemen a good glimpse of her décolletage. 'Did I not tell you I always win?'

He wanted to throw his coat over her chest. This woman was nothing like his wife, but she was Emily all the same. He was very certain. 'Indeed you did, my lady,' he replied.

'You must play with me some more,' she teased, her eyes filling with mischief.

Would Emily speak so provocatively? No, she would not, but he heard the words coming from her mouth. 'The night is merely beginning,' he said.

She grinned wickedly at him. 'Do you mean to say you wish to spend the whole of the night with me, Lord Keating? I assure you, sir, other gentlemen will wish their turn.'

His body lit like a rushlight touched to flame, the heat of raw carnal desire. But before he went completely up in flames, he struggled to consider that this wife of his now spoke like a skilled coquette. What games was she playing here besides whist? Nothing yet, if Sir Reginald's tale of a wager was true.

By God, these gentlemen were wagering on bedding his wife! He had half a mind to call them all out. He had half a mind to drag her away from this place this very moment. Drag her to *his* bedchamber at least.

That would not answer, however, no matter how much he craved it. What was she doing here? Why was she dressed in this disguise? Why was she flirting with every man in the place—even her husband?

He'd never discover her purpose by prematurely tipping his hand. She did not know he recognised her. She believed he thought her to be Lady Widow. He could play along for a while, until he found out exactly what she was up to. And, by God, he would be here every night to make sure none of these men collected on that wager.

After winning the next game, she yawned, stretching her arms above her head and declaring she must retire for the night. All three men jumped to their feet as she rose from her chair, Guy included.

'Now, I do not need all three of you to escort me to the door, do I?' She swept her gaze over the three of them, letting it light on Guy longer than the others. 'I pick…Sir Reginald!'

'Delighted. Delighted.' Sir Reginald nearly knocked over his chair to give her his arm.

Guy's fingers curled into fists. By God, he didn't care if Sir Reginald was on the far side of fifty and an old friend of his father's, the man was asking for a duel if he led Guy's wife to a room above stairs.

Trying to appear calm, Guy wandered over to the door a bit behind Sir Reginald and *his* wife. If they turned to the stairway leading above, Guy would not be far behind.

None other than Cyprian Sloane waylaid him.

'No need to draw daggers, Keating,' Sloane said, sounding as slippery a cad as ever. 'She'll allow Sir Reginald help her with her cloak and walk her to her hack. Nothing more. He's no rival.'

What the devil was that fellow doing here? 'Sloane,' Guy said, pushing towards the doorway. 'Didn't know you were in town.'

As he reached the hallway, Sir Reginald's voice sounded from down in the hall. Guy heard the front door open and close. Apparently Sloane had been correct. Guy bit down on a relieved sigh and leaned against the wall.

Sloane, who had followed him, eyed him curiously. Of all people, why should Sloane show up here? He'd been in Bath, and here he was again. Was this an accident? Had Emily come to meet Sloane in this place? She'd hardly given him a glance, however. Or was that because her husband had walked in the door?

'Have a drink with me,' Sloane said, bending his head to the supper room.

Guy's eyes narrowed slightly. What better way to discover what kind of fast shuffle the man was playing with Guy's wife?

The supper room was nearly empty. They sat at a secluded table where no one would overhear their conversation. Sloane ordered whisky for them both. After the pretty maid delivered it, Guy sipped and waited.

Sloane lifted his glass as if in a toast. 'Congratulations, Keating. You seem to have won the regard of our Lady Widow. I commend you.'

Guy gave Sloane a shrug. 'What concern is this of yours?'

'I lay claim to her. I saw her first.' Sloane's voice

dropped into a more menacing tone. 'Consider yourself informed.'

'Indeed?' Guy kept his cards close to his chest, but he certainly did so with effort. 'She has your *carte blanche*?'

Sloane did not break off his gaze, but Guy perceived a fleeting look of uncertainty there. 'Not quite.' Sloane paused before continuing, 'She's a wily creature, Keating. Not an easy win. I intend to be the first to bed her, however.'

Guy nearly rose from his chair to plant his fist in Sloane's face. With difficulty he adopted a calm demeanour. Could Sloane indeed not know he was speaking of bedding Guy's wife?

'Why are you telling me this?' Guy asked casually.

Sloane took a swig of his drink. 'Damned if I know,' he said. 'Maybe to make the game more challenging. No cards hidden.'

'The game?'

Sloane smiled. 'The game of who wins the lady. Have you put your wager in the betting book? Stakes are at four thousand, I believe.'

Guy's fingers squeezed the glass in his hand. This was his wife Sloane spoke of! His wife the men had bet on! He silently fought for control. They could not know Lady Widow was his wife. Even a man like Sloane would not speak in this manner to a husband of his wife.

Guy believed he discovered the gentlemen's interest in Lady Widow, but he still did not know why Emily engaged in this masquerade. He'd discover nothing if he unleashed his temper. 'Who the devil is she, anyway?' he asked instead.

Sloane's brows rose. 'No one knows. Makes the game more interesting. The winner removes the mask!'

Guy let that one pass.

Sloane glared at him. 'The point is, Keating, *I* claim her. I aim to win. Do not waste your money on this wager. She's mine.'

No, Guy thought. *She's mine.*

The air vibrated with tension. The two men stared each other down, like two Captain Sharps, each daring the other to accuse him of playing a dirty game.

Guy figuratively threw in a stack of coins. 'Seems to me the lady decides,' he said. 'You play your cards, Sloane, and I'll play mine. We'll see whose hand wins the lady.'

Guy would play his hand, yes, indeed. He'd return to Madame Bisou's, every night if necessary, until he discovered why his wife came there in a mask, flirting like a demi-rep. He'd return to make certain Sloane failed in his plan to entice Lady Widow into his bed. He'd return to make sure all of them failed.

No one would bed Lady Widow. No one save her husband.

Chapter Ten

Emily slept late the next morning. Or rather, she remained abed, until certain her husband would not be about. It was his habit to go out in the morning, off on some jaunt in town. Perhaps he'd go to White's to boast of meeting Lady Widow.

She rolled onto her side, hugging her pillow. Silly. No one would speak of Lady Widow at White's. Lady Widow's renown confined itself to one gaming hell. Not very auspicious fame, but more than Emily had expected to experience. She had aimed merely to be considered above reproach in every quarter. Ironic that by being Lady Widow she risked every shred of her reputation. Emily would be mortified if discovered.

But even her husband had not known her. Lady Widow's mask proved to be an effective shield. She could say and do as she pleased.

Even flirt with her husband, if she chose to.

Emily sat up and pressed her fingers to her temple. Why had he, of all gentlemen, walked into Madame Bisou's? It changed everything. She must not allow him to ruin her plans. She would make sport of him instead, show him how his desires could be shattered just as easily as hers…

She drew her knees up and wrapped her arms around them. No, she must not admit to any foolish notion that she'd hoped for anything more from her marriage besides an escape from her parents. She'd known from the beginning it was a marriage of convenience. She merely had not known that the convenience her husband sought was a fortune to gamble away. She'd thought he sought an heir.

What a lovely idea. A baby. A robust boy with hair as dark as mahogany and eyes as blue as the sea. She sunk her head to her knees. This was indeed foolish in the extreme. Her husband avoided her bed. There would be no baby from this marriage.

Do not think of that, she scolded herself. *Think of how he looked upon Lady Widow. Think of the sweet revenge when she spurns him.*

The clock struck noon. Had she ever stayed in bed this long? Dragging herself from beneath the covers, she summoned Hester to help her dress.

'You have slept late, my lady,' Hester remarked.

'I was out very late.'

Would not Hester's eyes grow round as saucers if Emily told her the disguise she'd fashioned worked so effectively that Emily's own husband did not know her?

She and Hester had created a more dazzling creature. Lady Widow made his eyes glitter with desire. The reprobate.

'Did you win the card game?' Hester asked.

Oh, she'd won more than a card game. She'd won the favour of Lord Keating himself.

'Of course I won.' Emily opened a drawer and removed four shillings, dropping them into the maid's palm.

'Thank you, ma'am.' Hester curtsied and, with a wide grin, thrust the coins in a pocket of her apron.

'And your brother received his share as well.'

Still beaming, Hester skipped over to the wardrobe. 'What dress today, ma'am?'

Lady Widow would undoubtedly have picked something bright and gay, but Emily Keating owned nothing of that description. 'My green and brown stripe, I suppose.' The stripe was about as dashing as ever-so-proper Emily Keating could manage, which was to say, not at all.

Hester helped her into the dress, tying the laces in the back. The looking glass reflected back a drab young woman in a drab outfit. Emily sighed. It really was much more fun to dress in something like the gold confection that had captivated her husband the night before. For the first time Emily appreciated her mother's madness for the latest fashions.

Hester arranged her hair in a simple knot on top of her head. Emily wondered how Lady Widow would wear her hair if she went without her hat?

Probably in a becoming cascade of curls.

When she finished dressing, Emily made her way down the stairs. As she reached the first floor, the Dowager Lady Keating called from the drawing room, 'Is that you?'

Not, 'Is that you, Emily?', which would make some sense, but, 'Is that you?', which avoided using her name, and could be answered affirmatively by anyone.

She took a deep breath. 'It is Emily.'

Her mother-in-law appeared at the drawing-room door. 'You slept the morning, did you not?'

'My apologies, Lady Keating. Did you require me?'

Lady Keating walked back into the drawing room, no doubt expecting Emily to follow. 'I have several calls to make and I need someone to accompany me. I hope you do not have plans.'

The word *plans* was emphasised, referring, Emily supposed, to the one day her brother had called upon her.

Emily lingered at the doorway. 'I shall accompany you, if you wish.'

'Good,' said Lady Keating, 'because Guy has taken Aunt Dorrie and Aunt Pip out in the curricle, and I have no one else I might ask.'

He'd taken the aunts out? How nice of him. The dutiful grand-nephew.

'Indeed,' she said.

A tension inside her eased. She would not run into him after all. Inexplicably, this easing of tension closely resembled disappointment.

Lady Keating went on, 'Aunt Dorrie got a notion she needed air and ribbons, so Guy took them to the shops.'

Good for him, Emily thought. She hoped they would make him look at every ribbon and engage him in a quarter of an hour's discussion of whether to buy the yellow or the blue. And which shade of blue? Would this blue perhaps clash with the shade of her bonnet? It would, Miss Nuthall would say. Lady Pipham would insist it would not. Finally Miss Nuthall would choose green, because her sister said green would never do. Emily had been to the shops with the aunts.

'When do you wish me to be ready?' Emily asked.

'Well, not now,' Lady Keating huffed. 'I could not leave for another hour at least.'

'Then I shall go see how Mrs Wilson goes on.'

Emily continued down the stairs, finding the housekeeper in the passageway outside her sitting room giving instructions to the maid.

What crisis would Mrs Wilson report today? A tiff between the maid-of-all-work and the kitchen maid? No partridges for dinner? Mice in the cellar? No difficulty was too small for Mrs Wilson to lay at Emily's feet.

When she saw Emily, Mrs Wilson shooed the maid away. 'Good day, my lady,' she said.

'How do things go on, Mrs Wilson?' Emily asked.

The housekeeper launched into a long discussion about the coal porter, how he meant to cheat them, how she, not knowing what her ladyship would do, worried her head off, but finally gave the fellow what-for and he'd done just as he ought.

'What else could I do, my lady? You were abed and like to never get up,' she concluded.

Perhaps Emily ought to sleep late more often.

'You did very well,' she assured her.

She walked back to the hall where Bleasby approached, begging to ask how he might serve her. She'd managed to reduce his duties to the lightest of tasks, but the old butler felt remiss if he did not do as much work as he'd done thirty years ago. She spent some moments convincing him his services were perfectly adequate, trying all the while to salvage his pride.

The door opened. Guy and the aunts had returned, Lady Pipham's and Miss Nuthall's shrill voices, bickering as usual, echoing into the hall. With the quarrel in full swing and the door open to the chilly air, Guy urged each of them over the threshold. He stood ready to remove their pelisses, but Bleasby beat him to it, silently assisting while the two ladies barely drew a breath between angry words.

Emily could have made a hasty retreat, but instead watched as Guy removed his beaver hat and caped coat, moving as always with a masculine elegance totally without affectation. He continued placating the sensibilities of each great-aunt, and successfully cajoled them out of their huffiness, making them each feel they had won the point.

They were in perfect charity with each other as they made their way up the stairs. With any luck, their truce would last until they reached the upper floors.

Watching Guy's solicitude towards the aunts affected Emily as much as it had the first time she'd seen it. She watched him through the whole exchange with the aunts, as if in a trance, his kindness still able to touch that needy part of her she tried so hard to ignore.

She stepped forward to take his coat and hat, but he did not hand them over. Instead, he lay them on a nearby chair.

'Good day, Emily.' He gave her a smile.

It almost seemed as if he'd really looked at her.

'Good day, sir,' she responded.

'You were not at breakfast,' he went on. 'Were you feeling unwell?'

She felt herself blush, knowing she'd stayed abed merely to avoid him.

'I assure you, I am very well.' She heard the edge of anger creeping into her voice. Beware, she told herself. Do not give him anything to wonder about.

She composed her most colourless countenance, but it seemed his eyes almost twinkled in response, as if he alone knew the answer to a riddle and was keeping it to himself.

What was the reason for his sunny mood? He had won a great deal of money at Lady Widow's table the previous night. Perhaps that was the origin of his bonhomie. Or perhaps it was meeting Lady Widow herself.

Her mother-in-law emerged from above stairs. 'I am ready,' she announced.

Emily turned her blank expression on her husband's mother. 'I shall get my coat and bonnet.'

Lady Keating gave her a quick nod, then came over to her son's side.

'Where are you and Emily bound, Mother?' He kissed his mother's cheek.

It occurred to Emily then that he did not kiss her in greeting. A dagger twisted inside her. She'd wager he would kiss Lady Widow if she let him.

Lady Keating patted her son's cheek. 'The daughter of my dearest friend is in town awaiting the birth of her baby. I sent a note round asking if I might call on her and her reply arrived this morning.'

'How nice for you,' Guy said.

Emily tried to keep her tread light on the stairs, though she felt like stamping her way to the next floor. It should not bother her that this gambling husband of hers cared nothing for her, but lavished all his attention on his mother and his great-aunts. It should signify nothing to her. She would soon leave them all behind.

She paused a moment, straightened her back, and continued up the stairs with more iron in her spine. By next spring, she told herself, before the Season was underway, she should have winnings enough to walk out of the door and say good riddance to them all.

Guy's gaze followed his wife as she ascended the stairs, her spine straight, her step purposeful. She walked with Lady Widow's dignity, he thought. With Lady Widow's grace, but in Emily both were held back, controlled, contained. There all the same, however. How could he not have seen it before in Emily? He felt like a blind man suddenly blessed with sight. Everything became clear. Everything except why. Why masquerade as Lady Widow? Why hide Lady Widow's vivacity the rest of the time?

The cloth of her dress caught between her legs, for an instant clearly outlining her pleasing form. This sudden vision rekindled the desire she'd aroused the night before. He had half a mind to follow her to her bedchamber, putting an end to that infernal wager once and for all.

Be patient, he told himself. *Don't rush the cards. Play out the full hand.*

He turned back to his mother. 'I am glad you are taking Emily with you.' He gave a glance back to the now empty stair.

Lady Keating sighed. 'I would not upset you for the world, Guy, but I still cannot like her.'

His eyes narrowed. 'She tries mightily to please you. She tries to please all of us.' And underneath her pleasing manners was so much more.

'I know,' his mother admitted. 'But her parents, you know. They are such wretched people. I'm convinced she cannot be as utterly correct as she seems.'

If you only knew, Mother, Guy said to himself.

'Blood always tells, Guy.' She gave a knowing nod, obviously overlooking the blood of a wastrel father in his own veins.

Was that it? he suddenly wondered. Emily's father was a sad gamester, even more ruthless in his play than the elder Keating's had been. How much of Duprey's blood flowed through his daughter's veins? As much as his own father's flowed through his? If Guy were always a hair's breadth from falling completely into the lure of the cards, why not Emily?

Lady Widow's eyes had danced with every winning hand. Was Emily at Madame Bisou's for love of gambling?

Eventually the gentlemen at Madame Bisou's would tire of letting her win, especially if the wager about her were won. What would be the result? If her opponents played to win, how long before she must present her husband with her gambling debts? She would not be the only woman to have succumbed to the lure of the card table. The Duchess of Devonshire had been known to bet deep, owing everyone throughout London. It was said she sadly damaged the Duke's finances with her losses.

The Duchess was also known to have borne another man's child. Surely Emily would not go so far?

His mother broke into his reverie. 'Besides, she is utterly lacking in charm.'

Guy almost laughed aloud. If his mother only knew how much charm Emily could display when she so chose. 'Emily's is a quiet charm, Mother,' he told her.

His mother rolled her eyes.

His temper flared. 'Do not roll your eyes when I speak of her. She is my wife, ma'am. Treat her with the respect she deserves.' He leaned towards her to imprint upon her that he was entirely serious. 'One word from her and you could be away from here.'

Lady Keating put her hands on her hips. 'There is nothing I should more desire. I am perfectly content to make my home at Annerley. I pine for a spell in the country.'

A short time ago she'd longed for London.

He shook his head in frustration. 'Annerley is her house as well, Mother. But you know even the dower house at Annerley is unfit for habitation, and the main house needs total repair.'

The dower house was under repair, thanks to a fat pot won a fortnight ago, but it would be spring before work on it could be completed. Guy planned to live in the dower house while Annerley was restored. He wished to be in residence for spring planting and to oversee the renovations. First, however, he needed to win the necessary funds.

'Surely it is not as bad as all that?' his mother said.

His mother was not privy to the whole of their financial distress. He'd taken care that none of his family were.

Guy gave her a steady look. 'It would be a great inconvenience for you if you were not welcome in your daughter-in-law's house, would it not? There is nowhere else to live.'

She glared back at him defiantly. 'She would not dare to toss me out.'

He did not falter. 'No, she would not be so cruel. Do not be so certain of me.'

Her face paled. 'You?'

'I would send you off, Mother, make no mistake about it, but only if you force my hand, only if you refuse to be civil to my wife.'

She began to wring her hands. Guy stepped closer and wrapped his arm around her shoulder. 'Now, do not fly to pieces. It is not so difficult a request, is it? As I have said before, all you need do is give Emily a fair chance.'

She slanted him a wary glance.

He continued, 'We have all underestimated her.' How true a statement that was. Had he underestimated her love of cards?

His mother buried her face into his chest. 'Oh, I will try, I promise.'

Guy had been as remiss as his mother in attending to Emily. Was it his neglect that sent her off wagering into the night? Well, she would soon have an abundance of his attention, both she and Lady Widow.

Half an hour later, Emily and the Dowager walked the short distance to Grosvenor Square, Rogers the footman accompanying them a few steps behind. Her mother-in-law actually attempted conversation, in a petulant tone, perhaps, the topics forced, but conversation none the less. Emily could not have been more surprised had the squirrel in the square begun to talk. What led to this sudden volubility?

Emily, however, acted as if it were the most natural circumstance in the world, responding exactly as she ought and even making an effort to advance the conversation.

Grosvenor Square was such a premier address, Emily wondered exactly who they might be calling upon. Lady Keating had not informed her. Who might the Dowager know well enough to visit?

Emily, of course, did not presume to ask.

'Here we are,' Lady Keating said.

They had stopped in front of one of the finest residences, the one house on the square Emily did not wish to enter, not with her family's connection to this one.

'Who—who do we call upon here?' Emily stammered to her mother-in-law.

'The Marchioness of Heronvale,' Lady Keating said. 'Do you not know whose house this is? She is the daughter of my oldest friend.' Lady Keating gestured for Rogers to sound the knocker.

Perhaps there was no cause for worry. Perhaps the Marchioness would not even remember Emily.

They soon entered a spacious hall more than twice the size of the Keatings'. The gilt in this hall was not chipped. Indeed, the gilt-adorned walls were painted Chinese blue. Huge Chinese vases held fresh white, orange and yellow chrysanthemums.

After they were announced, a footman led them above

stairs to Lady Heronvale's personal sitting room, where she lay on a yellow giltwood chaise, a perfect complement to her blonde beauty.

'Lady Keating, how wonderful to see you.' She extended her hand. 'Forgive me if I do not get up. The doctor insists I rest.'

The ethereal Lady Heronvale was quite obviously with child.

She clasped the older Lady Keating's hand warmly before glancing towards Emily. 'Oh, Miss Duprey!' She blinked prettily. 'Forgive me, I ought to have said Lady Keating to you, ought I not? We all read of your marriage. My felicitations.'

Emily took the Marchioness's delicate hand. 'Thank you, my lady.' The Marchioness *had* remembered her. From the after-the-fact announcement of her marriage, she had also probably surmised the wedding to have been a precipitous one. Emily focused on remaining composed. At least on the outside.

Lady Heronvale invited them to sit, assuring them she had requested some refreshment.

'How do you go on, my child?' the Dowager Lady Keating asked with an expression of genuine concern.

The Marchioness laughed. 'Never better! I feel amazingly well, as if I could walk from here to Westminster and back, but the physician and my husband refuse to believe it.'

'The Marquess dotes upon you, does he?' Lady Keating said.

How nice for her, thought Emily, *to have a doting husband*.

'Pardon me, Serena.' A lady's voice came from the doorway behind her. 'I do not wish to intrude, but Barclay directs me to tell you that Cook is out of lemon cakes.

She is preparing another confection for you, which will take a little time.'

Emily remained perfectly still. She recognised that voice.

The Marchioness waved her hand and smiled. 'Come in, dearest. Come meet my friends.'

Lady Heronvale sat up on the chaise, while the lady approached. Emily still could not see her face, but there was no mistaking her lovely figure, the elegant length of her neck, the natural curl of her dark hair.

'Lady Keating,' the Marchioness said, gesturing to Emily who rose to her feet.

The lady who entered stiffened.

Lady Heronvale continued, 'May I present to you my dear sister-in-law, Lady Devlin Steele.'

Her sister Madeleine.

Madeleine turned and regarded Emily with her wide blue eyes. 'Emily,' she mouthed.

Emily extended her hand, hoping it did not tremble. 'Lady Devlin,' she managed.

Her sister Madeleine clasped her hand warmly, keeping hold of it until Lady Heronvale spoke. 'And the Dowager Lady Keating...'

Madeleine turned, 'My honour, ma'am.'

Emily's mother-in-law did not rise from her chair, but limply accepted Madeleine's handshake. Lady Keating probably thought, as everyone would, that Lord Devlin had married a woman beneath him, a common sort, perhaps.

Madeleine was far from common, however.

Lady Heronvale made room for Madeleine on her sofa. Madeleine sat facing Emily, looking every bit as uncomfortable as Emily felt.

Correct pleasantries were exchanged, to which both

Emily and her sister contributed, but soon the Dowager and the Marchioness lapsed into a more private conversation about mutual friends and family members.

Madeleine leaned over slightly. 'Do you like books, Lady Keating?' she asked Emily.

Such an odd question. 'Yes—yes, I suppose I do.'

'The Marquess has a fine library. Would you like to see it?'

Emily immediately understood. 'Yes, I would. I mean, it would be my pleasure.'

Madeleine interrupted Lady Heronvale's conversation. 'Lady Keating desires seeing the library. Do you mind, Serena?'

'If it does not displease you, ma'am,' added Emily.

Lady Heronvale smiled. 'Not at all, but we shall serve some refreshment shortly.'

As if they were two little girls bent on mischief, the sisters rushed down the hallway, Madeleine leading the way. When Madeleine shut the library doors, however, they faced each other with sudden reserve.

Emily longed to embrace her sister, longed to show her how dearly she loved her, longed for that affection to be returned. They had not parted badly last spring, but their encounter had been so brief and much lay unsaid.

'Madeleine—' Emily's voice cracked '—it is so good to see you.'

'Oh, Emily!' Madeleine rushed up and threw her arms around her.

Both produced a quantity of tears that would have made their sister Jessame proud. They finally pulled apart, still sniffling and groping for handkerchiefs.

Emily blew her nose. 'How are you, Madeleine? Are you well? Are you happy?'

Madeleine beamed at her. 'Very happy. I do not much

like being in town, but the Marquess insisted Serena come here for her confinement. I could not refuse her request for my company.'

'I read the announcement of your marriage, of course. Is…is Lord Devlin well?'

A dreamy look came over her sister's face. 'Yes, he is splendid.' She smiled again. 'But you are a married lady, too. You must tell me of your husband! How did you meet? Devlin said he knew Lord Keating in the Peninsula, but he'd not had the title then.'

Lord Devlin had known Guy? Had he known Guy was a gamester?

'I met him in Bath.'

'Bath.' Madeleine sighed. 'You must have seen the Cresent and the Circus. Did you meet in the Pump Room?'

'No,' Emily said. 'In the Assembly Rooms.' Though that first glimpse of him had been in the Pump Room.

'The Assembly Rooms,' Madeleine repeated in awe. 'The announcement did not say where you were married. Was it at the Abbey?'

'No.' Emily paused. How much ought she tell her sister? 'We had a Scottish marriage.'

Madeleine's eyes widened and her gaze lowered to Emily's waist. 'Are you—'

Emily felt herself blush. 'No, I am not.' *Far from it*, she thought.

Madeleine covered her mouth. 'Oh, I am sorry. I did not mean to offend… It is that I know how easy it…I mean, it could happen to…'

Emily grabbed her hand and squeezed it. 'Do not fret.' She spoke softly. 'I remember, Madeleine. I remember why Papa sent you away.'

Madeleine looked away. 'I am not saying you are like me, Emily. You and Jessame were never like me.'

Emily put her arms around her sister again. 'No, we were jealous of you, Madeleine. You were so beautiful, even though you were the youngest. We ought to have looked out for you better.'

Madeleine put her fingers to Emily's lips to silence her. 'That is all in the past, Emily. It no longer signifies.'

But it signified to Emily. She'd puzzled out what her sister must have been doing in Lord Farley's room that wretched night. Their father's wrath had been terrible. The next day, she and Jessame were told that Madeleine had run away and that Lord Farley had been summoned back to London. Emily thought Madeleine had run away with the gentleman, but then, after several days, their father had produced the body of a young girl.

When they buried that body under a stone with Madeleine's name upon it, her father had declared that Madeleine's wild ways had led her to destruction. If Madeleine's spirit and vivacity had led to her death, Emily knew she must suppress any such feelings in herself. She had vowed to always behave with perfect propriety.

What had all that propriety gained her?

'I ought to have protected you,' Emily said to Madeleine. 'I was older than you. I ought to have done something.'

Madeleine gave her another quick hug. 'It is past, Emily. Think only of the life we have now. That is what I do. And I am so very, very happy.'

More tears flowed, more sniffles and wiping of eyes with damp handkerchiefs.

Madeleine had married well, Emily realised. She had a good life, a loving husband, a darling daughter.

'I forgot to ask about your little girl,' Emily said.

Madeleine smiled again. 'She is very well. She is above stairs, napping at the moment.' She patted her stomach. 'Next spring she will have a sister or brother.'

'How lovely for you!' Emily exclaimed.

If wantonness brought death, propriety ought to have brought happiness. What had gone wrong? Her sister had been like a vine grown wild, almost lost among weeds, but she'd managed to flower notwithstanding. What had Emily's strict adherence to correct behaviour gained her? She had all but withered, blossoming only when pretending to be Lady Widow.

There was a knock on the door and both sisters automatically dabbed at their faces again and fussed with their dresses. 'Come in,' Madeleine said.

In walked Lord Devlin Steele, Madeleine's husband.

'There you are,' he said, giving his wife a loving glance. He came directly over to Emily and grasped both her hands in his. 'Emily, it is so good to see you.'

Lord Devlin was more handsome than ever, his green eyes sparkling, his smile showing the dimple in his cheek. He was taller than her husband, but just as dark. At one time his entrance to a ballroom had set her heart aflutter. Surprisingly, she felt none of that now.

'It is good to see you, too, Lord Devlin,' she said, meaning it.

'And I realise I must also wish you very happy.' He grinned at her. 'Lady Keating.'

Emily felt herself blush again.

'I served with Lord Keating for a bit. He is a good man, Emily. A very good man.'

A good man? Yes, yes, he might have been, but the knowledge did not make Emily feel happy.

Devlin released her hands and turned to his wife. 'Serena wishes you both to return to the parlour for tea.'

'Wait.' Emily faced her sister. 'Madeleine, I have told no one of…of your true identity. No one. But you must know Robert is in town. Do you wish me to tell him about you?'

'Robert? Oh, how is he?' Madeleine shrank back. 'Oh, dear! What if I run into him?' She gave her husband a reproachful glance. 'I knew I should not have come to town.'

'You are not likely to see him if you do not wish it,' her husband said.

She turned back to Emily. 'No one knows of me. Only you, Devlin, and the Marquess.' She nodded her head firmly. 'I think that is best. I…I would not wish any scandal to befall our family…'

Had not their parents generated scandal enough over the years? Why should Madeleine hide? Emily's brows knitted together. Of course, she herself had dread of scandal. Why else had she gone into the gaming hell in disguise?

Madeleine went on, 'We must continue the deception, Emily. Please.'

'Very well,' Emily said, depressed. It felt like losing her sister all over again.

Madeleine gave a tentative smile. 'But may not you and I be friends? As Lady Devlin and Lady Keating? Now we are introduced, may we not see each other a little? Or write letters to each other?'

Emily stepped forward and enfolded Madeleine in her arms again. 'Nothing would please me more,' she whispered.

Chapter Eleven

That night Guy departed the townhouse as usual, but waited nearby to see who might pick up Emily and drive her to Madame Bisou's. He waited near the end of the court for more than two hours, providing Emily with plenty of time to retire, dress and escape.

Through the night mist he heard the watchman's call, 'Eleven o'clock and all's well.' The damp chill seeped into his bones. Perhaps she would not appear.

He waited another half an hour. No carriage came. Either she was not attending the gaming parlour this night or her means of transport was more inventive than he'd supposed.

Guy shoved his hands into the folds of his caped topcoat and walked a few streets to where he could obtain a hack. If Lady Widow did not put in an appearance at Madame Bisou's, at least he could try his luck at the tables. He still had a fortune to restore.

He found a hack and directed the coachman to Bennett Street. He'd seen some players who might give him the sort of sport he needed. He could attend to that matter, even if his wife remained at home.

His emotions were much altered when he now saw Emily at home. Speaking quietly to the servants. Seated at his dinner table. Playing cards with his great-aunts. All he could think of was her transformation into Lady Widow. Because Emily and Lady Widow were the same, his desire for her had more than doubled. He wanted this chameleon wife of his with all the bone and sinew of his body.

Guy went straight to the game room. It took him a mere glance to see her, seated at a card table. All the candlelight seemed to shine directly upon her. All sound became mere harmony to the melody of her laugh. He could feel the smooth blue silk of her dress beneath his fingers. Could imagine the scent of lavender lingering around her.

She looked up and his heart beat faster. She tossed him a welcoming smile and immediately turned back to her cards.

He felt like a green lad receiving his first smile from a lady. Before this night was over, Guy would indulge in his craving for her company, try to discover if the gambling was her passion, try to discover if other seductions were her aim.

Sloane was also present in the room, Guy noticed, his eyes narrowing. Sloane collected winnings from a table of gentlemen who were all rising to leave. He saw Guy and beckoned him over.

'Do you fancy a game of whist, Keating?' Sloane asked.

'I came to play,' Guy said with some hostility.

Sloane laughed. 'Ah, cards or for the lady? I beg you, let us not be adversaries for the time being. Shall we find two well-breeched fellows and deprive them of their money?'

Guy shrugged his assent. He'd seen Sloane play. He could do worse in a whist partner.

Sloane called over to two gentlemen standing at the

faro table. They came across and Sloane introduced them to Guy as two merchants trading in fine goods throughout the Continent, goods that had once been the stock of the smuggling trade during the war. Perhaps these well-breeched gentlemen of Sloane's had been breeched on illegal trade. In any event, they looked wealthy, judging by the cut of their clothes and the heavy gold chains dangling from their pockets. What did the source of their money matter as long as they had plenty of it?

Both he and Sloane took seats that afforded them an opportunity to keep Lady Widow in sight. A sidelong glance was all it took to watch her charming the fortunate gentlemen at her table, the ones who gladly lost their money to her.

Once the game started, however, Guy's attention was held prisoner by the cards. These gentlemen were serious players. It would be the best sort of contest, one of wits and luck. Guy hoped both were with him. That familiar pounding of excitement drummed through him, that sense of being at the edge of a precipice ready to leap to the other side. He would either fall or land on his feet.

Guy, Sloane and the two merchants were closely matched. Each game became a close-run thing. Guy's euphoria increased when he won. His anxiety reined free when he lost. The stakes were driven higher and higher, none of the gentlemen flinching with each increase. It had become as much a contest of who would bet the most outrageous amount of money as who would win the game. Guy felt that same burst of energy he used to feel when charging into battle, that same driving hunger to come out alive.

He soon found himself at the brink, ready to wager all his cash. *Do it. Do it. See how much you can win. The cards will come. Luck is with you.*

He was about to push his whole stack of counters to the centre when he heard Lady Widow laugh. He glanced over at her, a vision in her blue dress, her face shadowed by the netting of her elegant hat. She returned his gaze, creating a different sort of heat from the card fever that had almost stolen his senses. At this distance, he could not see the expression on her face, but he could tell she did not smile.

This was his wife! This alluring vision. Would she wish her husband to bet the whole? Lady Widow might laugh off such a reckless act, but he was fairly certain Emily would not.

He took a few coins from his stack instead, throwing them in the centre of the table. At the end of the hand, his opponents were the richer.

Sloane signalled for drinks, and the pretty maid who set down the glasses gave him an inviting look. Guy studied the man while one of the merchants dealt the cards. Women were aware when Sloane entered a room. He'd noticed it in Bath when Sloane singled out Emily for attention. Emily had resisted his charms then, though Sloane had briefly been one of her suitors, but she'd had the constraint of public censure to impede her. With Lady Widow and her mask, there were no such constraints.

After the next game, Sloane signalled for more drinks. Guy drank as little as possible when playing cards and his glass had remained full. So had Sloane's. The maid brought fresh drinks for their opponents. After the fellows' third drink, the betting became even more reckless. Guy's heart raced, and the blood rushed through his veins, as it had when he'd engaged England's enemy, testing whose sword arm was the strongest, knowing either victory or death would result.

Guy and Sloane had handily won the third rubber when supper was called.

'I've had enough,' declared one of the merchants, standing on wobbly feet and rubbing his hands.

Guy had won more this night than in a week's play at White's. The two merchants merely shrugged off the enormous loss. 'Good game,' they bellowed, speech somewhat slurred. 'Good sport.'

Guy's emotions plummeted, as was always the case after a close game, no matter if he won or lost. If he'd lost this one, however, he would not be laughing it off like these gentlemen.

'It was the whisky,' Sloane said.

'What?' Guy looked up at him.

'You kept your head, Keating. I much admire that.' Sloane gathered up his counters to give to one of the girls to exchange for cash. 'Our late opponents liked their whisky. Been drinking all night. I would not have bet on our chances if they'd been sober.'

Sloane addled them with drink? It was less than sporting, true, but a device that had given them an edge.

'Remind me not to play against you,' Sloane added.

Guy stood as the maid brought him his cash. 'Thought we were in it deep already,' he said. 'For the lady.'

Sloane laughed. 'Dear me, I'd forgotten her in the thrill of fleecing some very clever sheep. Shall we find ourselves cut out in the supper room, I wonder?'

Sir Reginald, who sat at Emily's elbow in the supper room, mumbled something she did not hear. She'd just seen Guy and Sloane amble in together, looking very much like schoolboy mates. Her heart skipped a beat.

They looked well pleased with themselves, so perhaps they had won after all.

While her whist opponents had played their cards badly, she'd stolen glances at Guy and Sloane at their game. She'd been enough at Madame Bisou's to recognise the two gamblers at the opposing chairs as the genuine article, the sort who would never bother with Lady Widow, preferring to engage in real play. She'd watched her husband's stack of counters rise and fall and had held her breath for fear he would lose his last groat.

With cards in his hand, her husband had no time to spare for Lady Widow. That should have pleased Emily, but Emily could not abide him loving cards so well.

And whether she played Emily or Lady Widow, she resented him so easily dismissing her. Emily pressed her fingers to her temple, as if the gesture might keep the two sides of her together.

She managed to paste on a radiant smile as Sloane and Guy approached her table. The gentlemen seated around her grumbled and shifted positions. They were no match for these new rivals and they knew it.

Sloane flashed his perfect set of teeth at Lady Widow. 'You are looking remarkably beautiful this evening, my lady.' He took her hand and kissed it, as usual keeping hold a little too long.

Would her husband take her hand? Would his lips touch its bare skin? She scarcely attended to Sloane, glancing past him to where Guy stood. Guy's face, for one second, looked grim, but when he caught her eye, he smiled. Not as widely as Sloane, but with much more appeal.

'Pleasure to see you again so soon, ma'am.' He bowed and the corner of his mouth took an ironic twist. He did not touch her, however. He also nodded to Sir Reginald. 'Good evening, sir.'

Sloane, however, was heedless of Sir Reginald and Lady Widow's other admirers. He picked up a chair from a nearby table and set it beside her. Guy remained standing.

Would he sit with her? Would he walk away? What should she say to him to entice him to stay?

Emily's smile remained fixed on her face, hiding the muddle inside. It was not like Lady Widow to be at a loss for words. Once she'd launched this performance of hers, she'd never lacked for confidence. Each coquettish flutter of eyelashes, each pert comment, each trill of laughter had come naturally, almost as if she really were this mysterious creature who wore masks and flirted openly with gentlemen.

But in the presence of her husband, she suddenly felt she'd forgotten her lines. She became Emily again, who relied on silence when she did not know what to say.

Sloane, without realising it, came to her rescue. 'How do you do this night, my lady?' he murmured in his overly intimate fashion.

She shook herself back into her role as Lady Widow, who pretended petulance. 'How might I be? You and your companion have had no use for me all the night.'

Sloane's eyes flicked over her. 'I assure you, Lady Widow, I shall always have some use for you. Any night.'

Sloane's words were shockingly suggestive. Emily shot a glance at her husband, but he'd turned his back to speak to the maid and perhaps did not hear.

She could not allow it to pass. 'Goodness! Did you hear him, Lord Keating? I have never been so shocked in my life.'

Her entourage of admirers chirped up like a Greek chorus, Sir Reginald barking louder than the rest. They all avowed they'd certainly heard the fellow. Shocking. Shocking.

Guy turned to her, the hint of strain peeping into the

corners of his eyes. 'Forgive me, my lady. I was not attending.'

Sloane looked amused.

Emily fussed with the sleeve of her dress. 'Well, I suppose it was all flummery.' She sighed.

Sloane's smile fled.

Emily glanced back at her husband. His penetrating gaze had not left her, and she felt caught in it. Sloane might undress her with a glance, but a look such as Guy Keating gave could steal a woman's soul.

She lowered her lashes and tried to slow the rapid beat of her heart. He'd been looking at Lady Widow, she must recall. Not his wife. Still, her breath had quite caught in her throat.

'I thought to fix a plate, my lady,' her husband said, his eyes unwavering. 'May I bring you anything?'

Her flock of gentlemen all assured her they would be happy to bring her her heart's desire—as if they could.

She gave Guy her most appealing smile. 'More champagne, perhaps?'

The others were half out of their chairs, but sat back down when Guy bowed to her and left to do her bidding. She watched him walk away, and the gentlemen around her watched her watch him.

Sloane spoke, his voice low. 'You seem much taken with Lord Keating, my lady.'

Emily blinked and turned her gaze upon him. 'Do I?' She glanced back at Keating, pretending to study him thoroughly. 'He is a well-looking man, is he not?'

Jealousy flashed though Sloane's eyes. 'A paragon,' he said.

At least she had the satisfaction of making Cyprian Sloane jealous. But what about her husband? Could she make him care? If not for Emily, could she make him care for Lady Widow?

She forced a laugh at Sloane. 'Come now, Mr Sloane, you will convince me you have a *tendre* for me, which I know is a mere hum.'

'Have I not been attempting to convince you of this these many nights?' He glared at the men around her until they all shifted in their chairs again. 'I wonder if you gentlemen might give me a private moment with the lady,' he said in a deceptively smooth voice. 'You have monopolised her company quite enough.'

Amazingly, the gentlemen at her table all rose and bid her pretty words of farewell.

Only Sir Reginald hung back. 'Feel I ought not to leave you alone with this fellow,' he said. 'Say the word and I won't leave your side.'

'Don't be silly, sir!' she exclaimed. 'This is hardly a private place, and your friend Lord Keating will be returning any moment. I shall be well chaperoned, I assure you.' It was not that she wished to be alone with Sloane, but rather she wished to limit the distractions around her when her husband returned.

Sir Reginald clutched her hand, kissing it with much more feeling than was comfortable. 'I am at your service, always, good lady.'

When he'd left, Sloane drawled, 'Can't see how you tolerate that encroaching prig.'

She affected a deep sigh. 'He is my gallant.'

Sloane gave a snort. 'Enough sauce from you, my dear…'

Lady Widow's brows rose at that familiar endearment.

'I wish to speak with you before your besotted Keating returns.'

She feigned mild interest.

'I won a small fortune this evening. Was unusually lucky.'

As was her husband, then. What a relief.

He went on. 'I'll give all my winnings to you—'

'To me?' She toyed with a morsel of food left on her plate. 'Do not be absurd.'

Sloane moved his chair closer. 'I was never more serious. Come above stairs with me tonight and it is all yours. That and more delights than you can imagine.'

She gaped at him, her cheeks burning with deep shock. What he asked of her was no less than Madame Bisou's gaily dressed girls were paid to do each night. Walk above stairs with the gentlemen and dispense favours for money.

What did she care that he was reputed to be an ideal lover, an experienced pleasurer of women? He had cast her in the role of harlot.

He did not know, of course, that she was the respectable wife of Lord Keating, his recent whist partner. She doubted he would have made such an offer to Lady Keating, in any event.

She glanced at her husband still at the sideboard. Would he care that his wife had been so propositioned by Mr Sloane?

Not his wife. She forgot. Lady Widow had been propositioned.

Sloane said, 'I await your answer, my lady.'

She swallowed and made herself give him a direct look. 'You misjudge me, sir.' She spoke in a serious voice, not like Lady Widow, but not like Emily either. 'I come to this establishment to play cards. Nothing more.'

At that moment, her husband, his expression alert, walked up and handed her a glass of champagne.

How had this encounter with Sloane appeared to him? Emily's stomach fluttered in anxiety.

She covered it with Lady Widow's grateful smile. She accepted the glass. 'I thank you, Lord Keating. I was quite pining for more champagne.' She sipped, gazing at him over the rim of her glass.

Sloane slumped back in his chair.

'My pleasure, ma'am,' Keating said.

His eyes captured hers, with a questioning look at first, then darkening with all the carnal desire she'd perceived the previous night. If he'd considered Sloane a rival, with such a look he was certainly placing himself in the game. His way of informing her was vastly more subtle than Sloane's, however. And much more powerful.

Emily rubbed the edge of her mask, where it almost moulded itself to her face.

Though Emily might resent his clear desire for Lady Widow, Lady Widow was thrilled more than she cared to admit. The mask concealed who she was, but it offered no protection against her emotions. Instead, sensations that had only twice known life again poured through her. The desire to have him once more unclothed in bed with her, joining himself to her body, creating a paroxysm of pleasure she'd never before dreamed could exist.

The blatant sexual invitation by Cyprian Sloane held no appeal, but this one look from her husband laid raw the aching wish to couple with him once more. She'd not known such sensuality existed within her, that a look from a man could elicit it, making her feel alive, giving her spirit a flight to the heavens.

From deep within her came another emotion as passionate, as consuming. The searing knowledge that the man she married would never give his wife such a look. He looked at Lady Widow, not Emily. She made a bold decision. If Emily could not have her husband in bed with her, Lady Widow would. She would do more than toy with his affections as first she'd planned. She would devastate them.

She favoured her husband with one of Lady Widow's most inviting looks. 'Mr Sloane tells me you won a great deal of money this night.'

'Luck was with us,' he replied modestly. 'Though it was a near-run thing.'

'Oh, I suspect you relish such sport,' she said, truthfully enough. He would discover in time that there could be something more enticing than cards. Lady Widow would see to it.

'Perhaps you would fancy to play at my table.' She fluttered her eyelashes and brushed her fingers across his sleeve. 'As an opponent this time.'

'Perhaps,' he said, with a gleam in his eye. The gleam of a gamester or a lover?

'You should like to conquer me, I fear,' she purred. 'Must I be afraid…?' Her finger drew a circle on the back of his hand.

'I might wish to win, yes.' His eyes reflected the exact seductive look she sought from him. 'I always wish to win.'

She laughed, and rested her hand lazily on his.

Cyprian Sloane glared at this exchange between Keating and Lady Widow, one foot swinging up and down at an irritated pace. She was definitely throwing out her lures to Keating.

None of the other gentlemen posed any real threat. Keating was his chief opponent. He had to admit Keating had played this particular hand with skill. Keating had kept his cards close to his chest, while he had impulsively exposed his whole hand.

What a fool he'd been to use money to entice the lady,

rushing his luck, playing his best cards first. Keating's game was obviously more to her taste.

'I'd be honoured to play you, my lady,' Keating was saying. 'Either as your partner or your opponent.'

Honoured, repeated Sloane in his head, mocking the words. *Either as your partner or opponent.*

Bah! Keating would deal him out of the game, if he were not careful. Again. Not that he cared that, out from under his nose, Keating had married the Duprey chit. Served the man right to be shackled to such a colourless creature. It would be vastly more entertaining to free Lady Widow of her mask.

He'd be damned if he let Keating beat him to it.

Sloane pushed his chair forward, creating a barrier between Lady Widow and Keating.

'Why don't Keating and I play as your opponents, Lady Widow?' he said. 'I warn you, though, luck has been riding with us this night.'

She turned her smile on him, just as he'd wished her to. 'But you have much to lose, don't you?' Her eyes were cold. He'd made her angry with his proposal. 'Perhaps your luck will run out.'

He needed to intensify his efforts to charm her, since his own mistake had created a setback.

Sloane put on an expression of deep regret. 'I fear I have made my own ill luck tonight with my rashness. For that I am deeply regretful.'

One thing was certain. He would do anything necessary to win. Anything.

Chapter Twelve

It seemed to Guy that the gaming room hummed with excitement when the foursome sat down to the game of whist Lady Widow had dictated. Certainly envious gentlemen in the room looked up to see whom she had favoured, but the real excitement was inside him.

How often had he sat beside his wife at the breakfast table, at dinner, in the parlour? At such times he had been conscious of an aching regret, because he did not know how to heal the breach between them, but this temptress incarnate stirred his blood. To have her arm so near his, her skirt brushing his leg, her face almost kissably close—how was he to attend to cards?

She smiled like the hostess of a Mayfair ball. 'Sir Reginald, you shall shuffle the cards. You are so skilled at it. Mr Sloane, you may cut them to see who deals.'

On the other hand, perhaps she was more like his company commander.

Poor Sir Reginald was obviously in as sad a state as he. The man's colour was high, his eyes bright. Sloane was harder to read, but Guy had no illusion Sloane would abandon his conquest or forgo the gentlemen's bet. He had seen Sloane speak privately to her, had seen her respond. What had Sloane said to her? What had she replied?

A moment later he'd reached the table, and she'd turned her charm fully on him, her husband. Sloane was all but ignored. Was that part of her game, or had she truly dismissed the man?

Lady Widow won the deal.

Guy's first hands were unremarkable and he had no difficulty adhering to the unwritten rule that Lady Widow must always win. She and Sir Reginald took the first game. But the next hand! The ace, king, queen and knave of trump. Two other aces besides, and four other face cards. He couldn't be an idiot and lose this hand, even if Sloane played like a gudgeon. He could not help himself. At ten pounds a point, it was sure to be a heavy loss for the lady. But the money remained in the family, did it not? What harm was there?

Sloane shot him a sharp glance when he caught on to Guy's hand. Guy returned it with an impassive expression. Sir Reginald fidgeted in his chair. Lady Widow, however, remained engrossed in the play, watching every card thrown on the table. At the end of the hand, Guy had won the honours points. Once scratched, the itch to win took over. Guy played the rest of the hands to win.

At the end of the game, Lady Widow's eyes danced with excitement. 'Well done!' she exclaimed.

Both Sloane and Sir Reginald raised their eyebrows in surprise, but Guy knew what she was about.

His suspicion had been confirmed. His wife Emily, Lady Widow, was mad for cards. The more challenging the game, the more she liked it. She, like he, could become lost in that thrill of luck, that intoxication of wresting a win from what might have been a loss.

Guy also played the third game to win. Sloane glared

at him half the time, but went along with it, apparently not so willing to let the lady win if it meant crossing a partner. Sir Reginald became as caught up in the fever as Guy himself, and Lady Widow was delirious with the play. What parts of her face were visible were flushed with excitement. Her eyes had a sparkling clarity. She sat erect, economising her movements to what entailed playing the cards.

Guy and Sloane won the game and won the rubber.

'Oh, that was fun!' Lady Widow said, reaching into her reticule for more coin.

'Allow me to cover your losses,' said Sloane, pushing his stack of counters to her side.

'I would be honoured to pay your debt as well,' Sir Reginald piped up, clearly upset that Sloane had thought of it first.

'No, indeed.' She laughed them both off. 'How shabby would it be for me not to pay my own gambling debts?' She counted out coins to both Sloane and Guy. Sloane pushed the coins back at her, but she ignored him and left them on the table.

'Thank you, gentlemen, for much amusement.' She looked directly at Guy. 'Perhaps you will allow me a rematch another night?'

'My pleasure.' He inclined his head, but was not so certain he was happy to discover she could become as deep in cards as could he.

When the more serious gamblers in this room caught on how much she loved the challenge, she would certainly continue to lose. How long before her debts became unmanageable? In spite of that worry, the game had invigorated him as much as it had her, bringing no credit to either of them.

She rose. 'I must be leaving.' Before Sir Reginald or

Sloane could interject, she added, 'Lord Keating, would you escort me to my carriage?'

Yes, he would certainly like to discover who transported her back and forth. More so, he'd like the time alone with her.

'Another pleasure,' he said.

Knowing Sloane's eyes shot daggers at his back, Guy threaded his wife's arm though his and walked her to the hall. He directed the footman to bring her cloak and his topcoat, and placed her cloak around her shoulders, enjoying having his hands upon her again, even if through layers of cloth.

When he stepped out into the night air with Lady Widow on his arm, fog muted the street lamps and swirled at their feet like smoke over a cauldron. Guy fancied it was like a blanket wrapping around them both, blocking out the rest of the world. He would much prefer they be wrapped in a real blanket.

As they neared the end of the street, a hackney emerged from the mist, its driver holding the horses and nodding familiarly to Lady Widow as she became visible. Guy could barely see the man, and the hackney looked like a dozen others that might pass by in the space of an hour. How had she managed this arrangement?

'Allow me to accompany you, my lady, to see you arrive home safely.' It was worth a try.

'Oh, no!' she said in all seriousness. 'That would never do. You might discover where I live, and my secret would be out.'

Her secret had been out with him within a few moments of seeing her. He helped her in to the hack, amused by the irony of her statement. 'Would I know you, Lady Widow? Have I seen you before this?'

'No,' she said, with a confusing note of sadness in her voice. 'You have never seen me.'

The hackney driver flicked the ribbons and the coach moved down the street, soon disappearing into the mist. Her words seemed to float back to him on the droplets of moisture in the air.

You have never seen me.

Emily slept late enough to hope everyone had finished breakfast. She heard the aunts' voices in the back parlour as she went downstairs. With any luck, Lady Keating would be with them or in her own room. Guy's room had been very quiet. He was either still abed—and she did not wish to reflect much on that idea—or he was up and away. At least she hoped so. She said good morning to Rogers, who passed her in the hall, and made her way to the dining room.

At first glance it was blessedly empty, but as she entered, a voice came from the sideboard. 'Ah, good morning, Emily.'

Her husband. She nearly jumped in fright. 'Good morning, sir,' she mumbled.

She had no recourse but to stand at his side to fill her plate. He seemed inordinately slow, choosing this or that, picking at the slices of ham as if one mattered over another. She was forced to wait or lean over him for a bit of toast.

'Allow me,' he said, interrupting his interminable selection process and putting a slice of toast on her plate. 'Or would you prefer a fresh one? I'll call for Bleasby.'

What was this solicitude?

'No, do not trouble him,' she said. 'I'm quite content with what is here.'

She took her slice of toast and hurried to a seat, busying

herself with spreading the jam. Her husband whistled a Scottish air while he finished filling his plate. He sat in the chair adjacent to hers.

She poured him tea, knowing from other mornings how he liked it.

'Thank you,' he said. His whistle became a hum. 'Did you sleep well?'

This cheerfulness addled her. She glanced down at her plate to regain composure. 'Very well, thank you.'

His humming recommenced.

She did not think she'd ever seen him in such a jolly mood. He had won at cards, both with the gentlemen he'd played first and later from Lady Widow. Had the sum been so large to precipitate this good humour?

Or was he cheerful because Lady Widow had singled him out? Once planted, that idea grew like a bramble, wending its way through her insides, prickling wherever it touched.

'I have some errands on Bond Street,' he said, interrupting his infernal humming. 'Would you care to accompany me?'

She shot him a surprised glance. Luckily he was busy cutting his meat and had not noticed. She swallowed. 'If you desire it,' she said, keeping her voice steady.

He raised his head, smiled, and resumed humming.

This attention seemed too pointed to be due to winning. It smacked of…guilt. That was what it was. Guilt.

Whenever her father had done something particularly reprehensible, like staying out for days without a word then waltzing in big as you please, reeking of rosewater, he always fussed over her mother, bringing her trinkets, plying her with treats, escorting her to the theatre.

The door opened and Lady Keating entered. 'Ah, there you are,' she said to Emily, then, seeing her son, swished over to him and gave him a kiss on the cheek. 'Guy, I did not see you at first.'

'Good morning, Mother.' He stopped humming.

'Yes, to you too, my son, but I came in search of...of your wife. To see if she may accompany me on calls today.'

Emily opened her mouth to reply, but her husband spoke first. 'Then I suggest you ask her. She is right here in front of you, Mother.' His voice had hardened.

The Dowager went red. With anger, Emily supposed. Or embarrassment. 'What do you wish of me?' Emily asked in a mild tone.

Her mother-in-law looked almost grateful. 'I...I do beg your company this afternoon. To accompany me on my calls.'

Emily glanced at her husband whose expression remained stony. 'I would be honoured to come with you, ordinarily, but I am not entirely certain I will be available...' Her voice trailed off.

Guy could renege on his invitation to her if he wished. It seemed his practice to indulge his mother whenever possible. Emily was certain Lady Widow would not tolerate having her wishes come second to another's, but Emily would not risk causing a scene. She waited to see what he might decide.

'Emily is previously engaged,' he said.

His mother's lips pursed, and Emily's jaw nearly dropped open.

He added, 'She is to accompany me.'

Her eyes narrowed. 'Indeed,' Lady Keating said. 'And where do you go?'

'I have a few errands on Bond Street,' he replied.

His mother brightened, 'Oh, well, that cannot be so important. She would do better to come with me.'

His eyes grew stern. 'She accompanies me, Mother. That is the end of it.'

Emily observed this exchange with more astonishment. It was nonsensical that her husband and his mother would vie for her company.

'Very well,' the Dowager said with a huff. 'I bid you both good day.' She flounced out of the room.

Emily gaped at her husband, but he seemed absorbed in spearing a piece of ham on his fork.

A pleasing autumn breeze had swept the previous night's mist quite away, bringing back bright colour to the town.

As they stepped on to the pavement in front of the townhouse, Guy asked, 'Shall we walk to Bond Street?'

It was not far. 'Very well,' agreed Emily.

She had become accustomed to walking with her mother-in-law on their morning calls. Her mother-in-law was a great walker and, in truth, it was a pleasure Emily shared, although she did not so inform Lady Keating. Emily greatly missed long rambling walks in the country. Her sister Madeleine had been mad for riding, but Emily always preferred the sedate pace of her own two feet. An autumn day at Malvern, the family estate, would not see the smoke of London chimneys quickly erase the blue of the sky. One might walk all day in its beauty.

'What a glorious day,' her husband said expansively as they left Essex Court.

It was glorious for the moment, still clear and bright. He tipped his hat to a lady passing them, one who lived on the Court. Emily nodded to her. Might the lady remark to others that young Lady Keating had been seen out walking with her husband? It would be a novel *on dit*, indeed.

'What shops shall we visit?' Guy asked.

Another surprise. She was unused to any Keating asking her wishes. 'Wherever you wish,' she replied. 'You mentioned an errand.'

'Ah,' he said. 'Nothing significant. I thought to stop in Hatchard's. I've a fancy for purchasing *The Naturalist's Diary.*'

Naturalist's Diary? This seemed an odd choice for a gamester's library. She'd be less surprised if he were in search of a copy of Hoyle's book.

'Very well,' was all she replied.

He stopped as they were about to turn into St James's Street. 'Now, you also must select a destination. Do you fancy a visit to a draper's? A milliner? I am at your disposal.'

This solicitude was rattling. What had provoked it? Did he desire her to have a new dress? Perhaps something as daring as Lady Widow? After his win the previous night, perhaps he could well afford to purchase a new gown for his wife.

Her mother's wardrobe always expanded nicely when her father was philandering. Perhaps Guy Keating was anticipating similar recompense due to his pursuit of Lady Widow. Was he about to make Lady Widow a shocking proposition such as Sloane had made? How might Lady Widow respond?

Emily made herself gaze impassively at her husband. 'I would not impose upon you, sir. Your mother would, I presume, be happy to accompany me to such shops. I shall wait upon her.'

He gave her a crooked grin. 'You make it difficult for me to indulge you.'

She met the direct glittering blue of his eyes, eyes a woman could fall into and never, ever escape. What might it be like to have this handsome man bent on giving her pleasure?

She swallowed. No, she was convinced he meant to appease her as her father did her mother. The pleasure belonged to Lady Widow. 'There is no need to indulge me,' she said.

With a tiny shake of his head, he started walking again. They reached Piccadilly, where a ragged boy ran up holding a broom. Guy tossed him a ha'penny, and the boy swept the street in front of them as they crossed.

When they reached Hatchard's Bookshop, Guy went in search of *The Naturalist's Diary* and Emily was free to browse the shelves. She spotted *Glenarvon*, the shocking novel everyone knew had been penned by the scandalous Lady Caroline Lamb about her affair with Lord Byron. Emily would never have admitted to following the whole sordid sequence of events, but she had.

She opened the book, her eyes lighting on a passage.

…Oh I am changed, she continually thought; I have repressed and conquered every warm and eager feeling; I love and admire nothing; yet am I not heartless and cold enough for the world in which I live. What is it that makes me miserable? There is a fire burns within my soul…

She slammed the book shut and replaced it upon the shelf, closing her eyes on stinging tears. *A fire burns within my soul.*

'Would you like the book?'

She opened her eyes. Her husband stood before her, eyeing her quizzically. *A fire burns within my soul*, she thought again.

She shook her head. 'I was merely passing the time. I desire nothing.'

He cocked his head, regarding her for a long moment. He finally said, 'I will make my purchase.'

Guy offered his wife his arm as they walked out. She'd gone so pale in the bookshop. What had happened to her in there? He wished she would open up her thoughts to him, her hopes, her desires.

Emily, the mask you wear conceals more than Lady Widow's, he said to himself. He wished they could cease this masquerade and bring the fresh air of honesty into their relationship.

But he was not ready to be honest, not until he'd secured their finances and her future. He owed that to her. Still, it would be pleasant to give her some enjoyment on this lovely autumn day. He must be more clever.

'I have a notion Aunt Pip and Aunt Dorrie might fancy some sweets,' he said. 'Are you too fatigued to walk to Gunter's?'

'I am not too fatigued,' she responded, agreeable as ever.

They walked towards Berkeley Square, the day warming in the afternoon sun.

Another gentleman was entering the shop as they neared it. He smiled at them warmly. 'Lady Keating. Lord Keating. Delightful to see you.'

Guy recognised him as Lieutenant—no, Captain, he'd gained a promotion—Devlin Steele. He had a brief acquaintance with the man in the Peninsula, but not enough to warrant this friendly greeting. Emily's grip tightened on his arm. She knew him? And was distressed to see him? Another secret, no doubt? Guy extended his hand. 'Lord Devlin. Good to see you.'

Steele accepted the handshake and turned to Emily. 'How nice we meet again so soon.'

Soon? What sort of secret might this be?

The man went on, smiling at Emily. 'Do you come for an ice? The day is almost warm enough for it. I beg you will bear us company. Madeleine is in the carriage over there.' He gestured to a fine shining vehicle bearing the Heronvale crest. 'She will want to see you.'

She was acquainted with the wife! Guy felt more than a measure of relief. 'Would you desire it, Emily?'

With an odd light in her eyes, she responded, 'Oh, yes.'

Steele insisted upon procuring the ices and shooed them over to the carriage. Emily almost ran to it. As they approached, a pretty face appeared at the carriage window.

'Emily!' she exclaimed.

'We have come to sit with you,' Emily said, sounding happy.

Her friend opened the door, and Guy assisted his wife in.

As Emily took the seat beside her dark-haired companion, she said, 'My lord, may I present Lady Devlin. Madeleine—I mean, Lady Devlin, my husband, Lord Guy Keating.'

Guy remained on the pavement. 'My pleasure, ma'am.' He shook the lady's hand.

Lady Devlin regarded him intently. 'I am very delighted to meet you,' she said.

Emily smiled at her friend, and the smile reached her eyes.

'I shall leave to assist Lord Devlin,' Guy said, aware of a small pang of envy.

He bowed to them and walked to the confectioner's. He'd wished to please his wife this day. He had not known he would do so by giving her a moment alone with her friend, a moment away from her husband.

Cyprian Sloane stood in the shadow of the tall green shrubbery watching Keating leave the carriage and walk back to Gunter's. He'd caught sight of Lord and Lady Keating walking down Bruton Street and on a lark decided to follow them. One never knew what useful information might be unearthed if one seized an opportune moment like this.

He'd watched Keating and his wife meet up with Heronvale's younger brother and thought it mildly interesting. When he saw a lady's face at the window of the Heronvale carriage, hairs stood erect on the back of his neck.

Had his eyes deceived him?

He'd moved closer, selecting this vantage point amidst the shrubbery. All he need do was wait for the face to appear again to be sure.

If he were correct, he'd need some time to ponder how to use the information to further his aims. The connection appeared to be between Lady Keating and the young woman he'd recognised. He'd need to discover how she came to be in the Marquess of Heronvale's carriage, in the company of the Marquess's brother, and on friendly terms with the respectable Keatings. Then he'd find a way to make this knowledge useful.

Sloane grinned. He'd spent the war years bartering in information, not too dissimilar to what he thought he'd discovered here. It felt invigorating to exercise his skills once more. All it took was a talent for being in the right place at the right time, patience to wait until all facts were revealed, and a little luck.

It was all a bit like a card game. Sloane would wait as long as it took. Then he'd see if he'd just been dealt a queen of spades.

Chapter Thirteen

After spending almost the entire afternoon together, Lord and Lady Devlin persuaded Emily and Guy to come to dinner that evening, Guy's mother and the aunts included.

The evening was a very cordial one. Heronvale was a generous host, his wife a warm and welcoming hostess. Steele and Guy had much in common, and Emily and Lady Devlin were inseparable.

When it came time to leave, Heronvale insisted upon ordering his carriage for them. During the ride home, Emily was very quiet. Aunt Dorrie rattled on about how well sprung the Heronvale carriage was, how delightful the company had been, and how delicious the food. For once Aunt Pip agreed with every word. His mother repeatedly reminded them she was the Marchioness's mother's dearest friend.

For once his family was entirely in good spirits. Guy's heart felt light. He'd wished for this, worked for it, faced the gaming tables for it. He wanted them all to be happy.

While the three elder ladies were busily trying to out-chatter each other, he leaned to his wife's ear. 'It was a pleasant evening, was it not?'

She turned, a startled expression on her face. 'Yes,' she said, her voice tightening. 'Yes, it was.'

His spirits dipped. None of his wife's happiness lay at his door.

When they were finally at home, Bleasby was there to greet them. His mother and great-aunts entered the town-house still clucking like chickens in a coop. Bleasby hurried to assist the ladies with their cloaks, his wrinkled face looking even more sunken than usual.

'Bleasby, what the devil are you doing up at this hour?' Guy asked. 'Where is Rogers?'

Arms piled with cloaks, Bleasby replied, 'I felt it my duty—'

'Duty—!' Guy began, but his wife interrupted him.

'Thank you, Bleasby,' she said kindly. 'It was good of you to take such care of us. You will retire now, will you not? And ask Rogers to take over?'

Bleasby bowed. 'As you wish, my lady.'

Guy stopped his wife in the act of removing her own cloak, assisting her himself. 'Thank you, Emily,' he whispered in her ear. 'That was much better said.'

She gaped at him with wide eyes. Her eyes looked grey this evening, he noticed, but he'd recalled them looking amber under Lady Widow's mask. Was her eye colour as mysterious as the rest of her, changing with her costume?

His hands lingered on her shoulders. He liked the air of mystery about her. It was frustrating, to be sure, but it also spawned more pleasurable senses.

Rogers rushed into the hall, a worried look on his face. 'Beg pardon, my lord,' he said in Guy's direction. 'Meant to be here before Mr Bleasby.' He quickly relieved Bleasby of the cloaks and waited for Guy to hand him Emily's.

Bleasby bowed and turned to leave, but stopped. 'I quite forgot, my lord. A note was delivered for you, and I was requested to put it into your hands tonight.'

He crossed to the marble-topped table and picked up a sealed paper from the silver tray.

Guy threw Emily's cloak on the pile in Rogers's arms, and took the note. He broke open the seal and read:

My dear Lord Keating,
Our wealthy sheep of last evening have begged for more shearing and are willing to increase the stakes.
I beg you would attend Madame Bisou's this evening around midnight, where I have reserved a private parlour.
Your faithful servant, etc., C. S.

Sloane

His heart accelerated. Midnight? It was nearly midnight now. He read the note again and barely attended the good-nights of his mother and great-aunts as they started up the stairs to their rooms.

'Is it bad news?'

His head shot up. His wife stood before him, looking almost concerned. He smiled reassuringly. 'No, not bad news at all. I…I must go out again, however.'

Her eyes narrowed slightly. 'Very well,' she said impassively. 'I will bid you goodnight.'

She turned and quickly ascended the stairs. He watched her, wishing he could tell her the whole, and worrying that she would attempt to go out in the night herself as Lady Widow when he would be unable to watch over her. A private parlour meant serious play indeed, and his attention would be commanded by the game. In spite of his concern for his wife and the bevy of gentlemen who'd wagered on bedding her, a thrill shot through him. This game would test his skill, nerve and luck to their very limits.

He ought to pen a note declining the invitation. Playing this sort of high-stakes game was a rash and ill-conceived idea, but still his blood burned to test himself in such deep waters, the same blood that had flowed through his father and his brother. That reaction alone should warn him to beg off, but could he afford to pass up this opportunity? The night before, those gentlemen had dropped five thousand pounds without a blink of an eye. How much more were they willing to lose?

Rogers stood waiting for his coat and hat.

'I'm going out again, Rogers. I beg you not to wait for me. I will be late.'

He ran into the library and removed from his locked drawer the envelope of banknotes he'd intended to send to Annerley. Stuffing it into the pocket of his coat, he hurried back out into the night, already late and hoping the players had not found another to take his place.

From the first-floor landing, Emily watched her husband rush out of the door.

Only a card game could be so important, she suspected. A note from Lady Widow might be treated as highly, but, of course, Lady Widow had not penned that note.

She gripped the banister before spinning around to climb above stairs to her bedchamber. She had all but decided to stay home this night, content after her lovely long visit with her sister, but if her husband could end such an evening with cards, so could she.

She'd have Hester help her don Lady Widow's costume and she would stay out just as late as her husband, if she chose.

* * *

When Emily entered the game room at Madame Bisou's, several gentlemen turned welcoming faces her way. Several, but not her husband. Holding her head erect, chin up, she smiled Lady Widow's smile and glided across the room with more feminine grace than she would employ as her other self.

No, her husband was not present. Nor was Cyprian Sloane, for that matter, but that was of no consequence.

Also absent were the two gentlemen who had played cards with Sloane and Guy the previous night, but that might be mere coincidence. Who was to say those men had not gone elsewhere to play?

She barely reached the centre of the room before Sir Reginald rushed up to her, grabbing her hand. Oh, dear, she must endure another wet kiss.

'My dear lady, how good to see you this night,' he said, planting his lips upon the back of her hand as moistly as she'd feared. 'I do beg you to play at my table. Shall I order you some champagne, or do you prefer something else?'

She gave him Lady Widow's smile. 'Champagne, of course.'

She might as well play cards with Sir Reginald as with any of the others, but she would wager none of them would provide the stimulation she'd experienced playing whist with her husband. He was a true gamester.

She allowed the older gentleman to lead her to a chair. Sir Reginald waved at one of the serving girls, who did not hurry to leave the side of the gentleman so blatantly ogling her cleavage. The East India man and the Duke's son appeared at the table, begging to play.

Madame Bisou wandered over. 'We have your company again this night, Lady Widow,' she said, adjusting the ribbons of a particularly atrocious salmon-coloured dress. The matching plumes in her flame-red hair bobbed with every word she spoke. 'You have been excellent for business, I must say, but may I inquire if your friend Robert is…?' Her brows rose hopefully.

'Not tonight,' Emily told her with sympathy. This *tendre* for her brother taxed Emily's ability to refrain from a fit of giggles.

Would it not be delightful to share the tale with her sister and have a good laugh together? But what might Madeleine say about her scandalous masquerade?

'If I see him, *madame*, I will convey your regards.'

Madame Bisou cheered a little at her words. Emily knew the *madame* would, in due time, select another gentleman and disappear with him above stairs.

Emily turned her attention to the game of whist she was about to play. By the time the first game had come to a close, she discovered a slight difference in the quality of the play. The East India man and the Duke's son seemed bent upon a win, but as the rounds continued, their card-playing skills deteriorated and ultimately she won the game. It was as if they'd attempted to deal from both the top and the bottom of the deck, wanting to give her the challenge her husband had shown her the previous night, but not daring to take it so far as to give her a loss. What did they fear if they won? That Lady Widow would not pay her debt? That she would turn to other partners? That she would search for another gaming hell?

The gamester in her hated that her skills were not further tested as they'd been the night before. The practical side simply counted her money at the end of the night.

When supper was announced, she permitted Sir Reginald to escort her. The East India man and the Duke's son stuck with them like porridge on a spoon. They'd all seemed perfectly content to pass their losses on to her.

When the East India man brought her a plate and seated himself close to her, she casually moved her chair before commenting upon the excellent selections he had made. After a few minutes more of watching the door, she could stand it no longer.

'I notice Mr Sloane and Lord Keating are not present this evening.' She gave a coy smile. 'Have I lost two of my most ardent admirers?'

'No, indeed,' blurted the Duke's son. 'They remain in the game.'

'Remain in the game?' She blinked at him, truly not comprehending.

Sir Reginald quickly interjected, 'He means they are engaged in a private party.'

Her amused expression almost fled. The only private parties she knew to take place at Madame Bisou's were between men and women. If her husband had another assignation besides his precious Lady Widow, how would she abide it?

With great difficulty, she feigned a knowing smile. 'I see. They have abandoned me for the favours of some other ladies. I am desolated.'

'Not so,' said the East India Man, who tended towards pragmatical speech. 'They bespoke a parlour for a private whist game. Been at it since half past midnight.'

'That is what I mean,' she responded. The man's explanation still did not inform her there were no women present. 'I am certain they must play more than whist, or why be private?'

'I assure you,' the East India man went on, 'it is a card game. A deadly serious one. The two gentlemen who lost to them last night challenged them to another match. They wanted no distractions.'

She knew it. The gentlemen who had been so seemingly unconcerned about dropping a small fortune the night before were bent on revenge. They would ruin Guy. How foolish could he be? Unlike her father, why could her husband not be content with one big win? Why did men forever have to go back to lose it all again?

She paid particular attention to a small square of cake on her plate, picking at it with her fork, hoping she'd disguised her utter fury at her husband's foolishness.

After supper, she played another two games, but had great difficulty paying attention. Sir Reginald and the Duke's son almost took the game, and at the end, she forgot to call honours, until Sir Reginald pointed it out to her.

Guy and Sloane still had not appeared from their private room. Surely they would stop in the card room when the play was finished.

It was late, later than she usually stayed. She must leave.

When she was riding home in the hack, it occurred to her that Guy might have finished earlier and might at this moment be home. If so, would he be waiting for her? Would he catch her in the act of playing Lady Widow?

But he was not at home. When Hester let her into the house, commenting that she'd worried because her ladyship was so late, she confirmed that Lord Keating had not returned. Emily climbed the servants' narrow staircase to her room and changed out of Lady Widow's costume, donning her own nightdress. She crawled into her bed and wrapped herself in the blanket, warming her feet next to the hot brick Hester had placed there for her. She lay awake as the minutes ticked by. He did not return.

At dawn she fell asleep. At ten o'clock she woke with a start. Climbing hurriedly out of bed, she rushed over to the door connecting her room with her husband's. Pressing her ear against the wood, she could hear nothing. She carefully turned the knob and pulled. It was not locked. She opened the door and peeked into his room. It was empty.

Next to the wardrobe, his boots stood at attention like soldiers. His bed was neat as a pin. He had not set foot in this room since dressing for dinner. Her heart raced so fast she thought she could hear the blood rushing through her brain.

Had some danger befallen him? Had he been set upon by footpads? Or had there been a dispute over the cards and duels challenged? Did he lay dying on some grassy knoll somewhere, some corner of Hyde Park, his life's blood flowing into the thirsty earth? She compressed her lips into a grim line.

Or had he lost so catastrophically that he had shot himself, like his brother? Her hand flew to her mouth, and her breath came quicker. She paced the room, trying to calm herself.

It was possible he had won. Perhaps he was celebrating. She stopped pacing and narrowed her eyes. When the big winners celebrated at Madame Bisou's, the girls she employed flocked around them, sometimes throwing their arms around the men's necks and kissing them on the mouth.

At least he would be alive, if that were the case. She would prefer he be alive, even if the one way she could imagine it made her murderously angry—or jealous, she could not decide which.

She strode back into her own room and shut the door before summoning Hester to help her dress.

'Oh, my lady,' Hester said, her eyes round as full moons. 'Mr Rogers says his lordship did not return home all the night!'

Of course the servants would know. 'Yes, Hester, I realised that as well. I do hope no one spoke of this to Lord Keating's mother or to his aunts.'

'I do not think so, ma'am,' she said. 'Mr Bleasby said we was to keep mum until he spoke to you.'

At least that was fortunate.

'He did right.' Emily forced a smile and squeezed Hester's wringing hands. 'I am sure Lord Keating was merely...detained. Unavoidably, I am certain, but we must save the Dowager and her aunts any distress.'

'Yes, ma'am,' said the girl without conviction.

'Let us dress me quickly,' she went on.

A few minutes later she hurried down the stairs. When she reached the first floor, her mother-in-law stepped into the hallway.

'You have developed a habit of sleeping late,' the Dowager said by way of morning greeting.

Emily clutched the banister to stop herself. She took a deep breath. 'Good morning, Lady Keating. Did you have need of me?'

'No,' she said in a desultory tone. 'But I have not seen my son this morning either, and I had cause to wonder...'

Wonder what? Emily silently asked. Wonder if your son and his wife had slept late together?

'I believe Guy went out quite early,' she said. Which, she persuaded herself, was not a lie. He'd gone out when the clock marked the new day. 'Did you have need of him?'

'No,' her mother-in-law said. 'I merely wondered.'

'If you do not object, ma'am, I will take leave of you.' She took a step down the stairs.

'Where are you bound?'

Emily stopped again. 'To speak with Mrs Wilson and Bleasby. To…to check the arrangements for the day. That is all.'

'I see,' the elder Lady Keating said, turning away and walking back into the parlour.

Emily expelled a relieved breath and hurried to find Bleasby. He was at the silver closet, a worried frown on his face while he counted the silver and polished odd pieces.

When he saw her he said, 'Good morning, ma'am,' and gave her his usual bow. 'I have no wish to distress you, but Master Guy—I mean, Lord Keating—did not return…' He could not finish.

She placed her hand on his arm. 'I know, Bleasby. But you are not to worry. It is due to that note he received, you see.' That might be true, she thought. 'Please spread the word to the other servants. Tell them to say nothing that distresses Lady Keating or her aunts.'

'I have done so, ma'am, but, if you must know, Mr Guy does not do such things. I am certain a mischief has befallen him.' His eyes were filled with worry.

Poor Bleasby. It would not do for him to become ill over this. 'Perhaps you can send Rogers out to ask some discreet questions. If there is bad news, there will be talk of it.' She tried to give him an ironic smile. 'In fact, if there were bad news, we should have heard by now. It is always the way.'

Not always. Not if he were lying in some alley with a stab wound or some such, but she must not think so.

'Very good, ma'am.'

The idea of sending Rogers out appealed to her, too. Perhaps he could discover something.

Where was Guy? Was he all right? Her heart started pounding all over again.

Rogers returned with nary a word. He'd inquired at all the gentlemen's clubs and some of the shops. No one seemed to have seen Lord Keating.

When dinnertime came and Guy still had not come home, Emily felt near frantic. She assumed her most placid façade and endured the constant comments and questions from the Dowager and Lady Pipham and Miss Nuthall. She invented a fictitious note that she'd received saying Guy would not be home for dinner and would be out until very late.

Because they had received no invitation for the evening, Emily expected to endure more of the same comments throughout the evening.

After dinner Bleasby asked to have a word with her. She excused herself from the other ladies.

Bleasby looked as if he'd aged another ten years, though that seemed hardly possible.

He spoke in a low tone, leaning close to her. 'I confess, I am sick with worry, my lady. It is not like Master Guy to do such a thing.' She did not correct him for forgetting his master's title. 'His father or brother might stay out for days playing cards, but not Master Guy.'

She shared every bit of Bleasby's worry. It was, she agreed, not like him at all.

Which was why her mind conceived disaster after disaster. She'd even wondered if he'd been conscripted,

taken off to sea, sold into slavery. Could it really be something so simple as a card game?

When the other ladies of the household finally retired
for the night, Emily hurried Hester to dress her as Lady
Widow. She was ready so early she had to wait for
Hester's brother to drive up with the hackney coach.

When she arrived at Madame Bisou's, she rushed inside, remembering, in time, to appear as if she were the
serene Lady Widow.

'Good evening, Cummings,' she said to the footman.

'Evening, my lady,' he responded in a voice that was
always two octaves lower than anyone else's.

She did not usually engage the large man in conversation. 'What is it like inside tonight?' she asked. 'Who
is playing cards?'

She hoped that was question enough for him to tell her
what she wished to know.

'The usual sort,' he replied.

She abandoned the art of subtlety. 'Are Lord Keating
and Mr Sloane still playing whist?'

'No, my lady.'

Her fledgling hopes were cast down to the depths. Vi-
sions of Guy bleeding in some alley returned. She handed
Cummings her cloak and, with a step as leaden as her
heart, climbed the stairway to the first floor.

When she reached the top step, a gentleman staggered
out of the supper room, almost careening into her. His
neckcloth was askew, his coat unbuttoned, his waistcoat
stained. His face bore more than a shadow of beard and
his hair stood on end.

It was her husband.

Chapter Fourteen

She grabbed the banister to keep from falling. Her husband swung around, tripping on the stair and winding up a step below her, his arms pinning her in place.

Her first thought was, *He is safe!* The second was, *He reeks of brandy.* While she'd been nearly sick with worry, he'd been here the whole time. Drinking.

He gave her a crooked grin. 'Em-m-m—Lady Widow!'

Trapped between his arms she could not move. He leaned into her, wrapping his arms around her and pressing her against the banister. Being a step below, his face was level with hers. He nuzzled her cheek with his stubble-covered one.

'Missed you, Lady Widow,' he said, chuckling as if he'd said something very funny.

'Unhand me,' she rasped, pushing against his chest. None of the gentlemen had ever pawed at Lady Widow. How dare he touch her in sight of anyone happening by? How dare he cause her to worry that he was dead somewhere, lying in the cold all alone?

'Don't want to.' He kissed her ear and, in spite of her fury, sent shivers of sensation riffling down her spine. 'Want to be with you, Lady Widow.' His lips warmed the sensitive skin of her neck. 'I did it,' he whispered, breath tickling her ear. 'I did it.'

She did not care what he had done. She pushed again. To no avail.

A laugh came from behind her. 'To think all I needed do was buy him a drink.'

She glanced up to see Sloane leaning against the doorframe of the supper room, looking as dishevelled and unshaven as the man now rubbing his hand down her back.

Her husband was behaving even worse than Sloane had done, treating her like she was no better than one of Madame Bisou's girls. The thought that they might have had more than Madame Bisou's brandy made her push with new force.

He merely held her tighter.

'You might get him off me,' she said, casting Sloane an irritated look.

Sloane grinned, taking a step but steadying himself with a hand on the wall. 'Jus' when he's doing such a capital job of ruining his chances with you? Don't be a nodcock.'

Her husband tried to lift a leg on to the step where she stood. His foot missed the step and he almost unbalanced them both from their precarious perch.

'Oh, do something,' she demanded of Sloane, grabbing the banister to keep from falling. 'Before we both tumble down the stairs.'

Sloane did not wobble as he walked, but his gait was very, very careful. She'd once seen her brother walk like that when he'd broken into their father's wine stores.

Sloane took each stair carefully. He braced himself and grabbed Guy's shoulder. 'Come on, Keating. Time t'take ya home. I daresay y'r wife'll be at daggers drawn, but it cannot be helped.'

'You are as drunk as he is,' Emily accused.

'We had only one little drink. To celebrate. Promise…'
Sloane made a gesture with his thumb and finger, to show
just how little the drink had been. He gripped Guy's
shoulders and pulled with more force. 'Keating, get on
with it, man. Go home to your wife.'

Guy released Emily and wound around to Sloane, using
Sloane to keep his balance. 'Home to my wife?' he snick-
ered. His mirth escalated until he was shaking with laughter so intense, no sound came from his mouth. Sloane
needed to hold him upright.

Emily gripped the banister so hard her knuckles turned
white. He dared laugh about his wife? She was some mon-
strous jest to him, was she? What thanks these were for
the hours and hours of worry she had expended on his
behalf. If someone handed her a dagger at this moment,
she might indeed draw it.

Her husband's laughter died with one long sigh. His
expression changed to alarm and he quickly patted his
coat pocket. 'Must take care,' he said shaking his finger
in the air. 'Don't want to be set upon by footpads.'

'Indeed,' Sloane nodded his head vigorously as if Guy
had said something profound. 'Footpads.' Sloane slung
his arm around Guy. 'On our way, man.'

The two men stumbled their way down the stairs.

At the bottom, however, Guy turned back. He gazed up
at Emily with an expression on his face so raw with desire
it surely belonged only in a bedchamber. 'Goodnight,
Lady Widow,' he called to her in a voice suddenly steady
and clear.

He remained there, gazing at her, his eyes searing her
skin with a lick of fire. It thrilled her.

And sickened her.

How dare he look at Lady Widow in that way, when
his wife was nothing more to him than an object of laugh-

ter? How dare he touch Lady Widow as if she were a common harlot, when he did not touch his wife? How dare he arouse those senses in Lady Widow, when he could not bear to bed his wife?

He might look at Lady Widow all he pleased in that lascivious manner. It merely threw more fuel on the white-hot furnace burning inside her now.

So hot with anger she could not move, she glared at him as the men fumbled into their greatcoats and stumbled out of the door.

Lady Widow had one advantage over Emily Keating. Lady Widow could hurt him. Give him some measure of the pain he so casually inflicted upon his wife.

She tapped her fingers on the wood of the banister railing. She would do it. If her husband was so determined to be unfaithful, she would oblige him. She could also inflict a jest upon him. Would not it be worth a laugh to know he'd been unfaithful *with* his wife, rather than *to* her?

At that moment, the East India man walked out of the game room. Spying her, he said, 'Ah, Lady Widow! I beg you to sit down with me for a round of whist.'

Playing Lady Widow, even winning at cards, would give her no joy this night. The fawning attention the gentlemen showered upon her suddenly gave her a great disgust. She could not bear their compliments, their oversolicitousness. Not when her husband behaved in so horrid a manner.

She did not give the gentleman a glance. Glancing instead down towards the front door, she said more to herself than to him, 'I must leave.'

She did not wait to listen to his protests, but ran down the stairs, begging Cummings to get her cloak. Without bothering to put it on, she hurried out of the door, heedless of the night's chill. It would take more than cold weather to cool the fury within her. She ran down the street to where the hackney waited for her, calling for her driver to take her home.

Her driver made excellent speed, and she ran through the mews to the servants' entrance in the back, realising at the last minute that Hester would not be there to let her in. She rapped on the locked door.

It was opened by a startled Rogers. 'M'lady!'

She said a quick thank you, gave no explanation, and hurried off to the servants' stairway. She made it up the three flights of stairs to the hallway of her bedchamber's floor when noise from below stairs reached her ears. She tiptoed down to the first floor where she could see the hall.

Her husband stumbled in, greeted by an obviously frantic Bleasby, who was repeatedly exclaiming, 'Master Guy! Master Guy! Are you injured, lad?'

Her husband's laughter reached her ears once more, though he stepped out of her view. 'No, Bleasby, I could not be better. I've done it, you see! No more to worry over now.'

Oh, yes, he had done whatever it was he had done, but worry would not escape him. She intended to give him plenty to worry about.

'I'm devilish tired, Bleasby,' she heard him say. 'It was a hellish long game.'

Card playing as well as drinking. She ought to have known. It sounded like something her father would have done. That and more.

Rogers's voice was added. 'M'lord!' he exclaimed in much the same tone as his greeting to her.

'Ah, Rogers,' her husband said. 'Be so good as to help me to m'room. I'm devilish tired. Devilish tired.'

He might well be tired from playing cards and drinking and whatever else all that time. Let him sleep all he wanted. She would plot her revenge.

Emily ran ahead of them, reaching her bedchamber before their footsteps sounded in the hall.

Guy woke to daylight, but with no conception of what time it was or even what day it was. He was somewhat surprised to find himself in his own bed. His last clear memory had been of his two whist opponents, heads on the card table, sound asleep in the room where they'd spent almost twenty-four hours straight.

He bounded out of bed. Where was his coat?

He found it brushed and folded neatly in the wardrobe. Bleasby's dedication, he suspected, but his heart pounded until he inspected the inside pocket and discovered the packet of banknotes.

He spread them on a table. One note signed over to him the total sum of ninety-four thousand pounds. Other notes were in denominations of one thousand pounds. Still others in lower denominations. Guy was not entirely sure how much he had won, but he knew he had succeeded. He had won enough to rebuild Annerley, to fix the tenants' cottages, to pay for spring planting. And he had plenty left over to invest in the funds. He'd won enough to make his family and Annerley secure.

He'd done it!

After carefully replacing the banknotes in their packet, he walked to the bureau and poured water into the basin. Splashing it over his face, he caught sight of himself in the mirrored glass. He looked as if he'd survived a battle rather than a bout of cards. He rubbed his cheek, the stubble of his beard scratching his hand.

A vague memory of Lady Widow invaded his mind, of him rubbing his rough face against her soft, smooth skin. Had he seen her, embraced her, as his memory seemed to tell him, or was it a dream? She seemed to inhabit many of his dreams of late.

Lathering his bar of soap and wiping it on his face, he scraped his cheeks and chin with the razor and then quickly washed and dressed. Still unsure of the hour, he chose a brown frock coat and trousers. If there were still time in the day, he meant to call upon his father's former man-of-business. The man had been wise enough to sever ties with his father and brother when they did not heed his advice, but perhaps he would be willing to take a chance on another, luckier Keating. Guy meant to tie up his winnings in safe investments as soon as possible.

The house was quiet as he made his way downstairs. It was deflating he had no one with whom to celebrate, but he supposed that was the cost of keeping their financial problems to himself. He wanted to tell the whole to Emily, wanted to share his good fortune with her, to see her changeable eyes dance like Lady Widow's, to swing her around in total happiness.

But he'd never explained to her how badly he had needed that fictitious fortune of hers. At the time it would have been like rubbing salt in her wounds to tell her she'd married a man one step from Dun territory.

He found Bleasby napping in a chair in the hallway, his chin bobbing against his chest. Poor Bleasby. Soon he could have a small cottage of his own on the Annerley estate and he could nap all the days through, not needing to serve anyone's desires but his own.

Guy tiptoed by the old butler and went into the library.

The clock on the mantel said four-twenty. He might make it into town to complete his business, if he made haste. He gathered some of his other winnings from the locked drawer and put them all together in the packet, tucking it safely in the pocket of his coat. Proceeding quietly so as not to wake Bleasby, he collected his greatcoat and hurried out.

Guy returned at dinnertime, rushing above stairs to dress, his heart light now his shoulders were free of the burden of debt. He dressed quickly, and finding no one in the parlour, headed to the dining room.

His mother and the aunts all looked up when he entered. Emily was not at the table.

'Guy, where have you been?' his mother cried. 'We have all been so worried. You should have told us you had business away from home.'

He gave his mother a kiss on the cheek. 'My apologies, Mother, I ought to have sent word.'

'But your wife said you did send word,' the Dowager said.

Emily had lied for him? Of course. She would have known where he'd been.

'Where is Emily?' he asked.

His mother fussed with the sleeves of her dress. 'Oh, she pleads a sick headache. She has retired for the night.'

Guy frowned. She'd never been ill. 'Does she require a doctor?' he asked.

'She does not require a doctor,' his mother responded in a peevish voice. 'I believe she has the headache in order to keep from accompanying me this evening.'

'Young people have no notion of manners these days,' intoned Aunt Dorrie.

He gave his great-aunt a stern look. 'That is unkind, Aunt Dorrie.'

Aunt Dorrie looked chastised.

Aunt Pip almost smiled. 'Young ladies do get headaches now and again. I am sure the poor dear needs a rest.'

From her late nights? Aunt Pip was correct. She must be exhausted with the hours she kept. He had not wished to postpone his interview with her.

Guy patted Aunt Pip's shoulder on the way to his seat at the head of the table.

His mother piped up, 'It is a wonder we are not all prostrate after the worry you gave us, Guy.'

'I do apologise, Mother,' he said again.

He let the rest of their conversation wash over him, mumbling occasional apologies for having worried them.

He wanted to see Emily. With the money safe and their future secured, he wanted to tell her the whole. From start to finish.

He wanted to tell her he'd known all along that she was Lady Widow. He wanted to tell her about the card game, how frightening it had been and how exhilarating. He wanted to confide in her his own weakness towards gambling and warn her to stop her own dangerous card playing before it ruined her like it had his father and brother. He wanted to confide in her what a shambles his father and brother had bequeathed to him, how many people would suffer if the estate went back into debt.

Most of all he wanted to beg her forgiveness and ask for an opportunity to begin their marriage again.

He was even willing to give up the intoxicating allure of Lady Widow. He wanted to put behind them Madame Bisou's and all it meant. No more secrets. No more masks.

But he should not inflict all this on her if she were ill upon her bed.

Guy stared at his plate, his appetite gone.

His mother's voice broke through his reverie. 'Guy? Guy!'

He looked up. 'Yes, Mother?'

'You were not attending to me,' she accused.

'Merely woolgathering a moment, what were you saying?' A change of subject might give a needed distraction.

'We are invited to a card party,' she said. 'And your wife has begged off. I am very desirous of attending.' She gave him a hopeful look. 'Will you escort me, Guy?'

He wanted to seek out his wife, not spend an evening at cards, but perhaps it would be cruel to inflict such a serious talk upon Emily if her head ached.

He might as well make one person happy this night. 'I'll escort you, Mother.'

It seemed he could not escape cards for even one evening.

Emily had arranged to arrive at Madame Bisou's early that night, departing before her husband and mother-in-law returned from the evening party. As soon as she handed Cummings her cloak, she asked to see Madame Bisou.

The madam attended her immediately, a hopeful look on her face. 'Robert?' she asked.

Emily shook her head. 'I have not seen him, *madame*.'

The henna-haired madam pursed her lips.

'I wished to request of you a private room,' Emily said.

Madame Bisou's eyes brightened. 'Ah, you have selected a fortunate gentleman? How very *superbe*!'

Emily affected her most haughty Lady Widow tone. 'I

wish a room in which to play a private game of cards.
You have such rooms, do you not?'

Madame replied, still sounding amused, 'I do indeed.
Will you follow me?' She grabbed a candle from the hall
table.

Emily followed her to the floor above the game room,
the set of rooms where Madame's girls took their gentlemen. Madame opened one of the doors and ushered her
inside. She lit a colza oil lamp above a small card table.

'Will this do, my lady?' Madame asked.

Emily looked around. The card table would do nicely,
but she also noticed a bed tucked away in the corner,
swathed in curtains and piled with pillows.

'It will do,' she responded. 'I should also desire some
refreshment. Some champagne, some brandy, and something to eat as well.'

'Certainement,' said Madame Bisou in her bad French.
She started for the door.

'Another thing,' Emily said.

Madame paused.

'Would you please ask Lord Keating to join me?'

Madame's eyes lit up as brightly as her hair. 'Aha!' she
exclaimed. 'So it is he! *Très bien.*'

'To play cards,' added Emily.

'Of course,' said Madame Bisou with a trill of laughter
as she swept from the room.

Emily wandered around, touching the furniture, checking the fire in the grate, avoiding the bed.

She supposed it would be all around the premises that
she had invited Lord Keating to a private party. It put her
to the blush, but as Lady Widow she must remain cool.

She turned towards the bed and stared at it.

Nerves fluttered in her stomach. What had happened to
her resolve? Did she not wish to carry off this new

scheme? It was revenge she was after, was it not? What other reason could she have for seducing her husband?

Emily closed her eyes against an image of herself and Guy in that bed.

No, not herself and Guy. Lady Widow.

How much clearer could he have made his desire for Lady Widow than he'd done the night before, holding her and touching her in so familiar a manner? He had not come into his wife's bed, looking for that sort of intimacy, had he? No, he'd gone to sleep alone. He'd not even attempted to give his wife one word of explanation of where he had been for two full turns around the clock.

Her revenge would be to give him what he wanted. Lady Widow. Perhaps even this night she would entice him into that gaudy bed. Perhaps she would engineer a long sordid affair. When she was ready to leave him, she would reveal her secret. He would discover exactly what he had lost by chasing after a woman in a gaming hell and ignoring his wife. By then she would be gone, disappeared into a new quiet peaceful life somewhere.

Alone.

Directly after Guy returned from escorting his mother, he hurried up to his bedchamber. He strode immediately to the door connecting his wife's room with his. He had thought about it all evening. He ought not to have let her headache impede him. He ought to have visited her and asked after her health and informed her he wished to speak with her when she recovered. He hoped it would not be too late. He could see candlelight from under the door. She would be awake.

He opened the door.

Her maid gave a shriek and dropped the dress she'd

been holding in her hand. Guy looked around. Emily was not to be seen.

'I am looking for my wife,' he said to the maid.

She turned very pale and stood as still as a statue.

'Well, girl? Tell me where she is.'

The maid trembled. 'She's…she's gone out, sir.'

Out? To Madame Bisou's, no doubt. Without another word he slammed the door. Grabbing his hat and cloak, he hurried back down the stairs to the hall. Rogers sat attending the door.

'I'm going out, Rogers,' he said, not even waiting for the footman to open the door for him. He flung it open himself and ran down the street to secure a hack.

By the time he arrived at Madame Bisou's he'd calmed down somewhat. She'd not done anything out of the ordinary—*her* ordinary, that is. She did not know he wished never to see this establishment again. If her headache improved, why would she not go gaming?

He asked Cummings if Lady Widow were present and Cummings said, 'Aye.'

He looked for her first in the card room, but she was not to be seen there.

He wandered into the supper room and was waylaid by Sir Reginald, who begged him to sit down for a drink. Guy obliged his father's old friend, because he thought the man could give him news of Lady Widow. He ordered a glass of port and sipped while the older gentleman launched into his latest plan for winning the fair Lady Widow, shutting out all the younger bucks and winning the wager for her favours. It took all Guy's powers of self-command to refrain from planting a facer on this old gent, who rhapsodised about the delights he expected to find when he finally won the prize. Guy's wife. He might have punched him if not distracted by the notion that he had also not seen Cyprian Sloane about the place. Guy began to worry anew.

Madame Bisou waved at him from the doorway, potentially saving Sir Reginald's long straight aristocratic nose, and Guy's sanity. He excused himself.

When he reached the flamboyant madam, she took his arm and led him out into the hall.

'She awaits you upstairs, *chéri*,' Madame Bisou whispered, somehow sounding more like a mother giving her son a treat than a procuress.

'Who?' he asked. Madame Bisou had occasionally attempted to interest him in one of her girls.

'Why, our Lady Widow, of course.' She smiled. 'You have won, it seems.'

His heart skittered. Lady Widow? She had arranged a room and invited him there?

He bent down to Madame Bisou's ear. 'Tell me the room, but do not refer to the wager about her. I am not a part of it.'

She gave him a sceptical look and directed him to a room near the one where he'd spent twenty-four hours.

He knocked.

After a pause, he heard her voice. 'Come in.'

Heart now pounding, he entered.

She stood in the centre of the room facing him, her posture stiff, as if she were a fox that had suddenly discovered dogs trailing it. She wore the blue gown, with a matching cap. Her face was blurred by the netting and obscured by the mask, but she looked to him like some goddess down from Mount Olympus.

He ought to stop right now and tell her exactly what he knew about her. He ought to, but he could not make himself form the words. He saw the card table set up with decks of cards and stacks of counters. He saw the bed in the corner.

Closing the door, he turned the key in the lock, and leaned against it, waiting.

This was her game and to know what card he should play, she needed to toss hers down first.

'Good evening, Lord Keating.' She relaxed her body and spoke enticingly in Lady Widow's voice.

'Good evening, my lady,' he responded.

She walked over to the card table and fingered its green cloth. 'I understand you have a penchant for private card games.'

'Hardly a penchant, but I did very recently agree to one, as you well know.'

'Yes, I do know.' She cleared her throat and looked him directly in the eye. 'I fancy a game of cards, and you are the only gentleman of my acquaintance who will honestly challenge me.'

He glanced again to the bed. If this were merely an invitation to a game of cards, she could have met him in the game room. The rise of excitement he felt had nothing to do with gambling. He moved closer to her.

She walked over to a side table. 'Would you like a drink? I will have champagne, but I took the liberty of ordering brandy for you, since you like it so well.'

What the devil did she mean by that? He raised a brow. This game became more and more intriguing. 'I had no idea my likes and dislikes were of interest to you.'

Emily had never spoken to him in such a seductive voice, nor moved with that surety he was seeing in her. Those behaviours bore the seal of Lady Widow and he was enticed.

She feigned a small laugh. 'A good gamester studies

the opponent, does he not? If desiring to win, that is.' She held up the bottle. 'Shall I pour for you?'

He gave a nod.

She poured brandy for him and champagne for herself and carried both glasses to the card table, where she sat down, her skirts rustling like the sound of bed linens.

He sat in the chair opposite her. 'What game do you propose, Lady Widow?' he asked.

'Piquet?'

A difficult game. It required attention, computation, memory and skill. And he was damnably rusty at it.

'As you wish,' he said.

She lifted her chin. 'What stakes?'

He took a sip of his brandy. If he wagered money and she lost, it might eventually support his request that she resist the lure of gaming. On the other hand, he could not count on his skill in piquet. He'd not played since being posted to the Peninsula.

She knew he would play in earnest. If she won from him, would it not further fuel her passion for the cards? He must choose stakes which would leave him at least even, should he lose.

'If I win the partie,' he stated, 'you will remove your mask.'

Her hand flew to her face, as if needing to ensure the mask remained in place. She checked herself and slowly lowered her hands to the table. 'That is too easy,' she said. 'Not exciting enough by half.' She cocked her head, her eyes suddenly brilliant from beneath the netting of her cap.

Her eyes were blue this night, he noticed, reflecting the blue of her gown.

She lifted a finger in the air between them. He wondered if it could gauge the palpable excitement in the air, an excitement which had nothing to do with winning at cards. 'I suggest...' she began, but then left a pregnant pause. 'I suggest the loser of each round must remove a piece of clothing. If you play well enough, I might be forced to remove my mask.'

'And the winner of a partie?' The blood already surged through his veins.

She gave him a most seductive grin. 'The winner of a partie does the removing of the article of clothing.'

He was ensnared. He'd surely lose this game by virtue of being too addled by carnal desire.

He made himself answer as calmly as she. 'And does the winner of the partie choose the piece of clothing to remove?'

She laughed and shook her finger at him as if he were a naughty boy. 'No, indeed. You will not win my mask in that manner, sir.'

He lifted his glass and she raised hers to clink against his. They both drank, gazing at each other, as the fire crackled in the grate and the lamp flickered.

'Your deal or mine?' he asked.

Chapter Fifteen

By the time the clock struck the next hour, Emily sat at the card table without gloves, without shoes, and with only one stocking remaining. Guy had handily taken all five rounds, once with repique, earning sixty points before she'd even played a card. One round he took all the tricks, earning a capot. Fully dressed, he dealt the sixth hand.

Her third glass of champagne calmed her nerves somewhat, but her eyes suddenly went out of focus. Opening wider, she made out too many sevens and eights and not one ace. Holding her breath, she made her exchange. Luck was with her. She picked up the high spades, giving her a sequence of eight, and two more aces.

She made her declaration with confidence. For the first time, the round was hers.

Her husband grinned at her. With exaggerated drama, he removed one shoe, lifting it high in the air so she could see it was off his foot.

'Do not gloat, my lady. I won the partie, you know,' he said with a wicked grin. 'Your rules require me to remove an article of your clothing. What shall it be?'

She was so vexed at losing the previous rounds, she had not much heeded this part of their bargain.

No matter. It was merely the first partie. The rest would be hers. Her luck would change.

'You may remove my other stocking,' she said. How bad could that be?

He grinned and rose, twirling his finger to signal her to move her legs from beneath the table. She turned in her chair, but without a shred of graciousness.

He knelt at her feet, which suddenly felt very exposed without shoes. She tucked her bare foot under her chair out of his sight.

He placed her stockinged foot in the palm of one hand and covered it with the other, warming it in his hands. Then slowly he kneaded her foot, fingers digging into the sole and thumbs rubbing her arch. Not only did her foot tingle and throb and melt all at one time, but the sensations climbed clear up her leg, spreading a blanket of pleasure throughout her whole body.

'This…this is removing my stocking?' she managed, hoping her voice did not sound as breathless as she felt.

His clever hands moved to her ankle. 'No, this is for my enjoyment…and yours,' he murmured. His hands worked their way up her leg, higher and higher, warming, massaging.

Once, what seemed so long ago, he'd touched her even more intimately. The shock and the pleasure of that moment returned as if a mere hour had passed. She could not help but slide down in her chair, straightening her leg and giving him easier access. A long sigh escaped her lips.

Would his fingers reach that very private spot? Would he dare touch her there again? Please?

He fingered her garter, untying it. Perhaps all he meant to do, after all, was roll down her stocking and pull it off her foot.

His fingers reached underneath her stocking, touching her bare skin. With his palms against her bare flesh, he pushed the stocking along. No matter, Emily longed to be rid of the lacy white silk. She wanted his hands to never cease this delight.

But too soon he pulled the stocking from her skin and held it out to her. She grabbed it and threw it to the floor where her other one lay.

He rose with a bit of difficulty and stood with his back to her for a moment while it seemed her whole body vibrated with an incongruous mix of languor and longing.

Throat suddenly dry, she took a long sip of her champagne. It never occurred to her this weakness of hers towards him would ever recur. She'd trusted her fury to squelch it. She squeezed her eyes shut and forced herself to remember that Guy Keating, Emily's husband, touched not his wife's leg, but Lady Widow's.

How could she have known it would be so difficult to care about the difference?

He walked slowly to his chair and poured himself more brandy. 'Shall we continue?' he said.

She dealt the cards.

This partie was much more to her liking. She lost only one round, giving up her hat, hoping he was too enamoured of Lady Widow to recognise Emily without the netting that obscured her face.

He, on the other hand, had lost his other shoe, his stockings, neckcloth, and coat. She kept a sceptical eye on his play, alert for any evidence he was giving her the win, but his play seemed as serious as her own.

What did not appear to bother him, though, was the cost of losing. When he removed an article of clothing, he made a grand show of it, his blue eyes twinkling and a smile twitching at his lips. As Emily, she would have tempered her mirth, even registered shock, but Lady Widow need not be so missish. She laughed at his nonsense, and let herself enjoy the fun.

'Now the partie is yours,' he said, crossing his arms over his chest and leaning back in his chair. 'I wonder if I should ask you to remove my waistcoat, or my breeches?'

Her face grew hot, but she quickly covered her embarrassment. 'You must choose, sir,' she said coolly. 'I am sure it matters not to me.'

He stared at her, one corner of his mouth turned up. Make haste and decide! she thought. The sooner done with the task, the better.

'My breeches…' he began.

No… She swallowed.

He grinned. 'My breeches would leave me a bit chilled. You, ma'am, may remove my waistcoat.'

She tried not to have her shoulders slump in relief. As she rose from her chair, he stood. Walking up to him, coming so close with her feet bare, reminded her too much of her wedding night and their first night in Bath. She took a fortifying breath and reached for his buttons, but she was so aware of his eyes gazing down at her, his breath caressing her, the scent of him filling her nostrils, her fingers fumbled.

The moment she freed the buttons and parted the cloth of his waistcoat, he grabbed both her hands. 'My lady,' he groaned.

He wrapped his arms around her, holding her hips flush against him. His head bent not an inch from hers. 'Kiss me, Lady Widow.' It was more of a demand than a request.

She wanted to heed it. She could feel the strength in his arms pressing her against him, could feel the bulge of his desire for her. She wanted to kiss him, to taste of him again, to let herself be transported to the time when she felt hopeful. It was so very, very tempting.

No! a small voice inside her said. *He does not want you. He wants Lady Widow.*

She forced her anger forward. She would not be weak. She would have her retribution.

She gazed up at him, and made her lips curl into a cynical smile. 'Why, sir, that is not in the cards, is it? You are preventing me from removing your waistcoat.'

He released her, so abruptly she almost fell backwards.

Somehow, winning this particular round of the game brought no delight.

It was not that she did not intend to bed him. She very much intended to do so. He desired that of Lady Widow and that is what she would give him. But on her terms, not on his.

He stood motionless, like a man awaiting his valet, giving no further hint of the passion that had previously provoked him. Surprisingly, his powers of restraint vexed her all the more.

She folded his waistcoat and put it on a side chair nearby, hanging his coat on the back of the chair as well. He watched her every move, standing there with his brilliant white shirt loose about him and his breeches moulded to his thighs. She realised too late that Lady Widow would have tossed his waistcoat carelessly aside, not caring where it fell.

'It is your deal,' she said, returning to the card table.

He dealt the cards.

She took another sip of champagne. Her fourth glass? She focused on her fury. She ought to be angry that he had attempted to kiss her, as though she were a common harlot. Never mind that it had been she who invented the stakes of the game for just such a purpose. He had started it, after all, with the silly notion she should remove her mask.

Lady Widow was of the quality, was she not? No man should trifle with her as if she were like whatever female company he and Sloane had entertained as part of their card party.

She gave a haughty sniff. 'I warn you, sir, I will not be treated like the other girls you've visited in these rooms.'

He glanced up. 'Other girls? There were no girls.' His voice was low and steady and his eyes fixed intently on hers. 'There was nothing but cards, I assure you. I have no interest in any woman but you.'

She could not look away. His gaze captured her and held her as securely as when he'd pinned her against the banister the night before. The fire she'd fed and stoked inside her, calmed to a soft glow. He wanted her.

No, not her. Lady Widow. The anger flickered back to life.

'Your exchange, my lady,' he said, breaking the contact and the spell.

Guy watched Emily as she arranged her cards. He ought to cease this charade forthwith, ought to inform her of his knowledge of her identity, tell her he had known all along. He no longer cared if he taught her a lesson about gambling. He no longer cared why she engaged in this folly.

He just wanted her.

By God, he'd almost taken her when she came so close, when she'd touched him. She was so alluring, so captivating in the back-and-forth struggle inside her. One moment she was cool and detached, the next as bound up in desire as he.

There was nothing stopping him now. He had the financial means to make up to her for tricking her into marriage. He had money enough for future generations to build upon. And he most definitely wished to risk conceiving an heir.

He finished the brandy in his glass, tried to pour another, but the bottle was empty. No, nothing impeded him from forging a future with his wife. Nothing but this masquerade. Devil take it, he wanted to bed Lady Widow, even if it were just this one time. He did not know why she, as Lady Widow, was intent upon taking him into her bed, but he wanted to experience this side of her just once.

He suspected, once the masquerade ended, Lady Widow would disappear.

She threw down five cards, picking replacements from the deck. Luckily, piquet had come back to him as effectively as jumping back on a horse after a fall. She wished for a challenging game and this had been one.

He exchanged his cards.

'Point of six,' she said.

'Good,' he replied. He did not have six cards of one suit.

'Quint,' she said.

She had five in sequence? 'Good,' he replied.

'Quatorze,' she said.

'What suit?'

She gave him a smug smile. 'Quatorze aces.'

All the aces? This hand was lost.

'Repique.' She grinned, automatically doubling her points.

He lost the round as was inevitable, but the loss might work in his favour. Perhaps she would play badly if required to stare at his bare chest. Slowly, knowing her eyes watched every flex of his muscles, he removed his shirt and tossed it to the chair where she'd placed his folded waistcoat and coat. Though bare-skinned, her eyes were heat enough. He felt no chill.

They played, speaking only declarations and points. Guy watched Emily drink the last of her champagne, her pink tongue licking a drop from her lips.

Dear God!

His breeches went next, removed without a flourish, best taken off under the table. His drawers, the only item of clothing left on his body, revealed too much from this arousing game.

He won the next round and his heart accelerated. Emily stood and seemed to unfasten her skirt, but only the top gossamer layer of cloth came off. Her modesty remained largely intact.

He won the next round as well, though he was amazed he could remember a knave from a ten. She removed a part of her bodice made of lace and ribbon.

Her hands shook as they played the next round and her voice quavered as she called out her scores. They were nearly even on tricks, but he won again by only five points.

She stood. 'I cannot remove my dress without assistance,' she said.

He went to her, forgetting his own dishabille. 'Allow me.'

She turned her back and he unbuttoned the row of tiny pearl buttons lining her spine. Her hair, swept up in a knot on top of her head, revealed her long graceful neck. It would be delicious to place his lips at the spot where her hairline met her neck, but it seemed like taking unfair advantage.

'All your buttons are undone,' he said, stepping back.

She let her dress slip from her shoulders and slide down

her body to the floor. She stepped out of the puddle of silk at her feet and turned to him, dressed only in corset and shift. From beneath her mask, her eyes beseeched him, but he knew not for what she pleaded.

'Do we continue to play?' he murmured.

She gave the ghost of a smile. 'One more hand.'

She played the next round badly, distractedly tossing down high cards when low ones remained in her hand. He could not say she intended to lose. Her choices seemed random; her mind elsewhere.

Perhaps her mind travelled in the same direction as his own, to the bed in the corner of the room.

The last card was played.

'I lost,' she said with little emotion in her voice. She lifted her head and steadily met his gaze. 'You may remove my corset.'

'Are you certain?' He found it hard to speak.

'Yes.' Her words were like a sigh. She smiled a Lady Widow kind of smile. 'We agreed upon these stakes, did we not?'

She rose and walked over to his chair and again presented her back to him. 'Undo my laces,' she commanded.

He stood. His fingers felt like clubs as he fumbled with the knot, finally untying it and freeing her of her garment. It seemed so familiar. He'd done the same on their wedding night, but without the emotions consuming him now. His feelings towards her were so altered, full of fascination, appreciation, gratitude.

She turned to him, that imploring, almost despairing look again on her face. Her sheer muslin shift revealed the shadow of her nipples, the dark triangle between her thighs. He gazed at her thirstily, wanting to plunder her, to take all his need of her in one glorious act.

But he could not. Was he not being as false to her in

this moment as he had been on their wedding night? He knew who she was. He must tell her.

'We must talk—' he began.

She covered his lips with her fingers and twined her arms around his neck. 'No talking, Guy,' she whispered. Her lips closed onto his.

Restraint vanished. Reason fled. He pulled her against him, deepening the kiss she offered, opening her mouth and tasting her with his tongue, savouring her sweetness, as effervescent as the champagne she'd consumed.

He ran his hands over her breasts, her abdomen, her back, wanting to explore every inch of her. He lifted her into his arms, while she rained his neck with kisses. He carried her to the bed.

She pulled the shift over her head and tossed it away. He made short work of his drawers, joining her on the bed, their naked bodies finally free of all barriers.

This was what he'd waited for, what he'd worked for all those nights at the gaming table, a prize he had not realised he wanted. This was something for himself. And for her.

He feasted upon the sight of her. 'You are beautiful,' he said.

Through her mask her eyes winced as if his words had injured her. 'Do not talk,' she cried, reaching for him.

This creature in bed with him was nothing like when he'd bedded her before. She had been quiet, passive then. Now she fully partook of the experience, touching him, kissing him, placing his hands where she wished him to touch.

He obliged her. Would do anything for her. His heart swelled with hope for their future. For countless nights like this one where their love could run free. He let her set the pace, let her climb on top of him and explore him, stroking and kissing. Whatever she wished, he would oblige.

His need grew with her every touch. Any coherent thought crumbled, until he felt only the desperate need to join his body to hers. He rolled them both over and rose above her. With her pliant and eager beneath him he entered her.

She gasped aloud and met his every move, catapulting him to the heights of ecstasy. With his last shred of will, he held back, waiting for her to reach the heights with him.

She did. With an impassioned cry she convulsed around him. He drove into her again and spilled his pleasure...and all his hopes...inside her.

Emily woke, tangled in bed linens and a masculine arm and leg. The clocked had chimed. What time?

She glanced at the room's window. It still appeared dark outside. Her husband was very soundly asleep next to her, his face as peaceful and untroubled as a young boy. As handsome as an Adonis.

What had she done? Somewhere in the last hands of the card game, things had gone awry. The more skin her husband exposed, the more her fury at him seemed to slip through her fingers, like so much water from a crystal pond. She had plunged in to their lovemaking as hungrily as a starving man would attack a long awaited meal.

No matter what, she could never regret making love to him, could never forget the glorious experience of being joined with him as one. Now she felt all at sea, no compass to guide her. What was she to do next? How could she return to being just Emily?

She slowly and carefully disentangled herself, wiggling out from under the arm and leg wrapped around her, freeing herself from the linens. She slipped out of the bed, the floor cool beneath her bare feet.

By the light of the dying colza lamp, she gathered her clothes and dressed hurriedly, buttoning what buttons she could reach, knowing she'd missed some. She stuffed her dishevelled hair beneath her cap. If she were lucky, no one would see her leave.

If she were lucky, her husband would not wake and profess his love for Lady Widow. She fingered the mask, still securely in place. This was the last night she would wear it. Lady Widow would disappear and somehow, someday, so would Emily.

Emily had already disappeared, however, and she, like Lady Widow, would never return. Who would appear in their place?

She smoothed her dress as best she could and tiptoed to the door. When she reached for the knob, she hesitated. Holding her breath, she glanced back at her sleeping husband, savouring one last look, saying a silent goodbye for what could never be.

She peeked into the hallway, glad to see no one there. She reached the stairs and hurried down the two flights, reaching the hall without encountering the night's clientele.

Cummings was at his post by the door. She begged him to quickly fetch her cloak.

He stared at her with a strange expression. 'Yes, m'lady,' he said and went off to do her bidding.

A moment more and she would be free of Madame Bisou's forever.

Cummings returned with her cloak. If he noticed her undone buttons while he assisted her into it, he gave no indication. She started for the door.

'Lady Widow!' a voice behind her called.

Reluctantly, she turned. It was Sir Reginald, looking painfully distressed. 'I beg a moment, ma'am.'

She did not wish to tarry, not even for a second, but she felt caught.

He rushed up to her and said, 'Let me escort you to your carriage.'

'Very well,' she agreed.

Once outside into the near freezing air, he fell to one knee, grasping her hands so tightly she could not pull away.

'Lady Widow, I know that Lord Keating has won the wager, but I beg of you—'

Her blood turned to ice. 'Wager? What wager?'

He gave her a look of chagrin. 'The wager of who would bed you first, but I beg you will—'

She jerked her hands away. 'You *wagered* about me?' Her voice escaped as cold as the night.

Guy and Sloane and Sir Reginald and the others took bets on who would get her into bed first? *Guy* did this?

He struggled back to his feet. 'A friendly wager, nothing to signify.'

'How…how…?' Words escaped her. She wanted to run. She wanted to know. Her voice dropped to no more than a rasp. 'Was it all about a wager?'

All the admiration, the flattery, allowing her to win at cards—that was all flummery? All aimed at getting her into bed, so one gentleman would win money?

Her husband's admiration of Lady Widow—was that, too, nothing more than…than…gambling?

'Don't quite get your meaning,' Sir Reginald said, dusting off his breeches. 'The odds favoured Sloane, to tell the truth, but, I must say, I retained my hopes. Would have won a bundle.'

He grabbed her hand again, but she quickly snatched it back and started for her carriage.

'Wait,' he called, hurrying to catch up. 'Want to tell you I have plenty of blunt to lay on you. Want to offer you *carte blanche*. A gentleman like me would be dashed more attentive than those younger fellows.'

She halted and spun towards him. He gave her a very hopeful smile. She swung her hand and slapped him across his cheek, the sharp smack resounding down the street.

Without another word, she ran to where Hester's brother waited for her with his hack.

Chapter Sixteen

Cyprian Sloane sat slumped in his chair in Madame Bisou's supper room, a whisky in his hand and three bottles on the table. He'd been there most of the night. He'd barely got in the door at Madame Bisou's when Sir Reginald accosted him and informed him he'd lost the wager. Keating at that moment was still occupied in a private room with Lady Widow.

That Greeking bounder.

T'think he, Cyprian Sloane, had taken the pains to invite Keating into that card game. Made the man's fortune, he had. Keating ought to have kissed his feet. Everyone knew the Viscount was nearly done up. Sloane had rescued him, plucked him out of Dun territory. This was his thanks?

Sloane downed another whisky. That bastard. That son of a whore.

Sloane laughed, the loud bark jolting the few other people in the room to look up at him. 'Son of a whore' best described himself, not Keating. No scandal attached itself to that paragon's birth, but everyone knew Sloane's father had not sired him. Nice gentleman, his *father*, saddling him with the name Cyprian lest anyone forget he was the product of cuckoldry.

Never mind that. Water over the dam. Water over the damned-if-he-cared. He laughed again, soundlessly this time, and placed his heels on the table. He folded his arms across his chest.

He'd told Keating how much this wager meant to him. Lady Widow was a tempting piece and the contest to win her had given him a vast amount of amusement. Until this night.

He cared nothing for losing the money. He had plenty of money, especially after that card game—the one into which he'd invited Keating. He was plenty rich, that was not to the point. He'd wanted to *win*, by damn, and Keating cut him out.

In his grandfather's time, he could have challenged Keating to a swordfight. He swished his sword arm through the air. A good fight would lift his spirits about now, especially if he could *win* it.

He crossed his arms again, staring dejectedly at the empty bottles on the table. No sense thinking of duelling. Only a fool risked his life for a bit o' muslin like Lady Widow. The way his luck was going, even if he won the duel, the scandal would run him out of England like that damned lame poet.

Curse the man! Keating, that is. Not the poet. At this moment Keating was fornicating with the prize when he, Sloane, was drinking bad whisky. He ought to have played his trump card. Not that he had any idea if the damned information was worth a farthing to Keating.

Discovering a drab of alcohol in one of the bottles, he poured it into his glass and downed it in one gulp. No sense staying in this damned place. He rose unsteadily to his feet. In his own rooms he could drink himself into oblivion with much better whisky.

Listing to one side, he made his way out of the room. As he entered the hallway, that devil Keating descended the stairs. 'Keating!' Sloane shouted. 'I'll have a word with you now!'

Keating scowled at him. In fact, the man looked dashed unhappy. How could any man not be happy after *winning* and bedding the mysterious widow?

Who the devil was she anyway? That was one piece of information he'd not yet discovered. Liked the mystery, frankly. Intended to peel that mask off her in a bedroom. Is that what Keating had done? Did Keating now know who she was? That would be another low blow.

'Well, what is it, Sloane?' Keating said.

That's right. He had something to say to Keating, if he had a moment to recall. Sloane wrapped his arm around Keating's shoulders and walked him over to a secluded corner.

Pointing his finger in the vicinity of Keating's nose, he said, 'The devil to you, man. You bedded her and you knew I had the first claim.'

'Do not speak to me of that wager of yours, Sloane. I will hear no more of it.' Keating shoved him aside.

Sloane grabbed the back of his collar. 'No, a moment, please. I have a plan.' He leaned into Keating's face, making the man wince. 'You…you tell them all it was a hoax. Just a card game, nothing more, and that the bet is still on. No one will be the wiser.'

'It is over.' Keating's voice rose. 'No more bets about the lady. I beg you would all forget her existence.'

'So you can have her?' Sloane gave a mirthless laugh. 'Mayhap I'll make a wager to be the man who takes her from you.' He raised a triumphant arm. 'Ha!'

'You are foxed.' Keating pushed him aside and headed towards the stairs.

'Tarry just a bit.' Sloane followed him down the stairs, grasping the banister to keep his balance. When Keating called to Cummings for his topcoat and hat, Sloane bade the man collect his as well.

'I'm going home,' Keating said.

'You will want to hear me out,' Sloane said, though he was not at all certain that would be true. In any event, sometimes you just had to throw a card on to the table and hope for the best. He trailed Keating out on to the street and kept pace, somewhat unsteadily, beside him.

'Speak up, Sloane, and allow me on my way.' Keating walked quickly. How could that be? He was half a foot shorter at least.

'Well, speak up,' Keating repeated.

'Give me a moment.' Damned soldiers always rushing to the charge.

They turned the corner before Sloane spoke.

'Your wife is acquainted with a lady, I believe,' he began. 'Sis…sis…sister-in-law to Heronvale.'

'What does that signify?' Keating slowed a bit.

'Patience, man. I'll tell you,' Sloane said, but paused, until Keating shook his head and resumed his pace.

'I met Lady Devlin some years ago,' Sloane finally said.

'I fail to see—' interjected Keating.

'Attend to me.' Sloane recomposed his thoughts into some semblance of coherency. 'I met Lady Devlin in a gaming hell run by Lord Farley. Remember him? Died earlier this year. Attacked by footpads, they say.'

'That means nothing—' Keating began.

'Nothing? She was Farley's prime piece, sir. She was the prize men won and plenty of 'em won her.' He rubbed

his chin. 'Not me, you understand. Farley gulled his patrons. I didn't fancy being cheated.'

The information must be hitting a nerve. Keating had
stopped walking. Luckily there was a lightpost to lean
upon.

'Why are you telling me this, Sloane?'

Capital question. Why was he? Oh, yes… 'Well, I had
the notion your wife's reputation might suffer if it became
known they were so closely attached; that is, if the tale
of Lady Devlin—the Mysterious Miss M, they called
her—became the latest *on dit*.'

Keating stood his ground. 'And?'

'And this scandalous *on dit* might fail to reach the gos-
sips' ears if…if you told the fellows at Madame Bisou's
the bet is still on.'

As trump cards went, this one sounded more like a two-
spotter, even to his ears. How much whisky had he consumed to induce him to think Keating would go for this
lame nonsense?

Keating glared at him, illuminated by the gaslight. 'I
took you for a different sort of man, Sloane,' he said, in
a low even tone. 'We part ways here. There's a hack
across the street and I'm off to hire him to drive me
home.' Without another word, Keating crossed the street
and, after a word with the driver, climbed in the hack.

Sloane watched him until the coach disappeared from
his sight.

Guy leaned back against the cool leather of the hackney's seat. Curse Sloane for giving him one more thing
to worry about. He needed to get home, to see Emily, and
explain what he ought to have told her from the beginning.

When he woke and found her gone, he'd known he'd

erred by not telling her the whole. Now he realised he had managed to deceive her one more time. Would it be too late to explain? Would she understand that he'd merely wanted to play out her masquerade?

He hadn't needed Sloane's extra bit of information. If Sloane were willing to ruin that poor lady's life, the man indeed deserved his reputation as a scoundrel. To think Guy had almost come to like him.

But Sloane was a petty matter at the moment. He would deal with Sloane's threat later. Emily was more important.

The hack delivered him home and he hurried inside, rushing up the stairs to his bedchamber, and only then shedding his topcoat and hat. He went immediately to the door connecting his room with his wife's.

It was locked. She had never locked the door against him. Temptation had often driven him to test the door, though he stopped himself before entering her room.

He could knock. He could break down the door for that matter, but would either of those actions gain him credit with her?

No, he was done with forcing her into situations not of her choosing. He'd respect her desire to keep him out. Morning was time enough to speak to her.

He fell exhausted into bed, but sleep eluded him. The memory of Emily in his arms tormented him, again and again drawing his eyes back to the door that separated them. Would he ever unlock that door? Would he ever find his way to her side?

With their moment of pleasure lingering in his mind, he finally drifted off into a fitful sleep.

When morning came, Emily dragged herself from her bed. She'd heard her husband return a few hours before, listened to him checking the door between them. What had he thought? He could go from Lady Widow's bed to Emily's?

She grabbed the bedpost as the pain of it shot through her. She'd thought she could treasure that one moment with Guy, even if he had been with Lady Widow and not his wife. She thought she could hold the memory close to her heart, to warm her on lonely nights. A brief memory of love.

It was all illusion.

It had been a wager, nothing more. He'd bet on bedding her. They'd all bet on bedding her, as if her heart meant nothing more than a horse running a race, a man in a bout of fisticuffs, a cock fighting to the death.

She could not even hold that one moment as precious. How false men were. How easily they trifled with a woman's affections, the lot of them. She'd never return to Madame Bisou's. She'd been a fool to step foot in such a place from the outset.

Hester entered the room. 'You are awake, my lady.'

Awake. Had she ever been asleep? 'Yes, I'm awake.'

She accepted Hester's ministrations as if by rote, caring not which of her drab dresses she wore or how her hair was arranged. The walls around her seemed like a prison cell, but she could imagine no other place to feel less captive.

The idea of continuing as Emily, so correct, so compliant, so uncomplaining, felt akin to death, but what had Lady Widow's world brought her?

She watched herself in the glass as Hester put pins in her hair to keep it in place, fancying her image dissolving like fog after sunrise. She did not know who she could be.

'There you are, my lady,' Hester said with her usual cheer.

Emily took a fortifying breath. She could make it through the day. She could walk and talk and do whatever anyone required of her. She was well practised in that skill.

Trying to erect a tower around her heart with each step, Emily went down to the breakfast room. The staircase, the rooms, the hall all looked the same, but she felt so altered it was like seeing them in a dream. One from which she would never wake.

Her mother-in-law was the only one at breakfast. Emily was relieved she would not yet have to encounter Guy. The Dowager barely glanced up when Emily entered.

'Good morning,' Emily said, though it sounded like the words came from someone else.

'Hmph,' Lady Keating muttered.

Emily shrugged, selecting her slices of toast and sitting down to pour tea. Amazing how one could act with a modicum of normality when one's insides seemed shattered to bits.

'You have slept late again,' Lady Keating said.

Emily had been about to take a bite of toast. Her hand remained poised in the air for a moment before she returned the slice to her plate and clasped her hands in her lap.

'Not late enough,' she said, not quite under her breath.

Her mother-in-law seized upon her words. 'What is your meaning, not late enough?'

Emily took a breath before meeting the older woman's eye. She felt like a vessel, already filled to the brim, into which Lady Keating had poured another pitcher full. 'Lady Keating, please inform me. Why do you dislike me so? What have I done to deserve this constant disparagement?'

Her mother-in-law gasped. 'How impertinent!'

Emily kept her gaze level. 'Not impertinent, ma'am. I truly wish to know what it is you object to in me. I have endeavoured to be pleasing to you.'

Emily would not take another moment of this treatment from her mother-in-law. She was done with being agreeable. She doubted she could abide another second of being agreeable.

'I am sure I have never—' Lady Keating began.

Emily interrupted. 'I am sure you have never called me by name. Do you realise that? You have never once used my name.'

She was not a vessel overflowing, she feared. She was a dam bursting. 'Why is that, Lady Keating?'

'This is the outside of enough!' Her mother-in-law threw down her fork and started to rise.

'No,' Emily said. 'Do not leave. Let us have this out. Tell me why you despise me so.'

Lady Keating's eyes flashed. 'You tricked my son into marriage. You have ruined him!'

A denial flew to Emily's lips, but she held it back. 'How did I accomplish this feat?' she said, keeping her voice even. 'How did I trick him?'

Lady Keating averted her eyes for a moment. 'I do not precisely know, but I can think of no other reason to marry a woman like y—' She clamped her mouth closed.

'A woman like me,' Emily finished for her. 'Exactly what about me?'

'You have nothing to give Guy credit,' the Dowager spat out. 'You have no looks, no charm, no fortune…'

Emily laughed and her mother-in-law gaped in surprise.

'No fortune, you have the right of it. Do go on, Lady Keating.'

The Dowager's face flushed red. 'My son ought to have married a woman of consequence, someone with money, connections. After…after his brother's death—my dear boy! God rest his soul—all Guy could talk about was money. We have no funds for this. There is no money for that. He wanted to bring Cecily home from school! He made us leave Annerley and go to Bath. I thought he was in search of an eligible match, not marriage to you! With your shameful family—'

'My shameful family!' Emily cried. 'How is my family more shameful than this one? Perhaps you ought to consider who may have tricked whom into marriage. If you think I sought a gamester for a husband, you are mistaken!'

Lady Keating shot back, 'My son is not a gamester! How dare you!'

As the Dowager shouted these last words, Guy walked into the room. 'What is this?' he asked hotly.

'She has been saying shocking things to me, Guy!' his mother cried, choking on a sob.

Emily stood, shooting a glare at both her mother-in-law and her husband. 'I will leave you to discuss how shocking I can be!'

'Emily, wait!' Guy pleaded, but she pushed past him and ran from the room.

Guy swung around to his mother. 'What have you done this time?'

'Now do not shout at me!' his mother sobbed. 'She started it.'

He gripped the back of a chair to keep from throttling her. How was he to make things right with his wife when his mother made it her business to be thoughtless and unkind? He did not need this from her! He needed to show Emily he could give her a good life with him. Financial security. A true partnership. Children. Most of all, children.

'Mother, I am going to end it. You have a fortnight to find other accommodations. I will give you an allowance and you may live where you please, but I'll not have you interfering in my marriage or making my wife miserable.'

'Oh!' she exclaimed in a horrified voice.

He did not wait around to hear more. He hurried out of the room in search of Emily. He met her in the hall, in bonnet and pelisse, putting on her gloves. Her maid was hurrying behind her. 'Emily…' he said.

'I am going out,' she declared. 'Hester will accompany me.'

'I will go with you,' Guy said. 'Hester, stay here.'

Hester, appearing quite alarmed, halted in mid-step, looking from one to the other.

'Hester will come with me,' Emily said.

'She will not,' Guy countered.

The maid glanced from one to the other.

'You will wait while I get my coat and hat.' Guy said.

As he turned to do so, she said, 'I will go alone.' She walked briskly out of the door.

Guy ran to get his coat. He quickly put the hat on his head and hurried after her, running to the end of the street, still struggling into his topcoat.

He quickly caught up with her.

'Emily, I desire to talk with you.'

She walked quickly, not giving him a glance. 'About your mother? I have no wish to converse on that topic.'

Her colour was high and her voice trembled with anger. In spite of himself, something inside him felt a prick of arousal. She was another new Emily. One he'd glimpsed that day when she threw the book at him.

'I am quite aware of my mother's ill-mannered behaviour towards you. I have spoken to her about it several times—'

'How well she heeds you,' Emily said with sarcasm.

He almost smiled, but thought better of it. 'I have asked her to find residence elsewhere.' If he'd hoped this would please her, he was mistaken. She stopped abruptly and faced him.

'And you think this improves matters?' She glared at him, the flashing of her eyes almost distracting him from what she was saying. 'What about your great-aunts? Your sister? Do you think I wish to be the cause of estrangement in the family? I think of my own family. Do you suppose I would be pleased to cause the same in yours?'

'What other recourse do I have?' he demanded. As difficult as it was to receive her anger, he was glad she did not mask it from him. 'My duty is to you, my wife.'

'Duty!' she said, as if it were a profanity. She started walking again.

He bolted to her side and kept stride with the brisk pace she set. They came to Piccadilly where the streets were busy with shoppers and tradesmen. This was not a place for him to engage in a private conversation. They had already received interested glances from passers-by.

Before he knew it, she darted through the traffic to cross the bustling street.

'Blast it, Emily,' he said, his heart still pounding in fright from seeing her nearly run over by a mail coach. 'Have a care. Where are you bound in such a hurry?'

'I have a fancy to call upon Lady Devlin,' she replied in a cool voice.

Oh, the devil, Guy thought. He'd nearly forgotten about

Lady Devlin. 'Emily, let us find a place to sit down a moment.'

'There isn't such a place,' she said.

'We could go to the park.'

Hyde Park was out of the way, but at least he could sit down with her in relative privacy and tell her about Lady Devlin. He didn't dare tell her the whole. That would have to wait until they returned home.

'I do not wish to go to the park,' she said.

He stopped this time and she kept walking several feet before resignedly stopping and turning back to him.

'Very well,' she said. 'The park.'

Though the day was chilly and rain threatened there was plenty of activity in the park. Soldiers exercising their horses. Grey-haired gentlemen taking constitutionals. The occasional couple looking more into each other's eyes than at the flora. He led her to a bench where she sat stiffly beside him.

'We are in the park,' she said unnecessarily.

He rubbed his face. How to tell her? He took her gloved hand and held it with both his hands. 'You should hear this information from me. I'll not risk you coming by it some other way—'

'Risk,' she murmured with a slight laugh.

'There is someone about who speaks of Lady Devlin's past,' he began.

To his surprise, she turned to him, her face turning pale.

'He…he says she used to be employed in a gaming hell—'

'No,' she gasped, rising.

He kept hold of her hand and pulled her back down. 'I thought you should know this. If this information becomes public knowledge, even being Heronvale's sister-in-law may not be enough for her to weather it.'

The distress on her face was much more than he expected. If he were not holding on to her, he was sure she would bolt.

'You may suffer by association to her,' he added.

'Are you forbidding me to see her?' Her voice was like ice.

'No,' he said, 'but you must take care. Our status could less stand such a scandal.'

She shot to her feet again and snatched her hand from his grasp. 'Our status? Do you think I give a moment's care for that?' Her eyes were wild, like a cornered animal looking for escape.

'Emily?' He regarded her with alarm.

People walking nearby stopped and stared at them.

'Who gave you this information?' she demanded.

'Calm yourself, Emily. Sit back down.'

'Who?' she repeated, looking wilder than the moment before. 'Who? Do not keep this information from me, I warn you.'

This was not biddable Emily who denied having any wants or desires. This was not the seductive Lady Widow, using feminine wiles to get what she wanted. This was someone entirely new. This was a mythological harpy— no—more like a mother bear protecting her cub.

'What is this, Emily?'

'Guy,' she pleaded, her whole body trembling, 'tell me who gave you this information.'

'It was Cyprian Sloane, but—'

'Oh!' She took off at a run, her skirts flying, and her bonnet blown off her head, held only by its ribbons.

Guy jumped to his feet and took off after her, heedless of the alarmed stares they received.

He caught up to her and grabbed her by the arm. Gripping her forearms, he held her firm.

'Guy, release me, I beg you. I must warn her, please.' She struggled to free herself.

'Not until you tell me why, Emily.'

They were both panting, but Guy was not certain it was due to the running or due to having her close to him.

She stilled. The surprise of it almost caused him to let go, when her struggles had not succeeded. She stared him directly in the eye. Her cheeks were flushed. Her eyes sparkled, but with pain. 'She is my sister,' she rasped.

He dropped his hands, but she did not run.

She held him with her eyes. 'Your mother called my family shameful this morning. Would you care to hear how shameful, Guy? Because, if you would, I will tell you now. I know you will keep what I say in confidence, because, having married me, you will not wish this to become known.' She gave him a haunted smile. 'If you think Sloane's revelation is a threat to the Keating name, you might wish to listen to me.'

She alarmed him. He had the notion that the walls she erected were tumbling down, but prematurely, before she was strong enough to do without them.

He reached over and put her hand into his. 'I am ready to hear you.'

Chapter Seventeen

He would despise her after this, Emily was certain. He would be even more regretful he'd married her than he'd been before. Not only did she have no fortune for him to gamble away, not only did she lack charm, as her mother-in-law said, but she also came from a family whose secrets could shrivel a person's soul.

She explained to him just how shameful her family really could be, leaving nothing out.

She told about her father bringing the body home, how she'd thought Madeleine had died alone outside in the cold. Tears flooded her eyes, and her voice caught on a sob.

To her surprise, he did not shake his head in disgust. He wrapped his arm around her and held her close against his chest until she was again able to speak.

'It is all right,' he murmured in a voice soft as kitten's fur. 'Your sister did not die.'

No, but that nagged at her too. Who was the poor girl buried in Madeleine's grave?

His arms held her close. The heat of his body warmed her, and the chill of the day disappeared. How was she to reconcile this kindness with all she knew of him? With all that had fuelled her anger?

Her mind refused to recall his wager on Lady Widow, refused to remember he'd tricked her into marriage, refused to accuse him of being like her father.

They continued on the park's path, her holding tightly to his arm. The trees in the park were already bare, their brown leaves scattered on the ground. Every so often the cold breeze stirred them into useless little whirlwinds.

She continued her tale. She told of encountering Madeleine in front of Lackington's Book Shop, on Devlin's arm, like seeing a ghost appear during the brightest part of the day.

She swallowed, her throat suddenly so dry she was unable to tell him she once had placed all her hopes on marrying Devlin Steele. This truth was too painful. She had been so eager to marry a good man. A man unlike her father.

Had she accomplished that goal by marrying Guy? Was he the good man he appeared to be at this moment, a man offering her no censure, no rebuff, merely comfort and understanding?

Whatever might happen in the days and weeks and years to come, she would never forget this moment with him. Her husband looked upon her with loving eyes. Her heart nearly burst with the joy of it.

In a halting voice she told him how thoughtless and selfish she'd been, and how jealous of the pretty Madeleine. If she had paid attention to her sister, guided her, looked out for her, Madeleine would have been safe.

'How could you have known, Emily?' he said. 'You could not have conceived of such events.'

Could she bear it? Could she believe it? She wanted to believe it. In this moment, walking with him and telling him the worst secret of her life, she wanted to believe she was not at fault. She wanted to believe he cared about her.

They left the park and walked to Grosvenor Square. She hated the thought of parting with him, but Madeleine would have difficulty enough in hearing the news from her. Besides, the longer he was with her, enfolding her in his kindness, the more foolhardy would the plan forming in her mind seem.

As they neared the Heronvale townhouse, she said, 'I wish to be alone with Madeleine when I tell her. I do not want you to be present. It will only distress her.'

Guy's blue eyes regarded her intently. 'Emily, I beg you not to tell her at all.'

'No! She must be warned! I insist upon it.' She could not keep this secret from Madeleine, not when her sister's whole future could be ruined by it. She would also tell Madeleine she would fix it.

His brow furrowed.

As Guy's wife she could do nothing for her sister. It would be scandalous for her to call upon Cyprian Sloane, even if she knew where to find him. Lady Widow, however, knew exactly where he would be that very evening. Lady Widow might be able to convince him to preserve Madeleine's reputation.

Her heart beat wildly with excitement. She knew she could resolve this! Lady Widow could convince Sloane, she knew she could! She could rescue her sister now as she had not done before.

She made her voice firm. 'Do not forbid me to do this, Guy. I have made no previous requests of you, but I am asking you now to allow me to warn my sister.'

They had reached the door to the Heronvale townhouse. He crossed his arms and bowed his head in thought.

'I will not forbid you,' he said at last. 'But it is a matter best resolved without her knowing of it, I am convinced. It would be far more effective if I spoke with her husband or with Heronvale.'

'No, Guy, you must not,' Emily begged. 'It is Madeleine's decision whether or not to tell her husband and the Marquess.'

She looked up at him, all turmoil inside. Wishing not to part with him. Not to become Lady Widow again. But excited and eager to rescue her sister.

'If this is what you desire...'

His eyes were warm and caring, their intense blue still having that melting effect on her bones and muscles. What she desired most was to throw herself into his arms and to feel his strength enfolding her, never letting go.

She must be realistic. She must take one more risk. For the sake of her sister. When she met his eyes, her gaze did not waver, even as the lie formed on her lips. 'I desire this above all things.'

What she truly desired above all things was for this moment with her husband to last forever.

He smiled at her and butterflies danced in her chest. He took her hand and lifted it to his lips. When he turned his back to her to sound the knocker, she rubbed where his lips had touched, her heart now aching with what she had decided to do.

For her sister, she would don Lady Widow's clothes one last time. She would wear Lady Widow's mask. She would return one last time to Madame Bisou's gaming hell and convince Sloane never to divulge this secret—no matter what it took. She would not fail Madeleine this time. She would right the wrong she had done, and her sister would be safe.

* * *

When a Heronvale footman opened the door, Guy watched Emily step over the threshold, and heard her ask for Lady Devlin. The door closed.

He had not wished to bid her goodbye. He turned away and stepped back on the pavement, remembering how it felt to hold her in his arms, to comfort her, to dry her tears.

The revelation about her family had been shocking in the extreme. He had not imagined how low her parents could sink. To abandon one daughter to such a fate. To treat the other like a mere encumbrance. Using them both as mere chattels to resolve gaming debts. Why, even his own father and brother had not been so lost to decency as that.

How had Emily come out of such a family with all her goodness? Her solicitousness of his mother, his great-aunts and the servants had been no pretence. If her father had passed on his love of gambling to her, Guy would help her conquer it. God knew, he understood all the temptations of a card table.

But first he must see her safe from this scandal. He must save her from the pain of seeing her sister ruined and banished all over again.

Guy turned towards Bond Street in search of a hack. He intended to stop at White's or whichever gentlemen's club might know where Cyprian Sloane could be found. He'd find Cyprian Sloane and do whatever was necessary to compel the man to keep his mouth shut. Then he would tackle all their other problems, including telling her he'd deceived her once more by pretending he did not know she was Lady Widow.

Guy spent half the afternoon searching before he finally located Sloane in a tavern near his rooms on Thornnaugh

Street. Sloane sat alone at a rough-hewn wood table, eating stewed partridge, drinking a tankard of ale, and looking like hell.

His bloodshot eyes only momentarily registered surprise before returning to their typical faintly mocking expression. 'Well, Keating. I must say, you are the last man I expected to see.' He added, 'Or wished to.'

'May I sit down?' Guy asked.

Sloane winced. 'Only if you promise not to shout. I have the devil of a headache.'

Guy signalled for the tavern maid to bring him some ale.

'To what do I owe this pleasure?' Sloane said with thick sarcasm.

Guy gave him a level stare. 'You shared some information with me last night. I am ready to discuss it.'

Sloane's brow wrinkled and he stared into his ale. Half a minute passed before the wrinkles cleared and he looked up again. 'Now I recall. Regarding Lady—'

Guy held up his hand. 'Do not say her name, if you please.'

Sloane shrugged. 'Regarding the "Mysterious Miss M".'

Guy gestured for him to be silent as the maid clapped down a tankard of ale in front of Guy and removed Sloane's dishes.

Guy took a sip before speaking. 'What would it take for you to agree to forget that piece of knowledge?'

Sloane's brows shot up. A slow grin came over his face. 'Did I not tell you what it would take? I want you to spread it around Madame Bisou's that you and Lady Widow merely played a private game of cards, and that the terms of the wager have not yet been met.'

Guy kept his eyes steadily on Sloane's as he again lifted the tankard to his lips.

Sloane continued, 'Then I want you to step aside, so I might have a chance with the lady.'

'I cannot do that,' Guy shot back. 'Tell me the stakes of the wager. I will pay you an equal amount.'

Sloane's brows rose again. 'Four thousand six hundred pounds?'

Guy did not move a muscle. 'Done. I will have a banknote in your hands tomorrow.' The amount would severely cut into the reserves he'd invested in the funds. It would strain his finances, and mean more years of pinching pennies so hard they would scream in pain.

Sloane laughed and shook his head, then pressed a finger to his brow with a wince. 'You miss the point, Keating. The money means nothing to me. I aspire to win the bet. Winning the bet is the important thing.'

Guy gave him a look of disgust. 'You would ruin that poor lady's reputation for the sake of a wager?'

'Well.' Sloane shifted in his seat. 'I confess not to have thought much upon that. I meant to induce you to my way of thinking by considering how your wife's reputation would suffer from the association. I thought preserving her good name would be the ticket.'

Guy slammed the tankard down on the table. 'Keep this matter of the wager between you and me. Why bring innocent women into it?'

Sloane leaned back, undaunted. 'Why, to compel you to agree to do what I want.'

Guy twisted halfway around, gripping the back of the chair so hard his knuckles turned white. He did not suppose a right hook to Sloane's face would persuade him to co-operate.

Sloane put on a horrified expression. 'Do not tell me you have developed a *tendre* for our Lady Widow?'

Guy glared at him.

Sloane took a drink and tapped his fingers against the pewter handle. 'Your heart is engaged. Fancy that.'

Guy ignored that statement. He leaned forward, putting his fists on the table. 'The point is, Sloane, why ruin the lady and her family? If you care nothing for her life, think of yourself. You would risk making powerful enemies. I dare say Heronvale's credit in the world exceeds your own.'

'I dare say it does.' Sloane laughed.

'Give me your word you will keep this damning information to yourself and never speak of it to anyone.' Guy looked him directly in the eye. 'I will pay you the money.'

Sloane did not so much as blink.

What would it take to make the man agree? Guy had no desire to challenge him to a duel, but it was beginning to appear that would be the next resort.

Sloane threw up a hand. 'Forget the money. You have more need of it than I.' He rocked back and forth on the hind legs of his chair. 'I'll give you my word, I shall never speak of the Mysterious Miss M.'

Guy peered at him, looking for any signs the man was not serious. He did not discover any. 'Thank you, Sloane.'

'Always felt sorry for her, to tell the truth,' Sloane added, draining the contents of his tankard. 'Didn't like that gulling bastard Farley by half. He got what he deserved.'

Guy signalled to the tavern maid. 'I'll buy you another drink to seal the bargain. What will you have?'

Sloane grimaced. 'Anything but whisky.'

A minute later they lifted two more tankards of ale.

Sloane eyed Guy suspiciously. 'Tell me, Keating. You accepted my word easily enough. Why? Why trust me?'

Guy smiled. 'I've heard you called many things, Sloane, but no man has ever said you do not keep your word.'

'What a shocking lapse.' Sloane took another sip. He put the tankard down and rested his elbows on the table. A triumphant expression suddenly lit up his face. 'I have it, Keating!' He grinned like a harlequin. 'If you do not agree to deny bedding Lady Widow, I will inform your wife of her existence. How would that suit you?'

Guy laughed. 'Too late, sir.' He took a long swig of his ale. 'My wife already knows all about Lady Widow.'

Emily rode back to Essex Court in the Heronvale carriage. She'd stayed with Madeleine all the afternoon, but contrary to what she'd told Guy, she did not mention Sloane's threat. As soon as her sister's eyes glittered with pleasure upon seeing her, Emily knew he had been right. She could not burden her sister with this worry. Madeleine would be better off never knowing of the potential hazard to her happiness.

She and Madeleine spent a lovely afternoon together, playing with Madeleine's daughter, chatting with the Marchioness, catching up on each other's lives, though their conversations by necessity left much unsaid. Madeleine glossed over her time with Farley, and Emily glossed over her marriage. Nor did she mention Lady Widow.

One more night to wear Lady Widow's mask.

As soon as she entered the townhouse, Bleasby informed her that the Dowager Lady Keating wished to speak with her.

'At your convenience,' Bleasby said.

At her convenience? Was that a nicety Bleasby added? She went first to her room to make herself more presentable. Before she could finish tidying her hair, there was a knock at the door. 'Come in,' she said.

Lady Keating entered. She had never visited Emily's room before. She looked much altered, smaller, paler, wringing her hands.

'Lady Keating!' Emily exclaimed.

'Am I disturbing you?' her mother-in-law said.

'Not at all.' Emily gestured to a chair. 'Do sit down. I was on my way to see you.'

The Dowager sat in the faded brocade chair, one of a pair that provided a nice place for comfortable chats. Emily had never had a use for the chairs before this time.

Her mother-in-law gazed off into the distance, looking very distracted.

Emily went to her side, crouching down to her level. 'Ma'am?' Emily took her hand. 'Are you feeling unwell?'

Lady Keating's hand was cool to the touch. She snatched it from Emily's grasp.

'I am not ill.' She took a breath. 'I came to beg you not send me away. Where would I go? I have no wish to be alone!'

Emily grasped both of her mother-in-law's hands this time. She peered directly into the older lady's eyes, forcing her to look at her. 'You will not be sent away. That is all nonsense.'

The Dowager's lips trembled. 'Guy says—'

Emily squeezed her hands. 'Guy will not send you away! Now let us stop all this foolishness. We need to be dressing for dinner soon.'

'I cannot eat a thing,' Lady Keating said dramatically.

Emily stood, giving a little laugh. 'You must regain your appetite, then. Besides, if you do not appear at dinner, your aunts will worry. You do not wish to cause them worry, do you?'

Her mother-in-law's eyes narrowed in suspicion, and her expression lost all its drama. 'Why are you being so agreeable to me?'

She had been fooled again, by a different Keating this time. She sighed. 'My lady, I have no wish to be your enemy. Nor do I wish to split your family. These are your decisions, not mine. But make no mistake. I am the lady of the house and I will brook no disrespect.'

The Dowager rose and raised her chin mutinously. Emily, however, did not miss the fleeting look of anxiety in her eyes.

Emily did not know if there was any chance for happiness between her and Guy. But she knew she would never leave her marriage. She would not be traipsing off to some other gaming hell to win money. She would not repeat such a folly.

If she indeed would remain in this household, as she must, she was determined not to be overrun by her mother-in-law.

Emily extended her hand to Lady Keating. 'Let us agree to be friends.'

Lady Keating stared at Emily's hand and lifted her head defiantly. Without a word, she strode past Emily and went out of the door.

Guy hurried in to the townhouse near the dinner hour. He and Sloane had consumed a third round before Guy had realised the time. He rushed to his room to change for dinner, all the time wondering if Emily were here, if her meeting with her sister had been difficult for her.

He tried to think of the best time to see her alone, hoping his good news about Sloane would earn him some credit in her eyes. He would need it if he was to tell her everything.

Unlike the previous night when he'd left Madame Bisou's, he was full of hope. Their afternoon, as difficult and emotional as it had been, had been a moment of unity between them. This night he hoped to strip off all the masks they wore and make love to his wife.

He found her in the parlour, standing by the window gazing into the street, now dark. His mother and her aunts were also present.

She turned her eyes upon him when he walked in. He met them briefly and smiled.

She smiled back.

His heart sang.

But for all that connection he felt with her, the room seemed to crackle with tension. He had forgotten the conversation with his mother that morning. Had his mother made things more difficult for Emily? He swore he would send her off by the morrow if she did not behave with more civility.

He glanced at his mother, who quickly averted her face. His aunts gave him the mildest of greetings and returned to their sewing. How much did they know? He hoped they had not been made a part of this discord.

The silence and tension in the room reminded him of a battlefield after the wounded and dead had been removed. Something of the horror always lingered. He glanced at Emily again and she returned a sympathetic look.

They were still attuned to each other! He nearly laughed with relief. The devil with the rest of them, he was happy to be in union with his wife. He took a step towards her, but, at that moment, Bleasby entered and announced dinner.

Emily walked over to him and took his arm. There was nothing impersonal in her touch. On the contrary, it stirred his senses as much as his hopes and he wished they could dispense with dinner.

He was eager for dessert.

When they were seated and the soup served, his mother said, 'You were gone all day, Guy.'

He glanced up. 'I had errands in town.'

The silence descended again. He ought to throttle his mother, who seemed unrepentant. With all their family had been through with his father and brother, she ought to jump through hoops like the horses at Astley's in order to achieve some measure of peace. The devil with her.

He turned to his wife. 'How was your afternoon, Emily?'

She gave him a meaningful look. 'I took your advice, Guy. I had a lovely afternoon with Lady Devlin.'

She had not told Lady Devlin then? Excellent! That was the best of all possible outcomes.

He smiled at her. 'I am very glad.'

'What d'you mean about Guy's advice?' Aunt Dorrie asked, pointing her soup spoon at Emily.

Guy opened his mouth to answer, but Emily spoke first. 'We walked through the park, and Guy suggested I call upon Lady Devlin.'

'Such a nice family!' sighed Aunt Pip.

Aunt Dorrie gave a huff. 'I should have liked to call upon the Marchioness.'

Emily gave her a kind look. 'Then we shall do so again soon.'

Guy's mother sat stiff and silent during this exchange.

To his surprise, Emily turned to her. 'Lady Keating, the Marchioness bid me to send you her very best regards.'

His mother glanced up. 'Did she?'

She returned to her soup, saying nothing more. Guy bit down on a scold. Rebuking his mother in front of them all would not improve the atmosphere. He'd not risk things worsening, when matters between he and Emily were looking up.

Rogers appeared to remove the soup bowls and to serve the fish. Side dishes were already on the table.

After a few moments, Guy's mother said, 'Emily, the menu you selected this evening is quite well done.'

Guy looked at his mother in great surprise.

Emily, however, seemed to take the comment as entirely natural. 'Thank you, ma'am,' she responded in a mild voice. 'I value your good opinion.'

Guy watched his mother favour Emily with a relieved, even apologetic smile. Guy felt like bursting into a triumphant song.

'Do we have any engagements tonight, Lady Keating?' Emily went on pleasantly.

'No,' his mother replied. 'The entertainments are getting rather thin. I expect many have returned to the country.'

Emily added, 'Have you read such announcements in the papers? There do seem to be many.'

Aunt Pip and Aunt Dorrie joined in the conversation, each declaring who they knew to be in town and who to be gone. Guy merely stared in wonder.

And in pride. Whatever had happened, he was proud of them all, conversing like one contented family. Just when he thought things couldn't be happier, something better transpired.

The good humour continued throughout the evening. Guy was loathe to interrupt it to request a private conference with his wife. He would wait until they all retired. He fancied, after all, talking with his wife in the solitude of her room, where they might be private, where they might go on as husband and wife.

She retired early, confessing to great fatigue. His mother and her aunts had insisted upon playing whist, and he was roped in to be the fourth partner. They were almost finished the rubber and he could beg off after that very comfortably.

The evening was still relatively young when he ascended the stairs. He would catch her before she gave any thought to dressing as Lady Widow.

He entered his own bedchamber and went quickly to the connecting door. Giving only one knock, he opened the door.

Emily's maid gave a shriek like before and dropped the dress she'd had in her hands. The girl was alone.

'Where is she?' Guy demanded.

She had never left the house so early. Surely she knew he wished to see her? Had he not sent enough messages with his inability to keep his eyes off her?

'I…I cannot…' stammered the girl.

'You can and must tell me,' Guy said, advancing on her.

He could not help his anger, it burned within him, trying to incinerate any hopes she'd gone to Madame Bisou's for a repeat of their night together. He tried desperately to cling to that slim, nearly ashen hope.

The maid took tiny steps away from him. 'I cannot.'

He backed her against a wall. 'You do not have to keep your lady's confidence,' he insisted, his voice firm and fierce. 'I know she goes to the gaming hell at night. I know she dresses in silks and wears a mask. Has she gone there early this night?'

The maid, eyes very wide, nodded.

Guy turned on his heel and stormed back into his room. Grabbing his topcoat and hat, he rushed down the stairs past a surprised Rogers, and out of the door.

Chapter Eighteen

Emily sat in the hackney coach as it clattered its way to Bennett Street. The risks she had taken before paled in comparison to this one. If Guy discovered her gone, what would he think? How would she ever explain?

She must meet Sloane. Once her sister was safe all her attention could turn to her marriage. And she would pray it would not be too late.

One worry teased her, but she tried to brush it away. What if Guy came looking for Lady Widow this night? What if his desire for Lady Widow had been more than to win a wager?

The idea made blood race through her veins, but it brought no comfort.

She hoped to arrive early enough at Madame Bisou's to catch Cyprian Sloane alone. Once involved in a card game, he might never speak with her. She must see Sloane tonight. After tonight, she would pack up her fine gowns and never appear as Lady Widow again. Her dress, the green silk she'd worn the first night she'd come to this place, seemed to chafe her skin, and the mask made her face so hot she wanted to rip it off.

Once she secured Sloane's promise not to divulge Madeleine's secret, she would run back to the hack and head home where she would try her best to build a life with Guy. To face whatever met her there.

Hester's brother dropped her off at the Bennett Street address. She knocked on Madame Bisou's door. It opened immediately. If Cummings was surprised to see her at this hour, he made no sign of it.

'Is Mr Sloane here tonight?' she asked.

'Not yet, ma'am,' Cummings replied.

'Be so good as to tell him I wish to see him.' Emily handed him her cloak.

'You wish to see Mr Sloane?' he repeated, with just a hint of curiosity in his deep voice.

'Yes,' she replied. 'I shall wait in the supper room.'

The first person she encountered was Sir Reginald. His hand leapt to his cheek, which still bore a red mark from where she had slapped it. 'Good evening, ma'am,' he mumbled, giving her a quick bow and a wide berth.

She refused to feel guilty for striking him. He had wagered for her and propositioned her as well. How would she ever act if again compelled to meet him as her mother-in-law's friend?

She peeked into the card room merely to assure herself Cummings had not been mistaken about Sloane. Her eyes swept the room. She jumped back out of sight.

Her brother Robert was wandering around the card tables, headed for the faro bank. Was he here looking for her? She certainly did not wish to see him.

At least Madame Bisou will be in transports, she thought wryly. She fled to the supper room, selecting a table as far out of sight as possible, but still affording a view of the doorway.

After a mere five minutes, Sloane sauntered in and scanned the room. When he saw her tucked away in her corner, he flashed his most charming smile and strode up to her.

'You wished to see me, Lady Widow.' He bowed, making the formality look ironic.

'I wish a private conference with you,' she said.

Interest kindled in his eyes. 'I am honoured to oblige,' he said. 'May I suggest one of the private rooms?'

Go into a private room with Sloane? She glanced away. Gentlemen walked in and out of this room. Serving maids brought them drinks. Someone might overhear them if they remained here.

She bit her lip. Stories of Sloane's conquests had abounded in Bath. It was said he had no scruples where women were concerned. Alone in a room with him, anything might happen, but what other choice did she have?

She lifted her chin, adopting Lady Widow's confident attitude. 'Very well, sir.'

He grinned. 'Let me attend to the arrangements.'

Sloane rushed out of the supper room, barely able to assimilate this unexpected turn of events.

He caught one of Madame Bisou's girls in the hallway. 'Procure me a private room and a bottle of your best champagne.'

She curtsied.

'Be quick about it,' he demanded.

She scampered away.

'Sir Reginald,' he cried, entering the card room. 'I have a wager to propose.'

Several gentlemen nearly knocked Sir Reginald aside as they hurried to Sloane's side and called for the betting book.

'One hundred pounds says I steal Lady Widow from Keating and remove her mask,' Sloane announced to the gathered throng. He had no difficulty finding takers, though he was a wee bit dismayed the odds were running against him succeeding.

More sweet the victory, he assured himself.

The girl returned with a room key, and Sloane left the men still arguing stakes back and forth. As he swiftly returned to the supper room, he caught Lady Widow looking unusually pensive. Well, if she were pining for Keating, he'd soon make her forget. Perhaps she was contemplating a comparison? If so, Sloane was determined to come out the winner.

He offered his arm, but she seemed not to notice. With a quick step, she ascended the stairs ahead of him. At the landing she tapped her foot impatiently until he caught up.

He opened the door of the room, extending his arm with a flourish to allow her to walk in first. He turned to lock it, but she said, 'I will take the key, please.'

His brows lifted, but he tossed it to her. What did he care if the door were locked or not?

She caught it and dropped it tantalisingly down between her breasts. *I'll retrieve that key later*, he thought smugly to himself.

She glanced at the bed in the corner of the room and, in a determined manner, turned her back upon it.

The champagne sat on the card table in the centre of the room. Sloane poured two glasses, handing one to her.

She took the glass, but placed it back on the table.

Did she wish to get right at it? Such eagerness. His luck was running high this night. He'd collect the winnings in no time at all. He took a step towards her.

She held up her hand, blocking his approach. 'I wish to speak with you, Mr Sloane.'

Not so lucky, perhaps. He sighed. Who would have

guessed she was the sort of female who demanded conversation first.

He folded his arms across his chest and attempted to look as if he had all the time in the world. 'I am your servant.'

She toyed with the stem of her glass, but did not pick it up. 'I will not mince words, sir,' she said finally.

Good! he thought.

She looked him directly in the eye. 'You have knowledge that could ruin Lady Devlin Steele. What will it take to induce you never to speak of it to anyone?'

He rolled his eyes. Not again.

He certainly had not expected this from Lady Widow. How many people knew this damned secret of his? Had Keating told her? If he had, it must have been after he'd left Sloane.

He tapped his fingers on his folded arms. Keating knew who she was! If Keating told her, he'd told her outside Madame Bisou's! Damnation.

'Well?' she asked, though her haughty voice quavered a bit.

Sloane peered at her through narrowed eyes. More had been going on with Lady Widow than he'd realised. This smacked of a mystery, and he hated mysteries. Much better to know all the answers. Unmasking her and revealing who she was would have been a particular treat. Second only to winning the wager, that was, but Keating had even ruined that moment. Blast the man!

One thing was certain. He would learn nothing if he scared her away. He'd play along with this game of hers. He gave her an engaging smile. 'I confess, I am astonished you possess this knowledge. I told only one person.'

She stood her ground, but her fingers left the glass and braced themselves against the table instead. 'Do not concern yourself with how I came about my information. Answer my question. What do you want for your silence?'

Oh, what a card to open with! The game was surely to be his if she played so recklessly.

He walked towards her, slowly, like a cat fooling its prey into thinking it posed no threat. When she threw up her hand again, he caught it in his and advanced so close his body brushed against hers.

'Lie down with me,' he whispered. 'Let me show you what delights I can offer, then let me peel that mask from your face and—'

'No,' she said, in a voice not unlike one of his old school masters. 'That is not acceptable.'

He was taken aback. She stepped away from his grasp and put a chair between them.

'Not acceptable?' His powers of seduction must have become rusty. From lack of use, no doubt.

'Such terms are not to be contemplated. I do have money, however. How much to pay for your silence?'

He felt as if he were dreaming the same bad dream twice in one day. 'Four thousand six hundred pounds,' he said in a resigned voice.

She gasped. 'I...I can offer you three thousand.'

If he estimated correctly, that would be about the amount she'd won at whist these past weeks, the amount her foolish suitors threw her way. She was making a sucker bet to wager all her money on one card.

He cocked his head. 'What is my silence to you, Lady Widow? Do you know Lady Devlin?'

She blinked rapidly, glancing away. Finally she said, 'Yes, I do know her. It would do great harm for her past to be public knowledge. It would be cruel in the extreme.'

'Which makes it information of value,' he added.

She looked at him hopefully. 'Will you accept the three thousand pounds?'

He stared at her, rubbing his chin.

Her confidence seemed to ebb. She nervously reached under the netting of her cap and adjusted her mask. The light from the lamp hanging above the table illuminated her face. He studied it.

It would make sense if she were Lady Devlin, but the hair colour was wrong. Lady Widow was taller and smaller-breasted, besides. But who the devil was she?

She seemed familiar, though that notion had never struck him before. That anxious look in her eye, that nervous gesture. Where had he seen her before?

She faced him again. 'You have not answered me.'

He walked a few steps to the side, examining her from another angle. He'd never really studied Lady Widow, he realised. He'd merely accepted her as a whole, delighting in a mystery yet to be solved.

He knew her. He just couldn't place…

She cleared her throat. 'Lord Keating told me you knew of Lady Devlin's past. It was kind of him to tell me, so I could try to make you see reason. To give your word—'

'My word?' Zeus. Where the devil had he gone wrong? It seemed the whole world believed he'd honour something as elusive as his word. He would, of course, but it rankled that it was so widely known.

'You know Lord Keating outside this place,' he stated, more as fact than question.

She did not reply, but she remained as motionless as a statue. He took a long sip of his champagne, watching her all the time.

Suddenly, he saw her. By God, it was so obvious he'd been a fool not to have recognised her right away! Did Keating know?

Of course, he did! It was all Sloane could do to keep from laughing. Keating had told him. His wife knew all about Lady Widow. Another mark on Keating's score-card.

'I…I know Lord Keating from here,' she said feebly. 'Nowhere else. But that has nothing to do with—'

He could not help interrupting. 'Surely you know him in the biblical sense, my lady.' *She's his damned wife!* He laughed to himself.

She glared at him and amazingly turned back into Lady Widow. 'Do not speak so crudely in my presence.'

'I beg your pardon.'

Oh, this is fun, he thought. He just hoped Keating did not show up and catch him with his wife. Sloane had no fancy for pistols at dawn. Besides, he'd started to like Keating.

'Tell me,' he said as casually as he could muster under the circumstances, 'does Keating know who you are?'

'He does not,' she said sharply and rather convincingly, Sloane thought. 'I have no intention of revealing who I am.'

He stifled another laugh. Difficult because this was too amusing. Her husband knew, but she did not know he knew. Delightful!

'Will you accept my money or not?' she demanded.

He waved a hand at her dismissively and dropped into a chair. 'The amount is but a trifle, and, I assure you, I do not need it.'

'I will not bed you,' she said.

Yes, that was certainly out of the question now, was it not? Another wager consigned to the dust heap.

'Then we are at a complete standstill,' he said, waiting to see what she would do next.

Her eyes bore into him, pained and fearful, like an animal caught in a trap. It made him consider abandoning the game.

She straightened her spine and her expression turned flirtatious. Good. She had recovered her bravado.

'But you are a gamester, are you not, sir?' She fluttered her eyelashes at him. 'Certainly you would not refuse the challenge of a game of cards?' She shoved the deck of cards towards him.

She certainly has my number, he thought. 'What stakes?'

She lifted her chin. 'If I win, I win your silence on Lady Devlin's behalf.'

Ha! She obviously did not know that prize had been secured earlier. Far be it from him to tell her and spoil the fun.

'And if I win?' he asked. What could she offer besides her body? And that was out of the question now as well.

'I shall remove my mask.'

He grinned. 'Name your game, Lady Widow.'

Guy pounded on Madame Bisou's door, his anger increased by winding up in the slowest hack in all of London. Cummings opened the door.

'Where is Lady Widow?' Guy demanded, thrusting his coat and hat into the man's arms.

'Supper room, last I knew of,' Cummings said.

Guy took the stairs two at a time. She was not in the supper room, he discovered. He hurried to the gaming room.

From the doorway, his eyes swept the room. She was not there. He looked again, more slowly and carefully. His gaze focused on one gentleman.

Robert Duprey hopped back with a shriek when he saw

Guy advancing upon him. There was no escape for him, however.

Guy grabbed him by the sleeve. 'I would speak with you, Duprey.' He nearly dragged Duprey out into the hall.

'Please, Keating…my coat…' Robert pleaded.

'Hang your coat,' Guy said. 'Where is Emily?'

'Em…Em…Emily?' he stuttered.

Guy grabbed the lapels of the young man's superfine garment and backed him into an alcove. 'Cut line, Duprey,' he spat. 'I know you are behind this Lady Widow business of hers. I ought to call you out.'

Robert struggled feebly. 'Oh, no! Not a duelling man. Not good at it at all.'

Guy shoved him against the wall and came within an inch of his face. 'Then why did you bring her here, you fool!'

'Made me do it,' shrieked Robert, his voice rising more than an octave. 'Forced me!'

'Emily?' Guy gave a dry laugh. 'My bet is you put her up to this charade and I demand to know why!' Guy let go of him with another shove and stepped back, waiting for Duprey's answer.

Robert cowered. 'Said…said she wanted money.'

Guy leaned menacingly towards him again. The young man raised his arms to protect his collar and neckcloth.

'Why did she need money,' Guy demanded. 'For gambling?'

'Y…yes,' stammered Robert. 'Fool plan, I told her. Couldn't win enough, I said. All of it yours anyway.'

'Explain yourself, man,' Guy said, again reaching for Duprey's lapels.

Robert tried desperately to protect his coat. 'Planned to leave you, she said,' he wailed. 'Told her it was not the thing!'

Guy dropped his hands. 'Leave me?'

Robert nodded vigorously. 'Said she'd buy a cottage where you'd never find her.'

The air filled with the pungent odour of too many hot-house flowers.

'There you are, *chéri*!' Madame Bisou's perfume had preceded her as she flounced in Robert's direction.

A relieved look came over the young man's face. Guy stepped away from him.

'I have pined for this moment,' Madame said, throwing her arms around his neck and crushing his coat and neck-cloth with her embrace. 'You will have time for me, no?'

'Y…yes.' Robert cast a wary glance at Guy. 'N…now if you wish.'

'I do wish.' She nuzzled his neck and pulled him towards the stairway.

Guy remained frozen. Emily had become Lady Widow in order to leave him. He ran a ragged hand through his hair, trying to reconcile the sweet, compliant, eager-to-please Emily with a woman plotting her escape. From him.

He could not blame her, to be truthful. It had been reprehensible of him to trick her into marriage in the first place, then to all but ignore her in his single-minded quest for money. But this day had offered hope for them, had it not?

He wandered absently to the doorway of the card room. The Duke's son nearly collided with him.

'The odds are three to one in your favour, Keating,' the man said excitedly. 'Have you placed your bet?'

'In my favour? What the devil are you talking about?' Guy asked.

The Duke's son smirked. 'Sloane proposed the terms. I suppose he did not like losing the other wager. The odds

are three to one he will fail to win Lady Widow
from you.'

'What?'

The man continued, 'But he's closed up with her in a
room at this moment, so there's some chance the odds
will change—'

Guy did not wait to hear the rest. He ran up the stairs,
pounding on two locked doors, and receiving shouts from
unfamiliar voices.

What did she think she was doing? Who was this
woman that she could bed one man one night and another
the next? Then it struck him. She was seeking Sloane's
silence. Would she do so with her body?

The third door was unlocked. He did not bother to
knock, but burst into the room. He saw the champagne.
He saw the cards. He saw Lady Widow and Sloane seated
at the table, each with a fan of cards in their hands. They
were, he was relieved to see, fully dressed.

'Guy!' cried Lady Widow.

'Damn,' cursed Sloane.

'What goes on here?' Guy demanded.

Emily felt the air sucked from her lungs. Her legs trembled beneath the table. Her vision blurred.

He had come in search of Lady Widow after all. She
could not speak.

Sloane answered him, his voice casual. 'Why, this is a
friendly game of cards, Keating. A private one.'

'The devil it is,' Guy growled. 'I hear otherwise below
stairs.'

The room grew dark and the men's voices echoed
through her head. Emily fought the impulse to faint. She
pressed her fingers to her temple. Of course, he would
presume Sloane brought her here for seduction, would he
not? The jealous rage inside him was palpable. Even a

gamester did not feel so passionately about a wager already won. His attachment had been to Lady Widow all along.

Where did that leave her? *Where does that leave Madeleine?* she thought in a panic. How was she to win Sloane's silence now? She must keep her wits about her. She needed to win the card game. After this, Lady Widow would never return.

Would Lady Widow linger in her husband's memory? she wondered. Would she always stand between Guy and his wife? No. She mentally shook herself. She must think of Madeleine.

Forcing herself to stiffen her spine, she said, 'I resent your insinuation, sir!' Her voice was Lady Widow's. 'This is a private game of cards, and I ask you to leave.'

She could feel the rage flaming inside him, putting more colour in his face, more sparks in his eyes.

He strode over to the table and picked up her nearly empty champagne glass, lifting it to the light, then sweeping his eyes over her. 'Is it indeed a mere card game, ma'am? It must have just commenced, for I see you are completely dressed.'

Emily's cheeks grew hot. 'You wrong me, sir,' she murmured.

Sloane broke in, losing only a tad of his composure. 'I don't have a jot of an idea of what you two are talking about, Keating, but, I assure you, cards were the only game played in this room.'

'Do not take me for a fool,' said Guy, his voice like a sharp-edged sword. He did not take his eyes off Emily.

'Alas, it is true.' Sloane stood, adding, 'I give you my word.'

Guy shot him a look.

'Tell you what. You play out my hand. Lady Widow

may explain the stakes. Tell me later who won. I'll honour my part, my word on that, too.' Sloane ambled towards the door. 'I must go below stairs. I suspect there are considerable debts to settle.'

He gave an exaggerated sigh. With an equally dramatic bow, he fled the room.

All was not lost, Emily realised. To save her sister all she need do was win the game with Guy.

If she failed, however, she must remove her mask and he would see who really played tricks with him.

'We ought to replay this hand,' she said, feigning a casual tone so unlike the emotions churning within her. She collected the cards and shuffled them. 'It is your deal.'

Guy grabbed Sloane's chair and sat in it. When she finished shuffling, she handed him the cards.

'What game?' he asked gruffly.

'Piquet,' she replied.

He stared at her for at least half a minute before he spoke. 'What are the stakes?'

She met his eye. 'I shall tell you when we have finished.'

He dealt the cards.

Chapter Nineteen

The atmosphere was like in a dream, looking real but unreal at the same time. Sound echoed as if far away. Light seemed excessively bright. Guy felt as if he were in a dream, acting as if it all was perfectly ordinary, sitting across the table from the alluring creature who was his wife and who likely had been prepared to bed another man.

'What is the score?' he asked.

She answered in a voice without emotion. 'The first partie was mine by one hundred seventeen points. This is the first deal of the second.'

'Do you play for points?' he asked, in like tone.

'The most points after the third partie,' she said.

Guy sorted his hand, estimating what was likely in hers. He chose his play ruthlessly, his anger intensifying concentration, wresting every possible trick from his hand. He did not speak and neither did she, except to make their declarations and responses, call out their points.

The anger boiled inside him with every play of every card, though he was not certain which fuelled it the most. Sloane for trying to bed his wife? Emily for risking her virtue? Plotting to leave him? Or was he angered against himself for letting matters reach this moment, when he might have put a stop to them that first night?

At the end of six hands, he won easily. Guy burned to win the third partie, to discover if he were correct in what he feared she offered Sloane. She would be playing to win Sloane's silence about her sister's past, that was obvious, but had she wagered what he feared?

He dealt the cards. Damn Sloane for accepting her challenge when the man had already given his word to Guy. Perhaps Sloane was no better than his reputation suggested, placing a new wager in Madame Bisou's betting book. Sloane had lost the first bet about Lady Widow. Guy had no notion that the man would create a second one—the seduction of Guy's wife.

But Sloane did not know Lady Widow was Emily, did he? He thought the two of them were competing for a woman who frequented a gaming hell and toyed with its patrons. Lady Widow dangled the gentlemen from her fingers like puppets in a Punch and Judy show. She'd not improved Sloane's perception of her when she played her private game of cards with Guy. If Sloane believed she'd bedded one man, why not another?

She exchanged five cards. He exchanged three.

No, he, Guy, was not innocent in this situation. Plenty of blame could be laid directly at his door.

He'd fallen under her spell as well, even knowing she was his wife. He had not refused her lovemaking. On the contrary, he had revelled in every moment of it.

She led an ace of hearts.

They called out their points as she took several tricks, he others. At the end, the round went to her.

He glanced up at her. She breathed a long sigh of relief, not at all like the gambler he knew she could be. The lines of tension at the corners of her mouth eased slightly.

He shuffled the cards.

She sat stiffly in her chair, gazing down at the table, avoiding looking at him, he suspected. This was nothing like the playful, erotic game of piquet they had played the night before. Even though she wore the gown, the hat and the mask of Lady Widow, this was the woman he had met in Bath, the one who sat across from him at the breakfast table, the one who faded from one's sight, who hid behind her mask of mediocrity. All liveliness gone. All charm vanished.

Only now he knew what events had forged her need to disappear from everyone's notice. If she'd given her parents any reason to consider her value, she might have risked being sold as they sold her sister.

A muscle in Guy's cheek twitched. Her father had sold Emily, in a way, by inventing a way to use her for collateral. Guy had fallen for the ruse, because he'd sought to use her as well.

His anger ebbed suddenly, but was replaced by a tide of remorse. If he had been thinking of anything but his crippling debts he might have recognised how out of character it had been for the colourless, all-too-proper Emily to agree to an elopement. The desperation to escape her parents must have been intense indeed for her to take a chance marrying him.

What had he offered her in return? He was her husband, the man who ought to have cosseted her and protected her. What neglect of his caused her to risk everything at Madame Bisou's?

He passed her the cards.

Emily reached for the deck, her hand brushing her husband's. The touch jolted her as much as if a spark of static electricity had jumped between them. Her eyes flew to his, but she quickly looked back to the cards, getting ready to deal.

She would rather have studied him, drinking in every feature, every nuance of feeling revealed in his face. She longed to see his lips widen into a smile, lighting up his eyes with happiness, but this was impossible. He was lost to her, as surely as this card game would ultimately be lost. Luck had long abandoned her.

Blinking back tears she realised three good hands might give her an edge. The point spread after the first two parties was only slightly in Guy's favour, but he was playing his cards with uncanny skill. The gamester in her marvelled at it.

She tried to steel herself for the loss, though what could be worse than failing her sister and removing her mask in front of him? The thought of unlacing the silk covering her face, peeling it from her sweat-dampened brow, and seeing Guy's shocked expression when she revealed herself, made her stomach roil with nausea.

If luck returned, she might win, but that hope seemed suspended on a very thin thread. Even if she won, she must invent a reason for gambling on the fate of Lady Devlin Steele. How would she explain to Guy why Lady Widow would care about Emily's sister? Or how Lady Widow had been informed of the threat to Lady Devlin's reputation? No matter what happened, she would lose.

The deepest ache, like heavy metal scraping her insides, was the knowledge that his regard truly belonged to Lady Widow. Why else be so furious at finding Lady Widow with another man?

She glanced up while he pulled out cards to exchange. How foolish a woman's heart could be! Once she'd been so eager to leave him. Now, even knowing he loved an illusion, she knew she would stay. She would run his house for him. She would economise when his gambling brought losses and debt. She would endure a thousand cuts to her heart if it meant being with him.

He'd shown her he was the man she'd hoped he would be, a good man, a man she could depend upon, no matter his love of gambling. She remembered his arms around her earlier that day when she so desperately needed his strength. He might never love her like Lady Widow, but perhaps they could find their way to become friends. If she could just last through this one final card game.

Her exchange was reasonably successful, adding a third ace to her hand. If she could just guess in what order he would throw his cards, she might have a chance to earn good points.

In the previous rounds, he had worked out what cards she held and in what order she would play them. In this round, however, that talent appeared to fail him and she beat him by twenty points. Like withered flowers greeted by rain, her hopes revived. She forced herself to clear her mind of everything but the cards.

Three more hands.

She won again. And again! It was down to the last round. He dealt and they exchanged their cards. She declared her points and her score climbed. She won trick after trick, until her score reached thirty.

'Pique,' she said, the word catching in her throat. Her points doubled to sixty, and her heart pounded in her chest. She had won.

They played out the rest of the cards, but she already knew she'd amassed the points she needed. Her whole body trembled with relief. Her sister was safe! And she would not have to remove her mask.

'Congratulations, Lady Widow,' he said as he lay down

his last losing card. There was an odd, melancholy expression in his voice.

It took her several seconds before she could breathe in enough air to speak. 'You…you wished to be told the stakes.' Like a good gamester, she would fulfil her part of the bargain, knowing it meant more explanation than she knew how to make.

He stacked the cards neatly and stood. 'Since I lost, it is not necessary. Unless something is required of me?'

Another reprieve? She rose, too, but did not dare take a step towards him. 'Nothing is required of you.'

She could barely make her legs hold her upright. Having prepared herself for the worst, she could not conceive of escaping all of it. All she wanted now was to leave this place posthaste and never return.

She looked at her husband, who seemed as immobilised as she. 'Would you inform Sloane for me? Tell him that I won? It is he who must keep the bargain with me.'

'You do not wish to tell him yourself?' He returned her gaze with pain in his eyes.

She felt the pain reflected in her own body. He would still be thinking Lady Widow wagered her body, that she had been willing to lie down with another man.

A knife twisted inside her. In the morning she would wake up alone in her bed, knowing he lay in the room connected to hers wishing he could be with Lady Widow. He would not know Lady Widow was about to disappear forever. He would not even realise Lady Widow had been faithful to him.

She raised her eyes to him one more time. 'I have had enough of cards for one night.'

He looked resigned. 'I will inform Sloane of your win.' He headed towards the door, placed his hand on the knob.

She could at least spare him the pain of believing Lady Widow had betrayed him. 'Lord Keating?'

He stopped and turned back to her.

'I would have removed my mask. If Sloane had won, that is what I offered him. That is all I offered him.'

He stared at her a long time, his eyes unfathomable. Then he opened the door and walked out.

Emily waited until he would have had time to reach the floor below. She hurried out of the room and down the stairs, hoping to avoid notice. From the stairway she heard the hum of voices. As she passed the door to the supper room, she spied her brother, seated with Madame Bisou, holding that woman's hand, looking as relaxed and care-free as he'd been as a boy playing tricks on his sisters. She walked past the game room, where she glimpsed Guy leaning over Sloane, seated at a card table with Sir Reginald and two of the others. With the cards to distract them, she supposed that, in the space of a fortnight, none of the gentlemen would even recall Lady Widow.

Except perhaps her husband. Would he pine for Lady Widow? When he regarded his colourless wife, would he wish for the charm of Lady Widow?

She hurried down the stairs to the hall, retrieving her cloak from Cummings and fleeing out into the night to where her hack awaited her. As soon as she was inside, she pulled off her cap and mask.

In no time she was home, let in the house by a waiting Hester, and soon back in her bedchamber.

She could not wait to remove the green silk dress. Hester could pack the dress and cap away in the trunk, and Emily would never open it again. Perhaps she could ask Hester to sell the clothes on Petticoat Lane and keep the profits. As soon as the maid left the room, Emily would throw the mask into the fireplace and watch it burn to ashes.

Emily took the pins from her hair, letting it tumble to her shoulders. She held her hair aside as Hester unbuttoned the dress. Hester pulled it over her head and she was free of it.

As Hester held the gown in her arms, the door connecting her room to her husband's opened.

Her husband stood silhouetted in the doorway.

'Hester,' he said in a mild tone, 'be so good as to leave. I wish to speak with Lady Keating alone.'

Hester gave a quick curtsy, dropped the gown on the floor, and ran out of the room.

Emily, dressed only in her corset and shift, stood awaiting him, sick at heart, but almost relieved at the same time. She'd had enough of masks. When he asked her where she had been, she would tell him everything, no matter what.

But he did not ask her where she had been. He walked up to her and handed her a paper. In the candlelight, she could barely make out that it was a banknote made out to her, allowing her to withdraw a huge sum from his accounts.

'What is this?' she asked.

He looked so much like he had in that private room at Madame Bisou's, but also so different. So sad, so determined.

'Your freedom,' he replied.

She examined it again and glanced back at him. 'I do not understand.'

His eyes flicked over her undressed state, but she did not have the presence of mind to reach for her nearby shawl. He finally gazed directly into her face, but did not answer her. At last it dawned on her.

'Do you wish me to leave?' She could barely hear herself, her words came out so softly.

'Is that not what you wish, Emily?'

'No, I—' Once she had wanted nothing more than to escape him, but everything had changed.

With a grim expression he reached over and took the banknote from her hand, placing it on her dressing table. 'Come,' he said. 'Let us talk.'

He led her to the set of chairs her mother-in-law had used earlier in the day. It seemed a lifetime ago.

Emily had draped her paisley shawl over one of them. She wrapped it around herself before she sat down.

'First,' he began, 'I know everything. I've known most of it from the beginning, from the first time I walked in to Madame Bisou's.'

Her mind tried to take this in, while her heart thudded painfully in her chest. 'You knew?'

'I recognised you almost immediately—'

'You knew!' It was not possible. When he had gazed upon Lady Widow with such desire in his eyes, he knew she was Emily? When she peeled her clothes off for him, he knew? When he made love to her, he knew he made love to his wife?

'Yes,' he said quickly. 'And I do not expect your forgiveness for not letting on until now.'

Her forgiveness? Was it not the other way around?

His words came out in a rush. 'I did not know until tonight why you came to Madame Bisou's. I thought it was for love of gambling. I feared it was…for other interests, as well. Tonight I discovered you were desirous of money—'

'Robert.' Robert must have spilled everything.

'Yes,' he admitted. 'I saw Robert. I was rather harsh with him, I'm afraid, but he told me you masqueraded as

Lady Widow to win enough money to…' he paused and took a breath '…to leave me.'

A dam of pain broke inside her.

'I have the money to free you,' he said.

He wished her to go! Of course. She'd shamed him, seduced him at Madame Bisou's as though she were as common as one of the girls employed there. If it ever became known that Lady Widow was in fact Lady Keating—

'You need not return to Madame Bisou's. In fact, I wish very much for you not to return to that establishment or any like it. It is too dangerous.'

Would he believe she had already decided not to return? Never to be Lady Widow again? 'I—' she began.

He held up his hand. 'No, let me finish.' He shook his head. 'I wronged you from the start, Emily. I deceived you so often, but I have no wish for more secrets between us. Do not think I have not seen how good you have been to me and my family. I do not know what I would have done without you, if I'd had to concern myself with my mother, her aunts or the household. You were better to me than I deserved.'

He had valued her all this time? Noticed her efforts to care for his family? Why did that not please her? She wanted more from him. She wanted what she'd had as Lady Widow.

Heart bleeding, she touched his arm. 'No, please, do not say—'

His eyes flashed. 'I am not finished.' He glanced down to where her hand rested on his arm. His other hand reached over and grazed hers, but she was uncertain if he meant to remove her hand or hold it there in place.

He looked back at her and continued, 'I do not blame you for wanting to be rid of me and my family.'

Be *rid* of him! She opened her mouth to protest.

'We do not deserve you,' he carried on, apparently willing to send her away with at least some pride salvaged. 'But you must not take any risks. I can pay for your freedom now. I have enough money.'

The money he won at gambling, no doubt, but she would never forgive herself if she accepted his money and later learned he was in terrible debt.

'No, Guy, you must save the money,' she spoke earnestly. 'Do you not realise you will have a streak of losing some day? You must always keep money in reserve. If you wish, I will hold the money for you, so you cannot put your hands on it to gamble away.'

He looked puzzled now. 'Gamble it away? Do you think I would keep the money to gamble it?'

She grasped his hand and held it tight. 'Oh, you would not plan to, I am sure, but I know about this, Guy. From my father. When gaming takes hold, a gentleman will risk everything. Please let me stay with you. I can help you. I know I can.'

He gave a dry laugh. 'You would stay under such circumstances?'

His laugh wounded her, but he must be made to see she could help him. 'Yes. I know you are not like my father, but the gambling is so very hard to resist.'

He gave her a cynical look. 'Gambling is hard for you to resist as well, no doubt.'

She felt her cheeks go hot. 'I cannot deny I like a good card game, but I am content with private ones. I have no wish to enter another gaming hell in my life.'

Guy peered into her eyes, looking so full of resolution. Her hand was warm, clutching his so tightly it was almost painful. She continued to believe him a gambler, but was willing to stay with him? She'd conceded he was not like her father, but believed him enough like that disreputable man to require her help? What a model for comparison. In his single-minded quest to save his family and Annerley—and her—he had never thought how his gambling might have appeared to her.

He dropped to his knees in front of her, taking both her hands in his, making her look at him. 'I am not like your father, Emily, and I am not like my father, or my brother. I...I do not claim to be immune to the lure of cards, but I swear to you, I only played to win enough money to keep us all from the poorhouse.'

'The poorhouse?' She blinked down at him.

He blew out an embarrassed breath. 'Another secret I kept from you. From everyone. When I inherited, there was nothing left but debt. Not a feather to fly with. The estate was in ruins, its people near starvation. My mother, my great-aunts, my sister—and, then, you—how was I to feed all of you?'

She gave him an intent look. 'That is why you married me, when you thought I had money?'

'Yes. For the money, I admit.' He squeezed her hands. 'I panicked when you told me there was no money.'

'So you gambled?'

'I needed a great deal of money and I needed it as quickly as possible. I could think of nothing else to do.'

He let go of her hands and stood, moving back to the chair and collapsing in it. 'What a mess,' he muttered. 'What a mess I've created.'

She sat very still. He shot a glance at her, wondering what thoughts ran through her mind. Forgiving him would not be among them. 'I am sorry,' he said in a tired, hopeless voice.

'How much did you win?' she asked.

'Above one hundred and fifty thousand pounds,' he said.

She gasped. 'Above one hundred...' Her voice caught.

'Take or leave a little. I've got an accounting. Much of it has been sent to Annerley, and all the debts I could discover have been paid. The bulk of the rest are in the funds.'

'Above one hundred...' she said again.

He could not bear to look at her. Could bear even less that she deserved to walk out of his life. 'So you see, I can well afford for you to live handsomely. There is no reason to be trapped here with me.'

Once more she fell silent. For so long, he started to squirm, feet and hands refusing to keep still.

When she glanced up, she returned his gaze with the blank expression he'd seen so often. 'I assure you, sir, I would be comfortable with half the sum on the paper. When do you require me to leave?'

Guy shot to his feet. How had he caused her withdrawal? He wanted never again to see that retreat in her eyes. He leaned over her. 'I do not require you to leave, Emily.'

Before he walked in this room, he'd been intent on giving up the game, as he had given up winning Sloane's game of piquet with her. He had decided to throw in his cards and let her go without taking any further risks, telling himself he was being honourable, not cowardly. But suddenly, he needed to play this game to the end. To give it his all. If he lost after doing so, the pain might be worse, but she was worth this one last wager. It was worth everything to bring her back to life.

He kept his gaze steady. 'I do not wish you to leave. I want you to stay, Emily. I want a chance to make something of our marriage, but I will not force you to stay.

You must decide what you want. You. Not what you should or should not do. Not what is required of you. Not what *I* want.' His voice cracked, but he forced himself to finish. 'What *you* want.'

She glanced away, but he took her chin in his fingers and forced her to look at him again. 'What you want, Emily.'

He had not known he could risk more than Annerley. These stakes seemed higher than that for which he'd braved the gaming tables. He risked his heart. Their future.

He let go of her and stepped away. 'You do not need to decide now,' he said. 'You have the banknote if you choose to use it. I will leave you to your sleep and perhaps…perhaps we may talk more in the morning.'

She remained in her chair. After a moment she nodded slightly. He walked to the door.

'Guy?' Her voice halted him. 'You wagered on bedding me, did you not? They all did.' Her voice trembled, but at least there was some emotion in it.

He turned around to her. 'Not I, Emily. Good God! I knew you were my wife. That wager was abominable to me.'

She blinked at him. 'You did not bet on me?'

He shook his head.

'The gentlemen who did, their interest was in the wager, was it not? That is why they flattered Lady Widow.'

This was an Emily he'd not glimpsed before. Insecure, woefully fearing she'd not been the sensational Lady Widow after all. He folded his arms across his chest. 'Emily, they would not have made the wager if they had not been…attracted.'

'And were you…attracted? Did you…like…Lady Widow? You must have liked her…to…bed her.'

Her questions unsettled him. He spoke of her leaving him, and she, God help him, talked of his bedding Lady Widow. This was a dangerous hand to play without knowledge of the rules.

He closed his eyes for a moment, willing himself to be as honest in this as he'd tried to be in everything he'd said to her in this room, even if it felt like he was showing all his cards. 'I admit to being captivated.'

Her head drooped. 'I see.'

His spirits drooped as well, but he persisted. 'Lady Widow captivated me. She and you were one to me, though I could not sometimes reconcile the differences.'

She gave him a pained look. 'I am not Lady Widow. I only pretended to be her. It was like a role in a play.'

He held her gaze. 'I know that,' he said softly. 'Do we not all play roles, Emily? Was I not playing the gambler, when I sat down to cards? I pretended, too, you see. Were you not likewise playing a role as my wife? Making yourself so—'

'Drab?' She sprang to her feet, eyes blazing.

He cursed himself for his careless words. Still, anger was better than no emotion at all, though scant consolation.

'Would you have me tint my lips and cheeks like Lady Widow? Do you wish me to dress as she does? Talk as she talks?'

He faltered. 'You mistake my meaning—'

She shouted, 'I am not Lady Widow!'

He strode back to her, grabbing her by the shoulders. 'Just as I am not a gambler! But both of those roles are part of us, are they not? I do not wish for you to bury that part of you who is Lady Widow, who is confident and sure of what she desires. Neither do I want you to hide that part of you who would risk everything for your sister. Or the gambler inside you. Indeed, the gambler inside me would much like to challenge you to another game.' He squeezed her shoulders, aware of how delicate she felt beneath his fingers. 'I do not wish you to feel you must hide any part of you from me. Good God, Emily, do not hide yourself, no matter what your decision. You have so much beauty inside you, so much emotion. You allowed me to glimpse it when we walked through Hyde Park—'

'Hyde Park?' she snapped, nothing but scepticism in her voice.

'Hyde Park,' he repeated. 'I felt as if I were seeing you for the first time. Do you not know how fascinating it is to know you conceal so much? It is like opening a package and finding more prizes the deeper one goes.'

He looked into her face, but it had gone blank. She had retreated from him once more.

'You are hiding again,' he said sadly. 'Though I suppose that is precisely what I deserve. It is what I have done to you until this night. I have hidden myself from you just as thoroughly as you have from me. You and I do not know each other, do we? I would like to know you, Emily. I would like it very much.'

He released her and rubbed his hands, the hands that had so briefly held her. 'I know the blame is entirely at my door, from the moment I tricked you into marrying me—'

'Your regret at doing so has been no secret.'

He froze, seeking her eyes. 'But I have not regretted marrying you.'

She laughed, a pained, forced laugh.

How much he had hurt her! At least, difficult as it was for him to witness, she was not hiding now. He wanted to get her to look at him. She would not. 'You have tried to be a good wife. You have tried to please me. It is I who have not been a good husband. If I had, you would not have become Lady Widow. You would not wish to leave me.'

'No, I—' she said, her expression softening.

He held up his hand to silence her. 'I cannot regret meeting Lady Widow, knowing that side of you, but I value her no more or less than the woman who has put up with my uncivil family, who has run my household with skill and economy, who has asked for nothing for herself, but who deserves everything. I cannot regret making love to Lady Widow, but neither can I regret those times I lay with you as my wife, how sweet you were—'

Her eyes flashed again. 'No more falsehoods, Guy. Until that night with Lady Widow you have taken pains to avoid my bed.'

Her words stung as sharply as a slap across the cheek. Fool that he was, he'd no notion that this too had caused her such pain. Her forgiveness for all his slights seemed impossible indeed. He turned and walked slowly to the door, aware of the sharpness of the glare she aimed at his back.

He opened the door, but could not make himself step through. He had promised himself to be honest with her and he would be so, even if he appeared to be making excuses for his behaviour.

He turned. 'You are correct. Until I won the money, I could not risk begetting a child. It was not an easy sacrifice, however, knowing you were just on the other side of this door.'

She stared at him, her silence giving him no reward for his abstinence, nor respite from his conscience.

He took a breath and tried to make the corners of his mouth form a smile. 'Another matter I ought to have explained to you.' He bowed to her and crossed the threshold, closing the door behind him.

Chapter Twenty

Emily picked up a shoe from the floor and flung it at the closed door, but it fell short and he probably did not hear it. She collapsed upon the bed, tears stinging her eyes.

What a fool she had been. He put the blame upon himself, but she knew better. She had deliberately withdrawn from him, deliberately avoided challenging him about his nightly absences, deliberately avoided challenging him in any way at all. Merely hiding herself from him lest he discover the biggest secret of all.

She loved him. She wanted him. And had from the moment she had seen him in the Pump Room at Bath.

She jumped off the bed and paced the room, tripping over her other shoe, picking it up, and throwing it against the wall.

How stupid she had been, so sure of the superiority of her unfailing correct behaviour, so certain he would not wish to pay attention to a drab creature such as herself. She'd had to transform herself into another person in order to have the courage to make love to him.

Now everything was ruined. He'd given her the means of leaving him and perhaps, for his sake, she should do it.

Not what I want, he'd said. *What you want.*

Lady Widow would have no difficulty telling him exactly what she wanted. Lady Widow would insist on having her way.

But she could not be Lady Widow, no matter how much he thought Lady Widow a part of her. She could not be so bold, so sure of herself.

She picked up the emerald green gown, recalling how well it had flattered her figure and colouring. She threw it across one of the chairs. On the table she spied the silk mask. She reached for it, crumbling it into her fist and striding over to the fire. She threw it at the flames, but it fluttered to the hearthstone as if thrown back to her.

She snatched it up again, suddenly knowing what she wanted. With all her heart, she knew exactly what she wanted.

And she knew exactly how to get it.

Guy had kicked off his shoes and thrown his jacket and waistcoat on a chair. He pulled the knot out of his neckcloth, letting its ends dangle down his shirt.

It would be nonsense to think of sleeping. He rummaged around the room until he found the bottle of brandy he'd brought there the other night when desire and need clawed at him. Sitting at the small table, he poured himself a drink and downed it in one gulp. He poured another.

She'd be a fool to stay with me, he thought, and he thought her anything but a fool.

The branch of candles in his room fluttered. In the doorway connecting their rooms she stood fully dressed, with a paper in her hand. Had she decided to leave him so soon?

She walked towards him. The light revealed her wearing the green dress she'd worn earlier that evening.

Though her hair was still loose about her shoulders, she wore Lady Widow's mask.

In Lady Widow's voice she said, 'If you like gaming so much, Lord Keating, perhaps you would fancy another game of piquet. It is what I want. A game of piquet.'

'Piquet?' A glimmer of hope kindled inside him. He gave her a slow, careful smile. 'So sorry, ma'am. I have sworn off gambling.'

She sidled towards him, so close her skirt brushed his knees, and waved the paper at him. It was the banknote. 'You do not wish to play for money? Very well.' She let the paper float to the floor.

Every sense in his body came alive, and he had thought never to feel anything again but pain. 'What stakes do you desire, then?' he asked, his voice husky.

'As before,' she purred. 'You win a round, I remove one piece of clothing. I win, and you remove a piece of clothing.'

He stood, so close he already felt the warmth of her body. He combed his fingers through her unbound hair, every bit as soft as he expected.

She placed her hands on his chest, the touch of her fingers stealing his breath.

'One condition,' he said, brushing her hair off her shoulders and reaching around to the ribbons at back of her head. 'No masks.'

As the piece of silk fell from her face, her arms encircled his neck.

'No masks ever again, Emily,' he whispered, letting his hands run down her back, eager for a lifetime exploring every curve.

She lifted her hand to his face, her caress so soft and full of promise it claimed his heart forever.

'No masks,' she said, her lips smiling as they reached to touch his. 'You may wager on it.'

* * * * * *

From reader-favorite
Kathie DeNosky

THE ILLEGITIMATE HEIRS

A brand-new miniseries about three
brothers denied a father's name, but
granted a special inheritance.

Don't miss:

Engagement
between Enemies

(Silhouette Desire #1700,
on sale January 2006)

Reunion
of Revenge

(Silhouette Desire #1707,
on sale February 2006)

Betrothed
for the Baby

(Silhouette Desire #1712,
on sale March 2006)

e**HARLEQUIN**.com

The Ultimate Destination for Women's Fiction

For **FREE** online reading, visit www.eHarlequin.com now and enjoy:

Online Reads
Read **Daily** and **Weekly** chapters from our Internet-exclusive stories by your favorite authors.

Interactive Novels
Cast your vote to help decide how these stories unfold...then stay tuned!

Quick Reads
For shorter romantic reads, try our collection of Poems, Toasts, & More!

Online Read Library
Miss one of our online reads? Come here to catch up!

Reading Groups
Discuss, share and rave with other community members!

For great reading online, visit www.eHarlequin.com today!

Coming this March from

MARY LYNN BAXTER

Totally Texan

(Silhouette Desire #1713)

She's only in town for a few weeks...
certainly not enough time to start an
affair. But then she meets one totally
hot Texan male and all bets are off!

On sale March 2006!

HARLEQUIN®

Super Romance

A compelling and emotional story
from a critically acclaimed writer.

How To
Get Married

by Margot Early

SR #1333

When Sophie Creed comes home to
Colorado, one person she doesn't want to
see is William Ludlow, her almost-husband
of fifteen years ago—or his daughter, Amy.
Especially since Sophie's got a secret that
could change Amy's life.

On sale March 2006
Available wherever Harlequin books are sold!

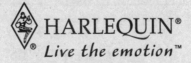

HARLEQUIN®
Live the emotion™

HARLEQUIN®

Super Romance®

OPEN SECRET

by Janice Kay Johnson

HSR #1332

Three siblings, separated after their parents'
death, grow up in very different homes,
lacking the sense of belonging that family
brings. The oldest, Suzanne, makes up her
mind to search for her brother and sister,
never guessing how dramatically her
decision will change their lives.

Also available:

LOST CAUSE (June 2006)

On sale March 2006

Available wherever Harlequin books are sold!

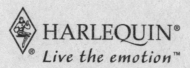

HARLEQUIN®
Live the emotion™